Finding Love on Whidbey Island, Washington

Finding Love on Whidbey Island, Washington

Washington Island Romance Series

by

Annette M. Irby

Dedication

Dedicated to Patrick Monroe, my dear brother. You have a giving heart. The Lord knows your sacrifices, and I pray He abundantly blesses you. I love you.

Acknowledgments

There's an unsung hero who has seen me through each of my books. Someone who offers unconditional support, input, helpful suggestions, prayers, and last-minute read-throughs. I'm grateful for the long hours, cheering, insightful advice, and love. Many thanks to my dear husband, Paul. I love you.

To my immediate family, we did it! Thank you for your sacrifices. Your support and cheering have made a huge difference.

And to friends and family who have prayed for me in this journey, thank you. Only God knows the impact you've had, and I appreciate you!

I haven't experienced adopting a child, so I'm thankful God brought SuLee Allen into my life at the ideal time. Thanks for answering my questions. Your cheerful, kind approach to life is beautiful. Any mistakes concerning adoption are mine.

I'm deeply grateful to the Christian writing community, especially teachers who give back by mentoring writers, like Susan May Warren, Rachel Hauck, James Scott Bell, and so many others.

My critique partners are a treasured part of both my writerly life and my friendship circle. Many thanks and fond memories of uproarious laughter and shared hearts to Dawn Kinzer, Ocieanna Fleiss, and Veronica McCann.

Thanks to Miralee Ferrell and Mountain Brook Ink for the opportunity to bring this series to readers.

To my readers and reviewers—thank you for reading and telling others about these books. I hope you enjoy these hope-filled, beachy reads.

*The L**ORD** has appeared of old to me, saying:*
"Yes, I have loved you with an everlasting love;
Therefore with lovingkindness I have drawn you."

Jeremiah 31:3 NKJV

CHAPTER ONE

Stepping in from the evening rain, Liberty Winfield entered the modern church building and followed the other late arrivals down the dim hall. Guitar chord strains mixed with the laughter of the rowdy group ahead of her, so she hung back and let them go into the chapel first. She'd rather enter the room alone, quietly sneak into the last row, and hide in case she changed her mind and gave up on this mission her therapist had given her.

Try attending a church during your visit, her counselor from Bainbridge Island had said last month. *Give God a chance to speak to you, to minister to you. If Sunday morning is too intimidating, simply go to the midweek service.*

The lights were low in the chapel as she passed the propped-open door. A tiny redhead in a princess dress shot out in front of Liberty, bumping into her legs. Instinctively, Liberty bent low and steadied the little girl. "Are you all right?" she asked, using a kind tone of voice.

The child turned wide brown eyes on Liberty and nodded without blinking.

No adults rushed over. Liberty stood and scanned the room, pushing down the ache in her sternum. She bent again. "Where's your mommy?"

The girl pointed, still not speaking. A woman stood across the room with several children, her family occupying one row of seating midway down the right aisle. She had red, flowing hair, like Liberty and like this little girl. Three active boys and a baby on her hip commanded the woman's attention.

"Let's take you over there." Liberty offered her hand and tried to ignore the churning inside when the child timidly accepted.

Together, they approached the woman while the room swayed with the guitar chords. The service hadn't officially begun yet. Folks spoke in soft murmurs, as if respectful of this place and each other.

The woman turned and noticed her daughter, who darted to her and threw her arms around her legs. "Oh, Isabella," the mom said. "You need to stay here with your brothers and me." She gave a sigh of frustration, then she looked up at Liberty. "Thank you."

Liberty could only nod. Of course, Isabella was too young to be the right age. She also looked so much like her red-haired, brown-eyed mother that Liberty guessed she hadn't been adopted. Liberty offered a weak smile and walked away.

The atmosphere returned to peaceful, but her heart couldn't relax.

What am I doing here?

If she decided to return to Whidbey, to live here like her friends were asking her to do, it could happen, exactly like that. Liberty running into a redheaded child so much like...

Why did You let me see a girl like her tonight, God? Didn't He know how much that hurt?

Whirling, she clutched her purse and eyed her escape. A large group of people crowded in, instantly lowering their voices and scurrying down the aisle toward empty seats. To avoid them, she backed toward the safety of the corner chair at the end of the last row.

Music carried from the front, and her soul stirred with something...intangible. Familiar from years ago, in a different building. She'd lost her mom and dad as a teen. In their will, they'd appointed a church couple as her guardians. The pair had been thrilled when she joined the youth group and served in various outreaches. They felt she could remain grounded, and perhaps spiritual, if she stayed involved at church. And for a while it had worked. But that hole in her heart seemed to connect with the same void in her boyfriend's life.

She shook off thoughts of where that relationship had taken her and zeroed back in on this moment. Shea advised her to stay focused on the present, to take charge of her thoughts whenever possible. She didn't need memories of Clay Garrison in her head or heart. Didn't need regrets surfacing. Or heartbreak to drag her back to her mistakes. It was enough that she'd braved a week-long visit to Birch Harbor on the northern end of the island. She'd do her best to resist the pushy memories.

Words appeared on the far wall, and the worship leader launched into a song. Everyone joined in, as if they knew the routine without the leader giving directions. Movement caught her notice as a man walked down the aisle on the other side and stopped. Through a gap between churchgoers, Liberty watched him worship. Was he a staff member? No one seemed to mind that he stood there. He was likely an usher or something.

He sang along, tipping his head back, lost in the experience. She should probably focus on God and that tenderness surrounding her with a deep longing.

She'd avoided church for years because she'd feared being vulnerable to God again.

The guy in the aisle, whom she could only see from the back, mesmerized her. Such vulnerability in his posture as he sang about God's unconditional love.

Right. Long ago she'd learned the sentiment wasn't true. *No one* loved you unconditionally. Something about this guy, singing toward the ceiling as if God Himself leaned in to listen intrigued her. What was his story?

She looked away. When she pictured her life going forward in this city, all Liberty felt was a hint of dread. Here in Birch Harbor, back where it had all happened—where she'd suffered losses that had broken her heart.

And where God allowed the people around her to take away what mattered. Even when those people forced her to relinquish the only fami—

Stop!

The leader finished the song and invited people to go around and shake hands. That's when the man in the aisle turned and smiled a warm greeting to those around him. He rushed over to help an elderly woman navigate to a seat with her cane.

And Liberty's world stopped.

Clay Garrison.

She'd purposely chosen this church in case he still attended their last one. And she'd come to a midweek service so the chances were even slimmer that she'd see him. But there he was—helping someone lean into him and find a seat. She didn't know what to make of that. The Clay she'd known had been self-absorbed. Like her, he'd pretended to have a deep relationship with God when they were teens to gain the approval of the adults around them.

At that moment, his head tipped up and he spied her across the room.

That was her cue to leave. She didn't want to talk to him. This—*he*—was why she hadn't wanted to move back to Whidbey Island. Halfway to the rear doors, she felt a tap on her shoulder.

"Libby?"

No one called her that anymore. Latecomers blocked the doorway. She was trapped.

"I can't believe it's you," he added in a careful tone, as if he was afraid of frightening her.

She could do this. She made herself meet Clay's green eyes. Familiar. Startling as they were the first time she'd seen them as a youth. And just as startling when she'd seen them in her daughter—*their* redheaded daughter.

"Clay." The name barely emerged. Words had a way of coming out strangled when you couldn't breathe. When you couldn't decide between fleeing or freezing.

The crowd cleared the doorway. Clutching her purse in a tight fist, she bolted from the room.

"Hey," Clay called from behind.

He'd better not follow her. If he did, he'd find she had one more option—fighting.

Self-centered Clay Garrison probably had no idea what he'd cost her. Had she been innocent in their relationship? No. But when she'd needed him the most, he'd let her down the hardest.

Steering her car out of the parking lot, all she could think was how not-so-churchy her anger and lack of forgiveness were.

And shame pressed on her shoulders like a cloak.

After the room had emptied, Clay worked with his fellow ushers and greeters to clean paper scraps from the floor. Liberty Winfield here. Alone. He'd never heard she'd gotten married, so he hadn't expected a husband. But she didn't come in with a nine-year-old child… all because of him.

Over the past decade, Clay had thought he'd come to terms with his mistakes. Tonight's encounter felt like a sucker punch. He'd rebuilt his life since then. Now, he felt drawn backward, drawn under.

If he could reverse time, he'd choose courage and say something less selfish. He'd draw her close and tell her they'd make it work somehow. That he'd find a way to support her and the baby.

How was he going to fix this? Would she give him a chance to tell her how sorry he was for his reaction?

All that light in her eyes, mixed with fear. *Clay, I'm pregnant.*

His response: *It's not mine.*

Then the hope in her expression faded to pain from his betrayal. But he knew her. Of course she'd been faithful to him.

He cringed on the way to his truck, a cloud of regret swallowing him up like the humid Northwest air pulling in a marine layer from the Salish Sea. Regret and loss.

If she'd stuck around tonight, he would have apologized.

He might have missed his only chance.

CHAPTER TWO

The parking lot was almost full at the smoothie shop when Liberty parked her car in a tight spot and squeezed out through the driver's side door. Bright green buds decorated tree branches overhead, and wind stirred the air this March morning. Noisy songbirds sang overhead as she locked her car. If she decided to follow through on the move, this would be her last sit-down with Shea Brown here on Bainbridge for a while. She'd been back from her visit up north for a few days, but somehow Bainbridge didn't quite feel like home anymore. But neither did Whidbey.

Liberty had met Shea a few years ago and had seen her for a year now, off and on. She knew many of Liberty's secrets. Yet Shea never judged her, only supported her. Since her schedule was packed, Shea had agreed to meet Liberty during a break, more as friends.

Few people stood in line inside, and Liberty ordered a pomegranate-berry smoothie while waiting for Shea to arrive.

Shea rushed into the store, her wavy brown hair fanning behind her. "Sorry I'm running a little late."

"No problem."

"Let me order, and then I want to hear everything about your trip to Whidbey." She rubbed her hands together, and her enthusiasm made Liberty laugh.

"Of course." Liberty found them a table by the window, sipping her cold, fruity beverage, with the perfect balance of sweet versus sour. Sounded like her coping mechanism for life—mix in humor to face the pain.

"So, tell me everything." Shea set her cup down and climbed onto her own stool across from Liberty.

"I took your advice during my week there and tried out a church." Shea's reaction made Liberty rush into her next sentence. "But before you get too excited about that, I need to tell you who I ran into."

Shea waited, but her eyebrows hiked.

"Three guesses."

"I assume your benefactors may have been there, yes? Since they were hosting you, their presence wouldn't be a surprise."

"True." She had stayed in Roy and Gloria Archers' home. Before retiring, they'd employed her for the past eight years in their orthodontic office. They treated her like their own daughter. "They weren't there. Someone else."

"An old friend then? You mentioned that Birch Harbor was your hometown and that you grew up there. That's where your guardians lived, the Kincades, right? Wait. Did you run into *them*?"

"Nope." The thought made her wince. She'd rather not see them again. "One more try."

Shea toyed with the lid on her cup. "I have a feeling I know where this is headed, but I can't remember his name. Something earthy...Mason? Dusty?"

"Clay." Saying his name left a sour taste in her mouth, and she slurped more of her drink.

"Clay. Yes." Shea leaned forward. "How did that go?"

"I didn't recognize him at first." Emotions rushed over her, transporting her back in time.

"That's understandable. It's been, what, a decade?" Shea grabbed a square napkin and set it under her drink. "Does this mean you've decided not to move back there?"

Liberty made what she hoped was a comical face. "This decision would be so much easier if he'd simply move away. Why hasn't he moved away?"

Shea laughed. "You know, you've convinced yourself your life would be better if you never saw him again, but what if talking to him is exactly what you need to do?"

Keeping her distance for years, making her own way, she used avoidance to navigate her life. The thought of interacting with Clay *on purpose* hadn't occurred to her until now. Leave it to Shea to throw a new idea in front of her.

"I mean, you wouldn't have to chat longer than it took to clear up the past."

"What if he hasn't changed? What if he still denies everything?"

"Then you've at least tried."

Or Clay could disturb her world, once he knew the truth. It was best to keep her secrets. "No, I don't think that would work."

Silence settled between them, with only the announcements of finished orders breaking the quiet.

"Perhaps you could live on the island and not run into him."

"I'm guessing he still lives in Birch Harbor." Why hadn't she checked his family's business web page? If they were still in operation, they probably had a group of staff photos. "Hang on." She grabbed her cell and found Seaside Greenhouse and Nursery's website. Sure enough, Clay was pictured. "Fear confirmed." She flipped her phone around and showed her friend.

"That answers that. But it's not like you'd have to work with him. You'll find a doctor's office, and he'll be out growing trees."

Liberty chortled at the picture Shea made with her hand gestures. "I may not have a choice about moving. Not with the cost of living going up here and no job leads."

"The Archers *are* waiting to welcome you."

"They invited me to move into their spare room until I get established, but I can't do that." Her hand felt cold from clutching her smoothie, so she let go. For once she'd like to trust that leaning on someone wouldn't backfire. "I'll take my camper."

"They're like honorary parents. They've always looked out for you."

Clutching her hands together in an impression of Gloria Archer, Liberty exaggerated her response. "'If only you'd have married one of our sons.'" She grinned at that thought. "Why is everyone always trying to marry me off?" If anyone understood that Liberty didn't trust others easily, and certainly didn't date lightly, it was Shea. "I mean, there's no stopping her. Imagine if I lived in her house. She'd line up a date for every day of the week." Liberty gave a mock shudder. "No, thanks."

"She means well. They genuinely care for you."

Liberty played with her straw. "I don't want to be a burden."

"You are *not* a burden, no matter what people may have once said or what you may have believed. You are loved. Many people care about you. And if you don't mind my saying so, God cares about you. A lot." Her voice sounded so sincere that the words slipped past Liberty's usual guards and settled deep inside. "Whenever those thoughts come, remind yourself that you are loved. You have a lot of skills and experience, and I'm certain you'll find another job." Shea turned thoughtful a moment. "Or you could pursue your dreams."

"What dreams?" Who had the luxury of chasing aspirations? Liberty only wanted a stable home life.

"Building fairy houses, for one. Working as an artist."

"That wouldn't generate enough to live on." Liberty enjoyed creating whimsical things based in fantasy. Gazing at them afterward gave her an escape. Her creations might help others feel less lonely or sad.

"You love flowers. You could work in horticulture or something."

"All my experience is in office admin."

"There has to be a way. If there is, I'm certain you'll find it."

Liberty tipped her cup to Shea's. "You're 'certain' about a lot of things in my life."

"I want you to thrive, to see your value and live in the freedom your name implies."

Liberty. "That sounds impossible." Her eyes went to one of several pictures on the wall. Could she find the courage to hope?

"Tell me more about running into Clay."

Liberty tapped the blackened screen on her phone. "He's still too attractive."

A light grunt came from Shea's direction.

None of Liberty's lingering attraction would matter if she hadn't noticed something in his demeanor at church that night. Before she knew who he was, she felt drawn, more than curious. "Not that I'm going to fall for that again." He could keep his muscles and masculine dimples, his dark brown hair and bright green eyes to himself.

"Of course not." Using a napkin, Shea wiped the condensation from her half-empty cup. "Did you talk to him?"

"Not exactly. He recognized me and came over, blurted something about not believing it was me, and then I ran." Gulping the cold beverage distracted her from the sense she'd acted cowardly. But she had hoped to avoid him while in town.

Over the years, she'd thought of all the things she'd like to *yell* at him. But more than anything she wanted to move on, to get past it all. Having her history thrown in her face, daily? Another mark against moving back there.

"Is this going to keep you from considering the Archers' offer?"

"Good question." Liberty didn't have the answer.

Shea finished her smoothie. "I need to get back to work, but I wanted to ask you something. I know you drive a tiny car. If you decide to relocate, how are you going to haul your camper?"

Liberty's travel trailer was about eighteen feet long, far too much for her sedan to handle. "Find someone with a truck and a free Saturday? I might have to pay to have it moved." Not that she planned to go.

"I may be able to help. I know someone with a truck. Could I text you later?"

"Are you forgetting I still haven't decided what to do?"

Shea pulled her purse strap over one shoulder. "You know, whether you return to Birch Harbor or not, I hope you can find peace with your past one day." Her voice sounded a little choked up. "I'd like to keep in touch, either way."

"Me too." Liberty stood. "I appreciate everything you've done for me." When Shea opened her arms, which she never did at the close of their appointments, Liberty stepped into her hug. Was this what it felt like to have a big sister?

"I'll be praying for you, that you'll know what to do and you'll find peace," Shea said, and then she released Liberty. "And I'll text you soon about my contact with the truck."

CHAPTER THREE

Clay hoisted the five-gallon potted Japanese maple onto the truck bed. *He's trying to get a reaction. Let it go.* But his dad's words rang in his mind.

Why can't you get your act together? That order was due yesterday. Do you want our business to fail?

As if the sight of Dad, leaning on his cane this long after the accident, after the surgeries, didn't eat Clay alive. As if he didn't already feel like he'd let him down, that he could never earn his approval. Dad hadn't given Clay the order until this morning, but Clay wouldn't mention that fact. He'd load the truck, drive to his mother's shop, swallow angry answers, and dream of working for himself far away from Dad.

After climbing aboard the truck bed, Clay shoved the container toward the cab, wedging it between two more maples. The high walls of this white and red F350 would protect the trees from the March wind during relocation. Shovels and rakes stuck out of their holding brackets, but those wouldn't be needed for this delivery.

The truck would hold several cherry trees and half a dozen dogwoods, along with the maples. He'd promised this load to his mother at the family's other business location—Seaside Florist on Main Street in Birch Harbor. This time of year, his mother, who ran the shop, liked to show off the nursery's best spring flowering trees, especially as folks started to plan for the growing season.

Kason, Clay's older brother, the one who lived on the Garrisons' tree farm and nursery with his own family now, hauled a dogwood onto the truck bed. "Hey, Mom called. I let her know we were on the job."

Clay shoved leaves out of his face as he stood. "Thanks. I wonder why she didn't call me."

"Says you didn't answer."

Clay hopped off the truck's tailgate and tugged his cell from his pocket. Oh, he'd set it on silent. He made the adjustment.

Kason jumped from the back of the truck and hooked a thumb toward the greenhouse. "I don't think he's trying to be mean."

Clay glanced toward the sky. Kason would never understand. "Sure. Listen, you wanna run this load to Mom, and I'll get that first order out?" Maybe that would appease Dad for a minute.

"He didn't even find that order on the workbench until this morning. Then I heard him muttering and limping through the barn, looking for you." Kason's expression said he didn't agree with their father's actions. "You could call him on it."

Clay snorted. "Great idea."

"Okay, fine, but just so you know—I hate it. I wish I could solve all this tension between you two." Kason rubbed the back of his neck, peering toward the greenhouse and barn, then back. "He's getting forgetful. No one has the courage to bring it up."

Clay wasn't a doctor. He knew Dad's injury affected his mood. Did his age affect his memory? Supporting his father in all the ways he could wasn't good enough. He'd work here until he got his own landscaping business off the ground, then he'd walk away and cheer Kason and the family on in other ways. And he'd always help Mom. But nothing was good enough for Dad.

Once he could afford to, he'd move out of his parents' garage apartment. Maybe then Dad would chill. At least Clay wouldn't be around for his moods.

"I can run that order in my truck," Kason said. "They only wanted three trees. You go see Mom. She specifically asked to talk to you today." Kason grinned like an idiot. "I have no idea why."

Clay punched his brother's arm, rolling his eyes. "You told her. Thanks a lot."

"Nah, I didn't have to." He rubbed his bicep. "The whole town is talking."

Great.

"Or, at least those who knew." Kason wagged his head. "I can't believe she's back. After all these years."

"She isn't *back*. She appeared at one midweek service. That doesn't mean she's back."

"She was the redhead from high school, right? Beautiful."

"Watch it, or I'll tell your wife."

Kason affected an innocent pose. "Brynn knows I only have eyes for her." They hiked back into the huge greenhouse where a sizable cluster of potted trees waited. No customers wandered nearby. "I still don't know why you broke up."

"Long story." Long, painful story full of idiotic choices Clay would *not* divulge to his older brother. No one knew. Especially not Dad. He already disapproved of Clay—no need to add reasons for his hostility.

Kason squatted and hugged a twenty-five-gallon potted maple. Standing, he pivoted and dropped it on a nearby rolling cart. "Mom is going to try to drag it out of you."

No doubt. Yeah, he couldn't wait to get over there and see her.

Clay finished loading the truck for the florist's shop and climbed aboard. He'd better face her and get it over with. Wasn't a big deal. Liberty would never move back to Birch Harbor. Not with everything that had happened.

A wind gust tipped Liberty's camper toward the left, and she braced herself, bending her knees with the motion. Was this what an earthquake felt like—this shaking? A quick peek through the small window over the kitchen sink showed the other campers in the mobile-home/RV park also swayed with the next gust. She sipped her mug of hot water and wished the heater worked better in here. Her travel trailer was built for summer trips, complete with romantic images of opened windows and balmy breezes. No thought toward surviving a blustery March windstorm in Western Washington.

The park's monthly fees would double at the first of April. A notice arrived the day after her bosses announced their retirement in February. They'd been excited to show her pictures of the new home they'd purchased on Whidbey, which would put them closer to their youngest son and his wife.

Last night when Gloria had called again, she'd mentioned a couple of job possibilities in Birch Harbor that Liberty could interview for if she was local by Monday. That gave her a few days to finalize the move and have her camper hauled up north. *If* she moved. But if not, how could she afford to stay here?

Another gust shook her home, and Liberty counted to ten before the force quieted down. Dotted throughout the RV park were several towering and scraggly pine trees. Who knew how they'd held up this long.

Shivering, she examined the small space. If the wind would let up, the trailer wouldn't feel so cold.

This place was all she'd been able to afford for housing. And it'd been home for a while now. The plastic countertops and wedged-in table were marred. The front end housed two small, stacked bunks, but she didn't use them because it felt like sleeping in a coffin, since the trailer curved and provided almost no headroom. She'd chosen to dismantle the table at this end and sleep on the bed it converted into. The kitchen filled one wall, and the bathroom—a toilet/shower combination—was snug against the parallel wall. She had everything she needed in here, except room to stretch out. And adequate heat.

Her pay-as-you-go phone vibrated on the scratched tabletop with a text, and Shea's face appeared.

Have you decided what to do? Because, I found someone for your move—me. ☺ And Liam. My boyfriend has a truck. Please let us help you.

The storm threw something at the camper, and it cracked against the outside wall. In past years, knowing the Archers lived on Bainbridge helped her feel less alone. Now they were gone and loneliness hovered, smothering her.

Maybe it was time for a change.

I've decided to move, she texted Shea back. Are you still free Saturday? I'll make a reservation for the ferry.

The reply was almost instant. Great! I'll ride with you if you want.

Thank you. See you around 8:30?

We'll be there.

Had she actually committed to moving back? The town was big enough that she could avoid the Garrison family, right?

Here's hoping.

She dialed Gloria's number and gave her the news.

"That's wonderful! Are you sure you must bring your camper? I understand it's been your home, but it'll be cold here on the bluff with the March winds. Let us host you. We can help sell the camper, if you want."

Liberty surveyed her space once again. She'd need a few boxes to pack up her dishes and belongings so they didn't bang around all the way to the other island. "As tempted as I am, Gloria, I need my independence." Keeping her distance protected her.

"Well, I'm happy you're on your way. I'm destined to worry about you, dear. And you know what my Roy will think."

Roy was a warm, teddy bear-type father figure, and suddenly Liberty looked forward to seeing them again. She might need caring people in her daily life after all.

"We'll gather a crew to help. What time will you arrive? Oh, I can't wait!"

"My friends and I will catch the late morning ferry." Providing the service could take her reservation, and they had room for a truck and travel trailer on board. "Can I call you from the boat?" Then she could give a better estimate.

"Sounds perfect. And I won't take no for an answer—I'm feeding you and your friends. I'll make homemade beef stew and my famous butter rolls. Perfect March comfort food."

The homey image wrapped itself like a ribbon around Liberty's heart, awakening a longing she'd almost given up on. Family. Home. Love. Maybe even peace.

CHAPTER FOUR

He should have known Mom wouldn't let things rest. After parking outside Seaside Florist's front entrance, Clay shoved his arms into the red and black flannel shirt he'd found in the truck's passenger seat. His T-shirt wouldn't stand up against this wind. A gust howled, bullying his truck. Time to face Mom.

He yanked the handle on his door and climbed out. The small businesses along Main Street lined up, welcoming customers with promises of coffee, pastries, books, art, and here, flowers and gifts. He'd begin his visit by positioning the trees the way she liked—flanking rows on either side of the walk leading up to the shop's entrance.

As he lifted the second tree off the truck bed, the bells on the door jingled behind him and Clay braced himself. Mom would give him an earful, pepper him with questions.

"Oh, Clay, I didn't know you'd be here today."

He didn't have to turn to place that voice. Jill O'Connell. Single and persistent. She craved attention and did workouts in the town's only gym. She was all about organic produce and juicing and chasing Clay. She kept up a good rapport with his mom, no doubt trying to get an invite to family functions.

"Do you need help with that?" she asked behind him when he didn't answer.

He grunted, setting the tree down three feet from the last one. "No, thanks." As if she would willingly get muddy. He straightened and faced her. "Hi, Jill." She wore skin-tight workout clothes and carried a green juice concoction as if she wanted people to see her with it. She eyed him up and down, and he barely kept from cringing. "Appreciate the offer. Have a good day." He marched back toward the truck. *Lord, give me patience.*

She moved closer to his vehicle. "I was just in talking with Elizabeth." Jill referred to his mother. "She mentioned searching for an assistant in the shop. You know I'd take the job if I wasn't already booked with classes at the gym."

Thank You for that, Clay prayed, his thoughts sincere. The last thing he needed was Jill popping out of the shop every time he made a delivery. "I'm sure she'll find someone. Don't worry about it." Why wasn't Jill taking the hint and taking off?

He lugged the next tree to the tailgate, wishing she'd move toward the bookstore so he could jump down and not be face-to-face with her. "I don't want to keep you."

"Good point." From somewhere she produced a cell phone and checked the screen. "Oops, gotta run. See ya later, Clay. Don't work too hard." She gave a flirty wink and strode away. He averted his eyes from all that she hadn't left to the imagination.

He'd rather see his mom. In fact, he'd rather face almost anything than have to chat with Jill again.

He'd just dropped the eighth tree into place and was shifting it to align it with the others when his mother appeared and opened the glass front door. "Come in when you're finished, Son. There's something we need to discuss."

Fantastic.

His phone buzzed. A text from Gabe Patrick, the music pastor at King Church.

New residents asked us to help their tenant move in tomorrow. Are you free midday for a couple of hours?

It wasn't his turn to cover the sales counter at the nursery, and he could handle his landscaping client first thing. Why not carry boxes for someone after that?

He texted back: Sure. Where?

Archer property on the bluff. I can't be there. Really appreciate it Clay!

Sure thing.

Clay hefted another tree into place. He was always looking for landscaping clients. If the Archers had moved into the house he was picturing, they could use yard work in the front and back. The previous owners were snowbirds and hadn't been here since October when they left for Arizona. They'd dropped back in for the closing, probably, but last he'd seen, hadn't touched the yard.

After unloading the final tree, Clay tugged open the front door of his mom's shop, gut tightening with apprehension. Bells signaled his arrival. Mom had the space decorated rather feminine, which probably appealed to her usual customers. Though, men did come in to buy bouquets for their girlfriends or wives. The dim lighting and glistening surfaces with shiny vases and floral arrangements were almost too much for him visually. Yeah, he'd stick to the greenhouse and farm. Or people's yards where he could work in the dirt and upgrade their curb appeal—make things better than when he'd arrived.

But for an unknown reason the space brought Libby to mind. Back when they were teens, she'd get stars in her eyes whenever they visited this shop, declaring aloud how she'd be surrounded in beauty one day.

Had she kept that promise to herself? He hoped so, but since she wouldn't be waiting inside with Mom, none of his daydreams mattered.

"Son." Mom waved him over to her spot near the counter. He scanned for customers. If he was about to get the third degree, he didn't need an audience. At least Jill had left. "Cecelia's in the gift section. She was hoping you'd drop by."

Cecelia. Young, blonde, single, recently returned from a cooking program in France. Like Jill—after him. "Then let's hurry this along."

Mom gave him a mock glare. "You can't help that you're so attractive. And available."

He crossed his arms and peered down at his mother, affection and irritation at war inside. *She* could help by not encouraging them. "What's up, Mom?"

She led him into the back room. "I can keep an eye on things from here." She fussed with her apron strings until she'd retied them. "Tell me about church last Thursday night."

Her goal was obvious, but he didn't want to cooperate. So, he'd not quite answer what she wasn't quite asking. "Great worship set. Small crowd of people, nothing like Sunday morning services." He knew where this was headed, but why give her anything she didn't already have? "Why?" He fiddled with an owl figurine on the cluttered counter. The white porcelain creature had lost an ear.

"Anyone specific drop in? Someone you haven't seen in a while?"

He quirked his mouth. "Like…?"

She scowled at him, though with humor in her eyes. "You know who I mean, and I don't appreciate these games. Everyone's talking about it. Now, what are you going to do about it?"

"About what?"

She puffed out a breath and perched her hands on her not-so-slim hips. "She's back, Clay."

He dropped the pretense and returned the figurine to the granite counter. "No, she's not." That thought both let him off the hook *and* dug a hole in his gut. But it was better that she had vanished again. One look at him, and she'd bolted off this island. That was for the best. "Have you seen her around town?"

"Actually, I haven't." Mom's brow scrunched. "You sincerely don't think she's back?"

He knew she wasn't. Maybe he'd humor his mom, play one more game. "If she were, I'd have invited her for dinner, you know that. Brought her right over to see you and Dad. Picked up a dozen of your roses to give her." Of course, he wouldn't do any of that. "In fact, I tried to talk to her at the service, but she had to leave." That part was true.

One eyebrow climbed toward Mom's dyed brown hair. "You're saying if you had another chance to see her, you'd make the most of it?"

"Yes." *Um, Lord, I might be in over my head here.* Except, if she ever gave him five minutes he would make the most of those, with sincere apologies.

The sooner he finished up with Mom's questions, the sooner he could leave.

Mom grabbed a paper towel and wiped down the workbench counter, gathering bits of baby's breath and chunks of foam into a pile. "I never did hear why you two broke up, but I always liked her.

And I didn't like how her guardians treated her at the end. I heard they kicked her out, though I never knew why." She tsked and frowned.

Cecelia passed the door leading to the rest of the shop, and Mom gave Clay a knowing look. Maybe he could buy himself space. "You know that's why I haven't dated much since, right?" Minus those few years where Mom tried setting him up repeatedly, not that she'd completely stopped.

"What do you mean?"

If pretending he pined for Libby, which wasn't quite pretending, caused Mom to back off, then his slight deception might be worth it. "Because I still have feelings for her." He realized his words weren't entirely untrue. *Oh, Lord, I think I'm going to regret that.*

Mom's hand came to rest on his flannel-clad arm. "Honestly? After ten years?"

He tipped his face down, not wanting to meet her eyes. Yeah, it was rather pathetic, wasn't it? He managed a nod and blinked to himself. How much of this was real and how much was a show? Even he didn't know. "I need to get going. I'm sure Dad has a million orders waiting."

She seemed thoughtful. "Of course, of course." She led the way to the door. "I'll see you later."

Clay darted toward the front while his mom ran interference for him, catching Cecelia as she called out to him. "Cecelia, hon," Mom said in a syrupy voice. "I wanted to show you something back along the gift wall."

In his truck, Clay pulled out onto the street and made for the farm. His conscience tapped a Morse code message he couldn't quite interpret. At the four-way stop, he replayed the conversation with his mom.

I only wanted a break from the constant matchmaking, Lord. I hope I didn't...

Did God sit in heaven, on a huge throne, and condemn him for trying to outwit his mother with a little game? Dad's face came to mind. Disapproval and anger and resentment, as if he'd never forgive Clay for the accident. As if he didn't even love him.

Clay knew God wasn't like that—condemning and angry. Still, he didn't have a license to sin. *If I blew it, I'm sorry.* Hopefully, Mom would now convince Cecelia, Jill, and anyone else who might be after him to let him be. It wasn't as if Clay gave them the wrong impression. He'd never encouraged their attention.

He made the last turn toward the farm, bracing himself to see his father in a few minutes.

The more he thought about it, picturing beautiful Libby, the more those old thoughts stirred up. He had never gotten over her. What he hadn't meant to do during their conversation was entrust Mom with his secret.

Heaven help him if Mom ever had a chance to use that information against him.

After three hours of traveling, including a rough ferry ride, and conversation with Shea, who sat beside her, Liberty pulled her car onto the Archers' property. A few vehicles were parked out of the way. Liam, behind them in his truck hauling Liberty's travel trailer, turned down the long driveway next, her camper bouncing behind him. She hoped it had fared well. Winds pushed banks of clouds in from Puget Sound and decorated the gray water with whitecaps. Just a bit north of Fort Ebey State Park, the view here missed the snow-capped Olympic Mountains in their majestic display because the Archers' property faced northwest, rather than southwest.

But what a view. In the distance you could make out a tiny, flat plateau of land known as Smith Island, and beyond that only water—the Strait of Juan de Fuca, which flowed out to the Pacific. Liberty had studied a map and knew Vancouver Island sat northwest of here, but it wasn't visible, given the vast distance.

In the neighboring lot, a towering bank of trees to the southwest leaned in the winds, and Liberty wondered again about her decision to not take the Archers up on their offer to sell her trailer and move into the house. A couple of trees posed a closer threat. Keeping her camper would allow her a quick, clean exit. This location was temporary. She'd make the camper work.

"What a picturesque setting," Shea said, her eyes bright.

"It reminds me of Bainbridge in many ways." Through her rear-view mirror, Liberty watched Liam park in the driveway, then she glanced around. The Archers' new property lay along the west side of the island, directly west of Birch Harbor, which occupied the eastern side of this narrow stretch of Whidbey. Here, along the coast, the large ranch-style house stretched in a square on a single level, with plenty of land to spare. The long driveway ended in a circle drive in front of a two-car garage. A branch of the driveway led to the RV pad between the main house and the woods in the vacant lot next door.

Roy emerged from the garage, smiling big in Liberty's direction before heading off toward Liam's truck. Together, the men could get her camper into place.

A timid and fragile sense of peace stirred in her heart upon seeing Roy's familiar face. She'd gotten used to her independence, but for the next little while, she wouldn't have to be so alone. She climbed from the car, Shea doing the same. Mist washed toward them on the wind. "I can't tell you how grateful I am," she told her friend, "that you and Liam would do this for me."

Shea walked around and put a hand on Liberty's arm. "We're happy to help."

Liberty gave her an answering smile. "Gloria must have called in a whole crowd." All they needed to do was back the camper into its new spot, level it, and ensure it wouldn't roll. They wouldn't need a mob to do that. Her attention landed on a landscaping truck... wait. A rig marked Seaside Greenhouse and Nursery withstood the next salty wind gust with barely a shudder. "Uh-oh."

There was no way the Archers knew the Garrisons, right? They'd only been here, what? A few weeks?

Shea followed her gaze and then zeroed back in. "What's wrong?"

Liberty fiddled with her bag. *Clay cannot be here.* "Gloria mentioned inviting a few folks over, but not the Garrisons."

"Deep breaths." Shea pointed. "Is that their truck?"

"Uh-huh." Her head ached. How would she avoid him if he'd come to welcome her home? His dad or brother could have used the truck to get here. *Please let that be it.*

"What if it's not Clay? Maybe it's someone else—hired help?"

Flashbacks hit her of that logo in the background as Clay unloaded potted blue spruce for the living Christmas tree lot. His dad, Jonathan, his siblings, Kason and Kourtney, even his mother, Elizabeth, all helping. Candy canes. Cocoa. Stolen kisses.

"I can't see him," she whispered. "I don't know what I'd say."

Shea moved in front of her, stealing her focus. "Listen. You've got this. You're not a teen anymore. You're a grown woman who has taken on the world and *won.* You're a survivor, even when everyone abandoned you. I believe in you. If, or when, you have to see him, you'll do great."

If only Liberty believed in herself like Shea did. "I'm not so sure."

"I am. Even if he is here, you wouldn't have to rehash the past today."

She tried to shake off the stress and think of a way to lighten her mood. "Let's go watch them back in the trailer. After that it's homemade beef stew for us." Which meant going inside. Thankfully she wouldn't have to face this alone.

Liberty hugged her jacket around her. The temps were probably mid-fifties, but the wind burrowed right through her jeans and raincoat.

Roy's short white hair stood on end as he directed Liam. Soon, they had the trailer parked. The camper didn't look any worse for wear. Neither did the heap in the back of Liam's truck. He'd tied the boxes down with bungee cords and a tarp.

"You seem cold, Liberty," Roy called from behind the trailer. He nodded at Shea. "Welcome. Why don't you ladies go into the house and warm up? We'll take care of this."

Liberty would rather not skip off when she could help, but Shea's shivering alerted her protective side. "Thank you," she told

Roy before waving at Liam, who gave her a salute from the cab of his truck. He was the perfect match for Shea. They seemed mutually honoring, and the looks they gave each other? Full of trust. Adoration. Love.

Shea linked arms with her. "Let's go. You can introduce me to your other benefactor."

"And she can introduce us to whomever she's invited over here today." Liberty pasted on a smile en route to the house as Gloria's face became visible through the kitchen window. She smiled from the sink, standing next to...was that Clay's mother? Liberty hadn't seen Elizabeth in a decade, though she remembered a kind, jolly woman. This was going to be fine. Her shoulders relaxed.

Slowing their pace, Liberty scanned the other windows left uncovered to let in the view. And there he was.

Clay stood near the dining room table, holding a mug. The unconcealed look of tenderness in his gaze made Liberty's heart thump. She hadn't seen that expression aimed in her direction perhaps ever. And coming from Clay? There was something different about it. Gone was the thinly veiled selfishness of his youth where he sometimes looked at her as prey. She'd label it lust now. Sure, he could be warm back then. But most often, he was in their relationship for his own benefit. And she'd only wanted someone to care for her. Especially after her parents died.

She pushed those thoughts away, collecting herself. She'd face this with courage. No one was asking her to divulge her secrets right now. Clay never needed to know everything.

"You can do this," Shea whispered to Liberty as they stepped into the kitchen.

"C'mon in!" Gloria called. "Come say hi to the Garrison family."

CHAPTER FIVE

Clay had been watching through the window since her muddy white Corolla first pulled in. *Libby.* He didn't need to grip this mug like he was cold, not with his palms sweating. But his throat was dry and sipping the coffee helped. She'd tied her red hair back in a ponytail, but the wind whipped the long strands around her face. Her black jacket hugged her trim figure over dark skinny jeans and black boots. Studying her as she chatted with her friend sent a sliver into his chest. A shiver went through him.

He'd been warned, but he still couldn't believe it. When the truck and trailer pulled in behind the Corolla, he knew he was in trouble. Pastor Gabe had asked Clay to be here to help someone move in. And the Archers, learning about his landscaping side job, had invited him to scope out the property and consider coming up with a redesign. He'd spent a couple of hours walking the yard. Then they'd invited him to lunch while they awaited the new tenant. His mom had driven out, leaving her shop in Brynn's capable hands.

Then Gloria had let them both in on the secret—the name of their new resident. Roy had asked Clay to stick around and warm up after tramping all over the huge, windy lot for two hours. There were still ideas to discuss, after a hearty bowl of beef stew.

Libby stepped inside and greeted Gloria, the newcomer to their little town, and their hostess, as Mom gave Clay a pointed look. *Get over here and say hi.*

He tried to control his pounding heart. Liberty. *Living* here. Back in Birch Harbor. Looking for work, according to Gloria. Staying.

The word wouldn't land, wouldn't process. He'd used Libby's name to call off the female pursuits, and his mom had been cooperative. Judging by the knowing look Mom currently shot his way, she was more on board than ever. Clay could consider himself trapped.

Mom greeted Libby with too much excitement, her voice too bright. She'd send the poor woman running back to her car if she didn't ease up. She must have gotten the hint from Clay's gestures, because she quieted down, backed toward the kitchen counter, gave Libby space.

Liberty's attention landed anywhere but on him. She introduced her friend—Shea—to Gloria and Clay's mother. Shea gushed about the granite countertops and gleaming hardwoods, the views, wide open spaces, and the ceiling's long planks painted in off-white. A gorgeous home, he had to agree.

Why wouldn't Libby look at him? She'd seen him through the windows, because they'd locked eyes. The sight of her finding him there, catching her breath, made his lungs lock up. She looked amazing, her red hair dancing in the wind behind her. A little frightened and pale. Vulnerable. He wanted to go hold her and reassure her. Calm those fears.

"You remember Clay," Mom said, pointing, as if Libby could ever forget.

Would Mom get the hint if Clay growled? Not that he would.

Libby was headed this way, her friend attached to her with linked arms. His hands sweated so badly he had to set the mug down before he spilled coffee on the immaculate floors.

She nodded at him. "Clay."

"Hi." His voice came out low.

"This is Shea Brown. Shea, this is Clay Garrison."

Clay endured Shea sizing him up. She didn't seem to evaluate him like the single women around town, but more as if judging whether he was fit to be near her friend. Protective. Did she know their history?

"Good to meet you." Shea stepped back. "The only other newcomer is my boyfriend, Liam. He's out working on leveling the trailer."

"Oh, that reminds me. I heard the new tenant"—he smiled in Libby's direction—"was bringing a camper. I have some easy leveling gizmos in my truck, complete with chocks. I'll run them out to Roy and Liam."

He made for the kitchen door. Outside, he dashed over and pulled the camper levelers and tire chocks from his truck's bed. He'd also brought a bubble level, in case they needed it.

On the RV pad, Liam and Roy were repeatedly driving the camper forward, then back. Measuring, eyeballing. They'd been at it for a while already. These tools should help.

He met up with the guys, introduced himself to Liam, and showed them the tools. Crouching on one side of the trailer and then the other, he positioned the levelers. The chocks would follow, once they got it right. He'd be vigilant about this job for anyone, but extra careful since it involved Libby.

This time around, he'd protect her. She seemed guarded, but strong. Not today, but he'd watch for a chance to apologize. No rush now that she was moving back. Then he'd try to ignore the fact that no one else had ever measured up to her. And she was living a few miles from him.

Mud splattered the old trailer. Was this all the housing she could afford? Clay searched the yard for the hose. Even clean, those rusty spots weren't going anywhere. The camper was dingy and aging fast, with worn out tires.

Roy gave Liam a thumbs-up, and Liam put his truck in Park and turned off the engine. Clay went around and placed the chocks under the levelers so the camper wouldn't roll. Roy disappeared inside and operated the slide out, expanding the living space. Then he reappeared.

Clay joined Roy while Liam unhooked bungee cords in the cab of the truck. "Hey, Dr. Archer," Clay said, coming up alongside the older man. The orthodontist reminded him of his father, only with a kind way about him. Roy was a bit older. "Thanks for hosting Liberty."

"Thank you for bringing those newfangled gadgets. Big help." Roy's blue eyes glinted as if he knew how to enjoy life, but then his expression sobered. "I wish we could've convinced her to move indoors. But she wouldn't have it. Says she must stay out here, remain independent. But honestly, I'm hoping she'll change her mind. This bluff is rather windy."

She hadn't seemed independent in their teen years. Perhaps living on her own had changed this part of her too. Who could change her mind now? "Let's wash this down before we unload the truck."

"Good plan." Roy pointed toward the hose mounted on the side of the garage, and Clay headed over.

Once the camper stood dripping, Roy strode to the truck bed. "Shall we?"

Liam nodded toward the house. "She may want to be here for that." He moved to the hitch. "I'll work on this."

"I'll lower the stairs," Roy said. "Why don't you go fetch our guest?"

"Sure." Like when they were teens, Clay still felt drawn to her. They had a shared history. But this new dynamic of not knowing the other person as each of them were today... this would take getting used to.

In the kitchen, he found her ladling drops of soup into a small bowl. Is that all she planned to eat? "Hey," he kept his voice quiet, so he didn't startle her. "We're ready to move your boxes into the camper. Want to join us?"

She set her dish on the counter and let her gaze bounce off him. "Yeah."

Shea stood from the table. "I'll come too."

"Your soup will get cold. Can't it wait?" Gloria asked them.

"It won't take long," Libby said, as if she wasn't in a rush to eat, though it was well past lunchtime and she looked like she could use the calories.

Clay held the door, and they preceded him out to the trailer. Roy worked on the hookups—water, power, whatever else. Liam had already disconnected his truck and pulled forward. He held a box in his hands. From Clay's approach, he could see about six or eight more.

"Can you grab that other large box, Clay?" Liam tipped his head toward the pile. "It's heavy."

"Sure thing." Glad for his height, he reached in over the side and gripped the box, grunting. Meanwhile, Shea worked inside while Libby returned. After loading up her arms, she passed him without a word. When she approached the door at the same time as he did, he stepped back, letting her go first. She reappeared half a second later, sans her box, and darted down the three steps past him as if he didn't exist.

Cold shoulder. Brush off. No indication they'd ever been more than enemies.

"Mind setting that on the table?" she called to him.

"You got it," he said, but she was already back at the truck. Once inside, his guess was confirmed—tight space with dinged surfaces. The slide out held the kitchenette—a sink, two-burner stove top, mini-fridge, and tiny oven. He toted the box to the table. That door on the left must be the minuscule bathroom.

Daylight came through the only window he could see. Claustrophobia would hound him living in here. No artwork or even interesting paint colors brightened the space, as if the Libby he'd once known didn't have room for that anymore, or didn't care. She'd once enjoyed an artsy day of visiting galleries in the touristy towns on the island, like Langley. How long had she lived like this?

Stepping out of his way, Shea gave him a face—part pity, part concern. She knew their story, didn't she? From her expression, she didn't necessarily agree with how Libby was handling this, but she also wasn't going to say anything. He could respect that. And he could give her space.

Minutes later, the small crew had transferred the boxes, and Roy appeared at the open door. "Great work, everyone. Lunchtime. Let's go eat."

The younger crowd made their way into the mudroom off the garage entrance and stripped off damp shoes and coats. The aroma of rich beef stew got to Clay this time. They found sinks—either in the main bathroom or mudroom—and washed their hands.

"I've warmed yours up, ladies," Gloria said from the stove. "Don't forget about the butter rolls. I've got homemade peach, strawberry, or blueberry jam. Help yourself."

Clay noticed Gloria had given Libby a large bowl with a healthy serving. He wanted to high-five her, but instead he silently thanked her for watching out for Liberty.

Reappearing from the mudroom, Libby rubbed her hands as if applying hand lotion. Afterwards, she hung back while everyone filled plates and bowls and poured glasses of ice water. She made an attractive wallflower. Her sky-hued sweater deepened her blue-gray eyes. Mom nudged his arm and tugged him toward Libby's spot at the table. He gave her a look. *Easy does it, Mom.* Subtlety wasn't her forte, and suddenly he hoped they all made it through this forced lunch without embarrassing Libby.

In the kitchen, Roy offered to help Libby find what she needed. He treated her like a doting father would, and Clay silently cheered their interactions. She gazed up at Roy as if he *were* her caring father. But there was a hint of self-protection in her eyes. Clay couldn't blame her after what her guardians had done—how they'd abandoned her. Rejected her.

Gloria's homemade stew settled like a lead weight inside. He'd rejected her too. Covering his condemning thoughts, he shoveled in more food.

Roy escorted Libby to the large table, and she sat in the chair he pulled out for her, next to Clay. She brought her peach lotion scent with her, and Clay tried not to close his eyes with pleasure. He'd missed her. More than he knew until right now. But that fragrance took him right back to threading his fingers through hers and holding her hand to his face, breathing deeply.

"Okay, everyone. Welcome!" Roy said, standing near the table. "Liam and Shea, thank you for seeing that our Liberty got here safely." *Our Liberty.* Yeah, Clay liked Roy more and more. Libby nodded and smiled at her friends. "And Elizabeth, thanks for coming and helping in the kitchen. My wife has found a new best friend." The two women beamed at each other, and Clay sensed trouble brewing, especially since Mom was capable of so many shenanigans.

"And Clay. Thank you for bringing those levelers. They made all the difference for making sure Liberty's rig doesn't roll away."

Clay chuckled. "No problem." He gave Libby a quick glance, but she studied her stew.

"And, precious Liberty, welcome." Roy's voice cracked with obvious fondness. Clay didn't think Libby would lift her head, but she faced Roy, her eyes wet. She gave Roy a nod, but no words, and Clay felt himself sliding off an imaginary bluff.

"Now," Dr. Roy said, pulling out his own chair at the table and zeroing in on Clay, taking the attention off Libby. "I wanted to talk more about landscaping. We are going to need a few projects done around here, if the Seaside Greenhouse and Nursery can spare you. I'm looking forward to seeing the plans I saw you sketching."

Clay was about to answer when his mom took a deep breath and shifted in her seat.

"Oh, he's free to help as much as you need." Mom nodded repeatedly. "As much as you need."

CHAPTER SIX

Shea volunteered to help Liberty unpack, so while Liam, Clay, and the Archers wandered around the yard, the two women worked on getting Liberty settled in. She hadn't missed the contrast between her tiny, ugly trailer and the wide-open gleaming spaces of the Archers' home.

"You're rather quiet." Shea pulled pillows out of a bag. "How are you feeling?"

Regret still rode her over how she'd treated Clay today. She'd almost bumped this box out of his hands when he'd stood at the bottom of the steps, carrying it in for her, waiting for her. Giving her space. That glimpse of compassion on his face, in his green eyes—the way it hit her? Ugh.

She ripped off the packing tape and yanked the flaps open to see her wrapped dishes inside. "I wish it didn't bother me to be near him." She frowned. "I treated him like he wasn't even there, as if that's my default when I don't know what to do. How immature is that?" All these years, Liberty had told herself she was over her past. That she'd faced her history and taken down the monster, but obviously she wasn't as free as she'd thought. And as settled as their history had once seemed, she might not be able to relax until Clay knew the whole story and agreed to let things alone.

Shea was quiet a minute while she stacked linens on the table. "Are you angry with him?"

"Yeah." Sometimes. Or at least, she liked hiding behind that answer. He *had* played a large role in the toughest season of her life. "Remember the story of how things ended?"

"Of course." They shared a look. "I recommend facing that anger."

She stilled from unwrapping another plate. "Forgiveness?" Had she never forgiven him? Her anger said no. Then there was the question of whether he could forgive her.

Shea's expression told her that's exactly what she meant for Liberty to do. "Of course, no one can force you. But God can help you, if you let Him, if you ask Him."

"I don't…" Liberty stalled, stretching her back muscles. "I mean, it's so childish, but I don't want to."

"That's natural. You're protecting yourself."

The insight clicked, as so many of Shea's intuitions did. Like tumblers in a lock that opened her thoughts and explained her motives. "I cannot afford to get swept back into his life, to let him get close again. I can't." She gripped her hand into a fist, more convinced with each second. "I won't."

"So, don't. But carrying around the pain he caused you all those years ago isn't healthy."

She placed a second plate into the sole cupboard. She only had two plates and a few cups. The bottom of the heavy box housed bottles of cleaning supplies and other liquids, like her favorite peach-scented shampoo, which matched her lotion—a single luxury she'd never given up. She surveyed the space, crowded with the two of them in here at the same time. "It's cramped." She was going for humor, but her friend didn't laugh.

Shea seemed to hold back her first reaction before offering a calm response. "I think the Archers would be happy to have you as their guest at any time, if you decide to take them up on their offer." She placed the folded sheets in their hiding place under the bench seating. "They—we all—respect you for being independent, but it's okay to let people take care of you."

Let people take care of you. The phrase pushed a lump into Liberty's throat. She could feel the Archers' fondness for her whenever they were together. Roy took such good care of her. Gloria always looked out for her needs. They'd begged her to move into the house with them and avoid the spring storms.

A gust pushed in through the cracks, shaking the camper. "They braced this trailer, right?" Shea asked, looking alarmed as she rocked on her knees and rubbed her upper arms against the chill.

Liberty giggled at Shea's exaggerated expression. "Yes. Roy

wouldn't rest until he did." She patted the nearest cupboard. "We've weathered worse than this."

"Of course you have. And I'm glad you're holding on to your sense of humor." She set aside the final box. "Roy thinks highly of you. I enjoy seeing that."

Not that she deserved his esteem. That concept—she'd never been able to accept it. And it kept coming up.

Ever aware of her moods, Shea stepped closer, pulling Liberty into a side hug. "You deserve love and care and kindness. I'm so glad Gloria and Roy are in your life."

"Me too." Knowing they were near gave her peace of mind. But now that she lived here, how was she going to handle the past? Sure, she'd discussed her history during her counseling sessions, but she was still stuck. Living here meant no escape. She couldn't pretend it never happened. Not when Clay would be out in the yard with his crew day after day for *weeks*.

She needed a job. Immediately. Then she could earn money while being away from Clay's jobsite. Someday they'd have to deal with the past. But she wasn't in a rush to do it.

Chatting with his father had never been Clay's favorite activity. And asking for favors? *No thanks.*

Not that this was a favor, exactly. Roy and Gloria had big plans for their yard overlooking the Sound. He would enjoy working with them.

Sunlight glinted off the sea view this March morning. Standing in his kitchen—or rather his parents' garage apartment kitchen— he poured another mug of coffee, splashing it on the quartz countertop. Dad expected him over at the farm by eight. He probably should have braved the house last night, talked to his dad then. He could only hope Mom, who'd been so on board with Clay working for the Archers, had brought it up with Dad and that the fight Clay predicted—dreaded—wouldn't happen today.

He wouldn't ask for full-time, only a couple of hours a day, beginning in two weeks. That seemed reasonable to Clay, but who knew how Dad would take it.

Coffee in hand, he passed the fireplace and leather sofa and headed to the slider and the view. A half-round window let in lots of light, which always made Clay glad his bedroom was on the other side of the unit.

He liked living here and he'd hate to leave, but part of him was weary of living on his parents' property. Dad made Clay feel like a burden to them, though he paid rent and helped with yard work. He was twenty-seven. It was time he made enough to afford his own house. Working at the family farm meant sharing in the profits and losses, and certain years there were more losses than anything else. The rent wasn't as high as it'd be elsewhere. At this rate, with a pathetic balance in his savings account, he'd need several more projects, consistently, before he would have the needed funds.

As a child, Clay remembered great interactions with his father, but about the time Liberty left, and especially around the accident, Dad had grown cold toward Clay. He no longer seemed to trust him. Clay hadn't had the courage to ask what had changed. Part of him didn't want to know. What if, after Dad told him, Clay couldn't fix it?

But for a chance to see Liberty often and possibly invite her out and finally apologize—that motivated him. He'd face his dad and a host of dragons to make it up to Libby. Whatever it took. Now that she was back, he should rehearse what he'd say if she ever gave him a few minutes of her time.

As he came up on the farm, the landscape filled with rows and rows of trees. There were acres of firs and pines back there, ready for Christmas. But this time of year, everyone focused on replanting their gardens. Clay had spent hours walking the greenhouse with customers and answering questions like, "Do hydrangeas grow well in the shade?" and "Can I buy a lilac bush that will bloom more than once a year?"

Clay's plan was to offer to find a part-time replacement who could cover several of his hours. That way Dad wouldn't have to take on all the visitors alone, while limping. Kason was often busy in the acreage, and Brynn chased their preschoolers while also keeping the company's books. They could try again to convince Dad to use his motorized wheelchair. He hated that thing, said the scraps of plants on the greenhouse floor got tangled in the wheels. Not to mention how the uneven floor slowed him down.

A familiar weight settled deeper inside Clay. Seeing Dad meant facing his other biggest regret.

"Clay!" Dad was already in a mood when Clay jumped out of his truck. Great. He locked the driver's door and counted to five while he turned. *Patience, Lord, please.* Dad stood in the doorway to the barn, leaning heavily on his cane.

"I thought we said eight," Dad growled.

The truck's digital clock read 7:57 when he pulled up. But to Dad, eight meant 7:45. Always had. Clay worked his jaw. He wouldn't point it out. "I need to talk to you."

Dad had already swung around and limped back into the barn. Clay followed. The greenhouse opened in half an hour.

"Your mother wants a delivery of five more vine maples and several daffodil flats," Dad said over his shoulder, pointing at the rows of plants. "We've got six new orders, and Kason blew a tire on the truck, so he's off getting that replaced." He stopped at the bench where an old desktop computer sputtered along, gathering emails, and an inkjet printer spit out pages. "You'll just have to run the deliveries out in your pickup."

"Dad, I need to talk to you." Clay tried again. It didn't look like Mom had found time yet to pitch Clay's new gig at Dad. Or was that why he seemed so ticked?

Leaning against the long table, Dad fisted a stack of paper. "Start with the Wilsons. They're farthest away. Work your way back."

"Dad."

He finally looked up. "What?" He seemed older lately. His white hair was shorter, as if Mom had talked him into a haircut. His pale gray eyes seemed less bright every time Clay saw him. His shoulders were more hunched than usual. Was he in that much pain these days? "C'mon, get on with it." His growl could wither the seedlings in the nursery.

"Did Mom mention the Archers' request? They're the new residents off Beachside Road. They live about two miles north of us."

Dad's expression hardened. "No. What request?"

"Our church asked us to volunteer out at the new neighbors' house Saturday. They have booked me to do landscaping for them. I'd like to hire someone part-time here to help you. And then I could spend a couple of hours a day out there." Clay braced himself, because in three... two... one—

"We can't afford to hire anybody. You've seen the books." Dad huffed. "You are not doing some harebrained landscaping thing during business hours. Now go load the truck."

Clay grunted before he could catch it, and Dad raised himself to full height. "You wanna say something? Say it."

"I wish I knew why you—" He bit his tongue to keep ugly words from leaking out. "Why you're so angry with me."

"Did you even think what your little agreement with these new residents was going to do to the family business?" Dad shook his head. "So like you."

His words wounded, and Clay tried not to wince. As much as he wanted to leave the accusation with his father and not ingest it, the words snuck into his mind and influenced his identity. Even this long after the accident.

"Of course I thought this through." Dad was never easily pleased, and he poked at Clay's last nerve, clouding his judgment. "I'll search for the replacement myself. I know a few teens at church who'd like a part-time job."

"No promises we can afford anyone else, unless you find someone who'll work for cheap. Until then, you'll give us eight hours a day." Dad thrust the order pages toward Clay. Then he stalked off, limping and mumbling.

Since the sun set around seven now, Clay wouldn't have much time after work, but he could go over tonight and finalize the plans he'd drawn up.

Would Liberty be there?

CHAPTER SEVEN

It was probably normal, in Liberty's situation, to study every redheaded girl she saw and wonder. Shea would say her behavior made sense. Now that Liberty had moved back into the area where it all happened, she felt closer than ever to her daughter. Of course, the little girl might not even live here now.

Liberty climbed into her scuffed Corolla and tucked the business cards into her purse before throwing her bag into the passenger seat. Not one medical office in Birch Harbor was hiring. She'd been to six clinics. A few office administrators mentioned that Gloria had called ahead and tried to find a position for her, but none had an opening. She'd rather not work in retail, but she might have to take anything so she could cover her utilities. The Archers wouldn't accept rent payments, but Liberty was determined to at least pay for her electricity and water.

The stores along Main Street seemed to shout at her as she drove by. Perhaps it was time to check for jobs there. Bookstores. Pastry and coffee shops. An art gallery. And the Garrisons' florist shop—Seaside Florist—still sitting where it'd always been. Glimmering vases under soft lighting decorated the shelves against the windows. Beauty. She slowed her car. A Help Wanted sign clung to the glass door.

She sped past. Work there? No thanks. Elizabeth was kind and cheerful, but she came with Clay. Jonathan and Elizabeth had been like second parents during Liberty's teen years, welcoming her into their home, encouraging her relationship with their son. There would probably always be a connection.

At lunch on moving day, Elizabeth spoke of their oldest son's kids. Liberty remembered Clay's brother Kason. In the last decade, he'd gotten married and now had two children—Mitchell and Muriel, according to Clay's mom. She gushed about her grandchildren. Did she know she had another grandchild, a girl who was several years older than Kason's kids? A redhead who, Liberty hoped, still looked like her?

Someone Liberty missed every day.

Help wanted. Why hadn't Elizabeth mentioned the position when Gloria talked about Liberty's job hunt? Maybe she thought it'd be awkward. No question. Especially if Clay made regular deliveries.

Whether Liberty worked at Seaside or not, how long could she avoid Clay? Should she? He knew about her pregnancy, and that she'd moved back to town without a child, so he must have a list of questions. Now that she'd seen him acting mature and kind, serving at his church, he seemed more deserving of learning the truth. Less of a threat to her secrets.

She pulled into the Archers' driveway and headed straight down the branch that ended at her camper. Knowing how much Liberty loved flowers, would Shea recommend Liberty try for the florist's position. How would they avoid the past?

She saw no sign of Clay or his truck on the property. Wasn't he supposed to start working here soon? She hadn't seen him—not that she'd spent every day pining away in her camper, twiddling her thumbs. Her vehicle was warm, so she'd been happy to travel around town, job hunting.

Roy met her in the driveway as she climbed from her car. "Come on over to the house, if you have a minute. Gloria and I have something to chat with you about." His warm, welcoming smile contributed to the overall impression he gave of being a teddy bear. She couldn't resist his invitation.

"I'll be right over." She'd stow her bag in her camper, then join them.

In the big house, Gloria and Roy stood near the dining table, each of their place settings sporting a beverage. "Help yourself to something to drink," Gloria said. "We've also got snacks here."

The picture windows framed the view. Sunlight glinted off the Sound like a million diamonds on a bed of blue. This time of year, you could catch a glimpse of clear sky. She'd seen rainbows over the Salish Sea this week when the sun hit the drops just right. If she looked for it, she might find symbolism there, or even hope.

A platter of cheese, crackers, grapes, rolled turkey lunch meat, and cashews sat in the middle of the table. Liberty's stomach growled. She hadn't been eating as regularly over the last few weeks; her mind was too preoccupied. Her clothes fit a bit looser—a reminder of her need to get back to a normal daily routine.

The kitchen was warm with the scent of Earl Grey tea and a hint of apple cinnamon as well. She joined them at the table, tea mug in hand, and let herself relax. Life in the lonely camper was cold, with plenty of emptiness for her memories to haunt her. The Archers' home was inviting and warm, not at all hostile. Here she could push off her doubtful, lonely thoughts. Here she could pretend she had family.

"How goes the job hunt?" Roy made himself comfortable across from her.

"Nothing yet." She tugged the teabag from her mug. The aroma of cinnamon rose on the steam. Though Puget Sound filled the forward view through all the windows on the west side of the house, Liberty's camper was visible to the left, with its backdrop of towering firs. The monstrosity didn't fit. It was almost laughable. She pointed toward her house-on-wheels. "Something's marring your view."

Wearing a grin, Roy peered over. "Perhaps, but we love the woman who lives there. Doesn't matter what the outside looks like. Though a For Sale sign might make it look even better." He winked.

She chuckled. "You could be right. But I think I'll hang on to it for now."

"Fair enough." Roy gave her a decisive nod. "But there are signs in the garage if you change your mind."

"Ha! You're prepared."

He gave her a wink.

"Have a snack." Gloria gestured toward the platter. She layered crackers and cheese onto her own plate, and Roy joined her.

Liberty chose a few foods too. In fact, would they mind if she made a sandwich? She wouldn't of course. Instead, she planned a shopping trip for essentials to stock her mini-fridge.

Gloria sat back. "We wondered if you'd like to go to Thursday evening service with us tonight. Pastor Gabe, the one who introduced us to the Garrisons, invited us, and we thought we'd try it out."

Liberty popped a green grape into her mouth to buy herself time. Her taste buds danced with activity. Hang out at Clay's church on another Thursday night? Sure. She'd commit immediately.

Gloria studied her. "You know we're here for you, right? Anything you need, we want to help." She reached across the table and placed a hand over Liberty's. "We care about you."

"Thank you. You've been very kind to me, and I wish I could repay you."

"No need." Roy waved off her words. "The offer still stands for you to stay in our guest bedroom for as long as you like." When Liberty started to object, he raised a palm in a peaceful motion. "I know, I know. You're independent. We respect that. We do. But we also worry about you. It's been so windy this month."

She couldn't deny that. "It's very important to me that I cover my expenses."

"Please don't worry about that," Gloria said. "I mean, if you had a double-wide parked out there you *might* use enough utilities to make a dent. I'm sure any usage will be negligible."

"Still..." Liberty toyed with the wheat cracker on her plate.

"So, come to church with us?" Roy's expression went hopeful.

If it meant avoiding her cold, depressing camper, she might try it. With the Archers beside her, she wouldn't be alone.

A flash came to mind of the sense of welcome she'd felt last time as God's presence settled into the room—as if He wanted her near Him. Would going tonight mean she could touch that again? She didn't deserve it, but oh, how she longed for that warmth.

"I wanted to tell you," Gloria began after taking a sip of her tea. "Elizabeth mentioned an opening in her florist's shop—for an assistant position. She needs someone artsy who can also handle the administrative work in the office. I told her you worked for us for several years and had both of those qualities. She said she'd love for you to consider the position, if you're interested."

Liberty almost choked on her tea. "That sounds like a job offer."

"You'll need to meet up with her for an interview. She may be at church tonight. You could talk to her there."

Another reason to attend. Hope docked in Liberty's mind, but she resisted getting on board. Her search couldn't end this quickly, could it? And what about it being with the Garrisons? Could she find enough courage to face that challenge?

Roy smiled in his gentle way. "This might be an answer to your prayers, and I know it would help the Garrisons out."

Did Elizabeth know the whole story? Back then, Clay demanded they keep their news secret. Had he changed his mind and let his mother in on it? If so, why was she so willing to have Liberty come work with her? No—chances were, she didn't know.

Either way, Liberty needed a job, and the courage to chase one down. "Thanks for the invitation. I'd like to go."

The two of them smiled at her from across the table. "Let's have an early dinner," Gloria said. "After that, we'll drive into town."

She didn't have the job yet, of course, but what if she got it? Working for Clay's mom would be fine, right?

CHAPTER EIGHT

As usual, Clay arrived at the church an hour early for Thursday night service. With his fellow usher-greeters, he helped prepare the room by straightening chairs and cleaning up anything left on the chapel floor from classes.

Being here reminded him he hadn't talked with Libby alone yet. He needed to, and soon.

The side door opened next to the chapel's platform, and Pastor Gabe came in. He wore a button-down shirt in navy blue with jeans. His short, dark brown hair, which was slightly receding, looked freshly gelled, and his salt-and-pepper beard, recently trimmed. The man's gray eyes radiated joy and acceptance, something Clay appreciated. Gabe was about fifteen years older than Clay and settled, with a family of three daughters. Clay wouldn't tell him, but sometimes he envied how comfortable Gabe seemed with his life. How at peace with himself.

Gabe pointed to a chair away from the other volunteers. "Have a seat, Clay. I can tell you've got something on your mind." He joined Clay in the same row. "She's *your* Liberty, isn't she?" He'd been Clay's mentor for a few years now, but he didn't know all of Clay's secrets. Only that Clay and Liberty had dated during high school, that Liberty's guardians had sent her away, and that she was back.

"Yup." Clay fidgeted while Gabe scrutinized him. He glanced around the room to ensure they had privacy. The other ushers were back near the sound board. Given the music they piped through the room, no one would overhear.

"Things are awkward, I imagine." When Clay didn't answer, Gabe must have guessed what he didn't say. "Here's a question for you. Did you ever clear the air? Chances are, you do that, you'll feel less uncomfortable near each other."

Clay groaned. "I agree. Except, she'd have to cooperate, and so far, she keeps her distance."

Gabe rubbed his whiskery jaw. "I wouldn't force a conversation. Sounds like you have some time to rehearse what you'll say." Gabe leaned forward when volunteers propped the main doors opened for the service, which would begin in fifteen minutes. "And, if you haven't already," he whispered, "forgive yourself." He met Clay's eyes and gave him an encouraging smile, then he rose to slip down the aisle and greet the early arrivals.

Clay rubbed his neck. Sure. No problem.

Ten minutes before the service began, Roy, Gloria, and Libby met Clay at the double doors. "Welcome, good to see all three of you here tonight."

Roy gave him a hearty handshake as if they'd known each other for years. Libby said hello, but then grabbed Gloria's arm and tugged her toward a row near the back.

After the main worship set, Clay helped pass offering plates to distracted churchgoers as they sang one more chorus. Across the room, Scarlett Tompkins, all four years and red curls of her, darted toward the platform. Where was her mother, Jan? Suddenly Libby was there, retrieving the redhead. Wow, they looked alike. Head down, Libby frowned, but he read deep sadness rather than criticism in her expression. He watched as she found Jan at the back of the sanctuary.

Stationed near the back door, Clay looked up to see Libby striding down the aisle, holding Scarlett's hand. He couldn't move as the two of them approached, looking like a mother with her daughter. She seemed to need something, so he stepped out into the hallway with them.

"Hey, Clay." Libby gently swung Scarlett's hand between them. "She wanted a drink. Is there a fountain out here?"

"Absolutely." He pointed. "Right around that corner. There's even one low enough for little girls to drink from." He ducked his head and watched Scarlett's face light up.

"Thanks, Greeter Garrison."

He chuckled at her nickname for him and offered his knuckles for a fist bump. She obliged, and Libby watched them. She pressed her lips together and followed Scarlett down the hall.

How had Libby gotten placed in the role of babysitting?

They reappeared before he had a chance to decide whether to return to the sanctuary or wait them out. They stopped near him again. "I see you're still serving at church."

He nodded. "A lot of other things have changed, but not that." He followed them back into the chapel and took a spot near the sound board.

After the final song, Clay wished folks a good week as he offered fist bumps and handshakes at the door. When the room had cleared a bit, he cleaned the floor and strengthened chairs. At one point, he glanced up and saw Liberty strolling toward the front, buttoning her peacoat over her slim middle. She made a beeline to his mother, who stood near the stage, chatting with one of the young, single women from church.

Clay moved closer, not so he could eavesdrop. Mostly. He jumped onto the stage and cleaned up.

"Mrs. Garrison—" Liberty fidgeted as if she was nervous. Clay felt glued in place as he listened, though he straightened music and mic stands. If he drew attention to himself now, Mom would call him over. He shifted to put more of his back to the room. Occasionally, he peeked at them.

"Please, call me Elizabeth."

Libby's face creased into an anxious smile. "Okay, Elizabeth. May I speak to you a moment?"

"Certainly." Mom faced Clay, a movement he caught out of the corner of his eye. "Son, you're my ride."

"Sure thing."

Jill—the leader of his church-going admirers—ambled up onto the stage, joined by Cecelia and two other women. "Clay, do you know where Pastor Gabe went? We wanted to ask him something."

Clay searched the room. "He's probably in the hallway." He bent to pick up a lost guitar pick. Anything to avoid those flirty looks. *This* was why he'd given his mother that line about pining for Libby.

The group drifted off, and Clay's attention shifted to Liberty.

Not a lie exactly. He hadn't let himself analyze it very closely.

Mom and Libby chatted for several minutes. He caught phrases about the florist shop. He knew they needed a new employee. Was this about that job?

Later, sitting in the truck with Mom on their way home, he had questions he wouldn't ask.

"So, God answered my prayer tonight," Mom said, smoothing her long jacket over her legs. "I have a new full-time assistant." He felt his mother's scrutiny burning a hole into his right ear. "And you owe her a dinner invitation, if my memory serves."

Oh, that. Two things to talk to Libby about. No doubt his first topic—apologizing for being a self-centered idiot ten years ago— would make her eager to accept an invitation to come spend an evening with his super dysfunctional family. Why not share the love and joy?

He frowned at the road ahead of him.

"Shall we set it up for this coming week?"

He groaned, but Mom spouted meal ideas as if she didn't hear him.

Sure. He'd get right on it.

CHAPTER NINE

From her parked car, Liberty studied the rainwater running down the street while she waited for Elizabeth to arrive at the shop. The hour was still early. Phone to her ear, she listened for Shea's response to her news.

"I'm glad you took the job, Lib," Shea said. "You're brave and strong to face his family, even voluntarily choosing to work with them."

Like in their counseling sessions, she gave Liberty a moment to absorb her affirmation. Liberty didn't think this was so voluntary, with her gas gauge camped at E. "I'm looking forward to earning a paycheck again."

"Without that financial burden, you might even feel like creating more fairy houses. Do you think Elizabeth would be willing to sell those in her shop?"

The possibility hadn't occurred to Liberty. She'd been artistically dry for so long. "I haven't gotten that far." Still no sign of Elizabeth this morning. "Honestly, I don't want any more ties here than necessary. I'm not staying in Birch Harbor. I'm only here to figure out what's next. I might apply to college and study marine biology or ornithology." She laughed to let Shea know she was covering her anxiety with humor.

"Both good fields. You like fish and birds." Liberty could hear her smile through their phone connection. "Oh, I'm next in line," Shea said. "Let's talk after your first day, okay?"

They disconnected, and Liberty searched the street once more. Nothing. She'd better check her phone again in case her new boss had tried to reach her somehow.

A tap on her window gave her a jolt. Clay stood looking in at her. Rain ran in sheets down the glass, but she lowered the pane a bit anyway when he motioned. Drops splattered in.

He shivered, which made him look vulnerable—an appearance

he didn't usually have, and one that touched something deep inside her. "Sorry, Mom's running late. She asked me to open up. Are you ready to go in?"

Liberty nodded, unable or unwilling—she wasn't sure which—to talk to him.

His long strides carried him between the two rows of waterlogged trees toward the front door. There was a slight overhang for a little protection from the rain. She met him under that, wishing she had an umbrella so she could put more space between them as he bent toward the lock. From here, she could see the fresh razor job the barber had done on the back of his neck during a recent haircut. The view seemed intimate, and she pulled her attention away and watched a car splash by. How was she going to spend one-on-one time with him?

Nightly, she lay awake, worrying how he'd react when he learned what had happened. Did she have the courage to tell him? How would he take it? And what would he do with the information? Liberty didn't know this Clay—who he'd become. She could only guess if he was the type of person to trust with her secret.

And she couldn't keep it from him forever.

Clay bent even lower and fiddled with the key. "It's not working. Sorry about this." He muttered words about the storm, rambling, but the noise of the downpour on the metal overhang drowned them out. His hands shook. Did she make him nervous? "Huh. Maybe Mom changed the locks."

Watching him struggle drew compassion to the surface. "Take your time."

He looked in her direction, gave her a companionable once-over, and the corners of his emerald green eyes crinkled with humor. She held her breath. That smile. "Sure thing," he said. "Another gallon or two of rainwater couldn't hurt."

She chuckled. Her leggings were wet, but her coat had done a pretty good job of protecting her upper body.

The key finally turned. "Got it." He held the door for her and she entered, crossing directly in front of him. Close. He emitted warmth and he smelled good, though unfamiliar. He wasn't wearing as strong of a scent as he had in high school—more evidence she didn't know this version of him. Something about his aroma reminded her of Earl Grey tea, though she wasn't sure why.

He flipped light switches here and there, highlighting displays of glittering vases and knickknacks. Then he clicked an arrow on the wall thermostat several times, and Liberty hoped he was turning on the heat. Walking toward the center of the shop, she took in the colors and beauty, and sighed. Gleaming hardwood floors, shelves full of violet and green vases and décor items. Banks of glass-doored refrigerators housing colorful arrangements.

Clay stopped nearby. "Mom mentioned this was your first day."

"Mm-hmm." She kept her focus from landing on him. "I'd forgotten how lovely it was in here. The color scheme—that soothing green on a few of the walls. The creamy paint color over here." She was babbling now. Disengaging, she walked closer to the gift area of the shop, which housed stuffed animals and small paintings in lovely frames—perhaps the work of a local artist? A soothing blue shade enclosed a side room. The gridded French doors to the space were painted in bright, glossy white. A sofa and two plush chairs before a gas fireplace suggested this was a meeting place. Perhaps Elizabeth met with party planners in there. Or rented it for book club meetings or some such.

She stepped inside and turned slowly. It'd be a joy to relax with friends in a space like this, perhaps with cups of tea and novels. If she remembered correctly, the Garrisons had an event venue in their greenhouse out at the farm as well, suitable for family gatherings or small corporate workshops. The local retreat center used to lend them business a decade ago. Was that place still in business?

She'd need to return to the main shop area soon, where Clay waited, as if letting her take in the store's changes. With no sign of Elizabeth to train her, what would happen next? Was Clay planning to guide her through the first day? Suddenly, her coat felt too warm, and she shrugged out of it.

Clay appeared at her side. "Mom loves this room. So do the

brides and wedding planners who come in. In fact, you two will be preparing for a wedding this weekend. Lots of tulips. We've been coaxing them in the greenhouse. I'm on my way to pick those up next." He was rambling now, and rain from his coat dripped on the floor. He'd shoved his fists into his pockets. "I don't know what Mom wanted you to get started on. She didn't mention that part. The shop doesn't open for another hour." His attention fell to the wet jacket in her arms. "Here, I can at least show you the employee's room where you can store your stuff."

She followed him toward the back. He chattered about something and seemed as uncomfortable around her as she did around him. If they had a speedometer to measure their word speed, perhaps they could have a good laugh.

Last night at church, she'd imagined telling him everything. Was it time? Didn't she owe it to him?

She licked her lips as she followed him. Since they rarely had moments alone, this might be her chance.

He opened a door to a room with one window, a table, and a few kitchen appliances. He flicked on a light switch. "Here you go." He gestured for her to enter. "You can hang your things in one of the lockers. We keep this secure during business hours."

She put her gear away and closed the metal door. Addressing the past might help them both feel more comfortable. Facing the bank of gray storage cubbies, she organized her thoughts. Now or never. She forced herself to meet his eyes. "I need to tell you about our daughter."

He gasped like he'd been punched, and then he went still over there between the sink and fridge. Somewhere in the otherwise silent room, a clock ticked loudly. The table separated them now, and she preferred it that way. He swallowed loud, and she waited for him to speak. Had her time at the service last night made her brave? Suddenly she was determined to tell him what happened, so she could let it go.

"Yoo-hoo! I'm here," Elizabeth's voice carried from the front of the shop. Clay's focus snapped from the floor toward his mother, then back to Liberty. Their time was up.

His green eyes met hers, and she almost gasped at the raw pain there. The questions, the emotions. "Daughter?" he whispered.

"Hey, there you two are." Elizabeth stood in the doorway to the breakroom. "Good. You let her in." She peered between them. "Everything all right?"

He rushed past his mom. "I'm sorry. I need to go—" He rattled his keys. "Tulips."

The bell on the front shop door gave a cheery jingle as if nothing monumental had happened in the last few minutes. Too bad she hadn't been able to tell him more. Compassion urged her to rush outside and chase after him, which she couldn't do.

"How are you this morning, hon?" Elizabeth hung her jacket in one of the lockers. "I hope you don't mind if I call you that. You're more than an employee, you're an old friend of the family. Goodness, it's pouring buckets out there. I'm soaked. Let's go enjoy the gas fireplace in the sitting room and try to get our bearings, shall we?"

She led the way into the blue room Liberty had admired earlier. Using a remote control, Elizabeth clicked on the fireplace, which took a moment to light with a *whoosh*. The glass front washed over with condensation before heat seeped into the room.

"Doesn't even need a fan. It radiates without one." Standing there, Elizabeth turned every few minutes, exposing her clothes to the warm air at different angles.

Liberty joined her, staying in one position while the fireplace blazed hot against the back of her legs. She should move. But the image of Clay's broken expression after she'd blurted news of their daughter into the room glued her into place. She needed to talk to him alone, for as long as it took to answer his questions and ease that grief in his green eyes. If only she'd approached the topic gently minutes ago. As much as she blamed him for the void in her life, she didn't wish him ill now.

Elizabeth nattered on about procedures and the wedding coming up the following Saturday and how she'd pay overtime if Liberty wouldn't mind coming in, but Liberty only caught some of what she said. This wasn't the type of employee she wanted to be—

inattentive and unprepared. Suddenly she realized Elizabeth had been quiet for several moments, which was unlike her. "I'm sorry. I missed that."

Using a tissue, Elizabeth polished an empty vase. "I'm hoping Clay asked you to dinner."

Liberty paced away from the fireplace. "Dinner?"

As if she hadn't tipped the world upside down, Elizabeth fiddled with the unlit candles on the mantel, repositioning them. "Clay didn't mention it? We'd love to have you over, as our guest. Does Sunday evening work?"

Clay sat in his truck down the street from the flower shop, gripping the steering wheel so tight his fingers cramped.

I have a daughter. Or had...

Where was she?

He wanted to tromp back inside and ask all his questions. But, his mom. Was Liberty in there telling her everything? As far as Clay knew, Mom had never heard the news of the pregnancy.

How did Liberty know the baby was a girl? A late miscarriage? Or if Liberty kept her, had she then... died? His fingers went numb from the even tighter grip.

His cell phone buzzed in his jacket, and he took it out. Probably Dad, wondering why he wasn't back at the farm.

His mother's face showed up on the screen. His gut sank. He clicked to accept the call. "Mom."

"I can't believe you didn't ask her."

"Wha—"

"Over to dinner." Mom tsked. "Doesn't matter. I did. Sunday night." Mom gave him two seconds before adding, "Now, where are those tulips?" The occasional bride asked for a mock-up of the bouquet a week ahead, especially if the flowers weren't too expensive.

He turned the key in the ignition. "I'm on it."

Dinner? Mom was obviously scheming. Clay wanted to protect Libby, who probably felt coerced since she now worked for Mom. He'd have to let her know she didn't have to come. He'd make up an excuse for her to his mother. Plus, Dad wouldn't appreciate the hubbub of Clay bringing over a "date."

He pulled onto the farm road.

Libby's face today when she'd mentioned their daughter—the determination, the courage. She'd grown into a strong, independent woman. She impressed him. She'd obviously suffered a huge loss, given that their daughter wasn't present anywhere. What tragedy had she endured? His lungs tightened as if gripped in a fist.

He had tulips to deliver, and then he had to find a way to get Libby out of this dinner plan. So much for his ridiculous promise to Mom that he'd invite Libby over and pick up where they left off. Why had he said that? Something else he'd better fix.

Then he needed to talk with Libby, if she was willing. Because somewhere, at least for a while, they'd had a daughter.

CHAPTER TEN

She'd told him. That should be reason to celebrate. It had taken courage and perhaps a little foolishness to blurt it out. The expression on his face. She cringed recalling the shock. Not finishing that conversation seemed cruel. She shouldn't have brought it up at work. Was it possible he'd never told his parents? Elizabeth didn't seem awkward around Liberty. Given how talkative she was, there was no question she'd have said something already if she knew.

Sitting in her camper that evening, Liberty texted Shea: I THINK I BLEW IT.

No response followed, which left space for Liberty's mind to fill the emptiness with doubts and second-guessing herself. And a dose of condemnation.

Her phone buzzed on the cheap Formica tabletop. I'D LIKE TO TALK TO YOU. CAN I CALL?

The text wasn't from Shea, but from a local number. Fingers shaking, she texted back: WHO IS THIS?

HEY LIBERTY, IT'S CLAY.

She stared at her phone, barely blinking.

OR I COULD COME OVER.

She couldn't avoid him. WHAT'S UP? Her thumb pressed Send before she realized how stupid that must sound. Of course they needed to talk. Unless she'd blown something at work, and Elizabeth was letting Clay mention it.

I WANTED TO CLEAR UP MOM'S DINNER IDEA.

Oh, that. Yeah, she wasn't looking forward to a family meal with them either. But she didn't answer before his next words appeared on her screen.

YOU DON'T HAVE TO COME. I CAN LET MOM KNOW. I'M SORRY SHE PUSHED FOR IT.

SHE NEVER KNEW ABOUT THE BABY, DID SHE? Liberty hadn't

planned to go there, but had he literally never told anyone?

Now he went silent for several minutes. Then, CAN I COME SEE YOU?

She'd put this off too long since getting back to Birch Harbor. They couldn't discuss their secrets in a restaurant, though. KNOW OF A PRIVATE LOCATION WHERE WE COULD MEET?

NO ONE'S USING THE FARM'S EVENT SPACE. HOW ABOUT THERE?

Sitting here debating wasn't going to resolve this. She typed the words: HALF AN HOUR.

I'LL BE THERE. THX LIBBY.

The nickname took her back ten years, but she couldn't dwell there now. Instead, she'd coax her weary self out into the damp March night and figure out a way to face this. As long as Clay, who loved to fix things, didn't try to fix this, they'd be fine.

There wasn't a way to make this right. There was only the chore of finding a way to live with it, like Liberty had done.

Clay pulled into the family farm's driveway and went straight to the house's back door. Libby would be here in about fifteen minutes, and Clay didn't want his brother or his family to worry about unscheduled, after-hours lights in the event room. Kason met him at the door. "Hey, bro."

He stepped inside where the scent of strawberries and angel food cake filled the kitchen. A dome covered the spongy dessert on the counter. "Looks like I missed happy hour."

"Happy hour" was how his young nephew referred to anytime the health-nut family indulged in sweets.

"Want some?"

"I can only stay a few minutes." Clay looked around the kitchen, peeking through the doorway to the living room. "Is your family around?"

"They're upstairs. Bath time. I'm supposed to go help." That explained the towel draped over his shoulders. "What's going on?

You're antsy."

Without Brynn around, Clay could speak freely. He trusted Kason, appreciated his occasional older-brother insights. "I'm meeting Libby in the event room in ten minutes. I wanted to give you a heads-up."

"Okay." Kason leaned against the counter and crossed his ankles. "Libby, huh?"

"She uh…" Clay rubbed the back of his neck. He'd keep a few of his secrets. "She has news for me, about the past. Man, I hope I'm ready for this." He paced.

"Dude."

The words *I have a daughter* rose up, but Clay stuffed them back down. "I can tell you more later. Anyway, FYI."

"Unka Clay!" A naked streak zoomed through the doorway and clamped onto Clay's leg.

"Hey, Muriel, how's my favorite niece?"

The three-year-old was soaking wet, her dark blonde curls dripping on her tiny shoulders. His heart melted. He loved his niece and his nephew, Mitchell, who was six. He'd always had a soft spot for kids. Kason put the towel to good use and lifted Muriel, who freed her arms and raised them to Clay.

He scooped her up, towel and all, and snuggled her, snorting pig noises into her wet hair until she squealed. She smelled of strawberry shampoo and baby soap.

"Kase! Pre-schooler on the loose," Brynn called from upstairs, and the men chuckled.

"Got her."

"Thanks." Footsteps followed his sister-in-law's words before a door clicked shut up there.

"How's my Muriel today?" Clay asked the imp in his arms.

She clapped her hands together. "Splashy-splashy time."

He chuckled at her dimples and cheerfulness. He'd given her bath toys on her last birthday. She calmed and rested her head on his shoulder with a deep, comfortable sigh. Such trust. He cherished it.

Was this what it was like to have a daughter? Snuggles and

sharing of her life? The thought sunk in. With Mitchell, Clay pretended to blow up tanks and shoot finger pistols. They roughhoused and hid behind sofas for shootouts. With Muriel, there were hugs, tea parties, and strawberry shampooed curls.

The microwave's red digital numbers flipped over and brought him back to reality. He'd better head out.

Kason watched him for a second, then he snatched up the cake in its carrier dome. "Trade ya. Take this out there." Kason set it back down and accepted his daughter, who snuggled into his shoulder this time. She seemed ready for warm jammies and bed.

There was something peaceful about the routines over here this time of evening. What must that be like? Family rituals with little people who looked up to you? Muriel's wet hair matched her father's now, but when it was dry, she'd match her blonde momma. Clay had had a normal childhood, but seeing Kason as a settled dad… Clay was missing out.

"Good night, you guys." He reached for the dessert.

With a free arm, Kason opened the back door and then stepped out of his brother's way. "You got this, bro." He clapped Clay's shoulder on his way out.

In the greenhouse, Clay flipped on the light switch for the chandelier over the grand round table. The sun had set early, given the cloud banks at the horizon, darkening the room. He lowered the level on the blinding chandelier. But now it might seem intimate, which was the opposite of what he wanted. With a spin, he nudged the level up a notch. They'd only need a couple of these chairs. He questioned putting out the cake with the fancy plates and silverware Brynn stored here. The image didn't work with what they had to discuss tonight. No, he'd set the cake on the counter and leave it there. The space was already so fancy with the chandelier and dental molding around the table. If he pulled two chairs off to the side for a less formal setting, that might seem too personal. He'd leave them.

"Hello?" Libby's unsteady voice called from the entrance. He'd left the door unlocked out front.

"Back here." He owed her an apology, no matter what else

happened. *Please give me the words, Lord.*

Libby came into view wearing her black peacoat over jeans. She met his eyes and waved a mitten-covered hand. "It's colder than it looks out there."

Except for her quavering voice earlier, she didn't seem as anxious as he felt. Or she was covering.

"Please, have a seat." He pulled a chair away from the table. "Hang on, I'll be right back." He dragged a space heater from the corner and plugged it in, cranking it to High.

Rocking in the dining chair, Libby hugged her coat to her as if she was more than chilled.

Of course she was. How could he ease her stress? "Would you like a bottle of water? We have a mini fridge over here. Might have juice too. I haven't checked in a while."

"Apple juice, if you have it. I'm suddenly thirsty." She murmured that last part, and he wasn't sure if she'd meant to say it aloud. He grabbed two juices—one orange and one apple—and joined her at the table.

"This is crazy." Her hands trembled as she set the cap down. "I mean, I volunteered for this little chat."

She'd been through so much. He gulped OJ. *He'd* rejected her. He winced. He'd *blamed* her.

To her face.

"I'm sorry." He leaned closer, forced himself to look her right in the eye, see her tears, feel their impact in his bones. "It was selfish of me to treat you like that after you found out, after you told me."

She blinked, and teardrops spilled down her face. He reached for the box of tissues on a nearby cabinet.

They'd begun the conversation with his apology. Now he hoped she'd open up with answers.

CHAPTER ELEVEN

For years Liberty had assumed she'd never hear Clay admit he could have handled things differently back then. She dabbed her face with the tissue. "Thank you for apologizing. Honestly, I didn't expect that. It means a lot."

He gripped his juice bottle so tight that it crinkled. "I should have called you that weekend. But then, you were gone. No longer at school. I thought it was morning sickness keeping you home. When you didn't come to church with the Kincades, I got worried."

She hadn't let herself consider what he'd gone through after she was sent away. Overwhelmed with all the changes and losses, she'd barely been able to cope. Survival and the baby filled her concentration.

"I wish I could relive that conversation or fix it all somehow."

Though she'd guessed he'd want to solve things, sadness pressed in like fog on a fall morning. "There's no fixing any of it."

He pushed his juice away and leaned toward her. "How can I make it up to you?"

There was one thing he could do, and she'd get to it, after she answered his questions. One promise he could make, and if he kept it, everyone would be better off. "First, tell me what you want to know. I'm sure you have questions." She reached for the hand lotion in her bag while she waited for his curiosity to take over. Once they discussed everything, she might finally have a sense of closure. Or a few of the nagging thoughts might relent, because given the same circumstances again, she'd probably make similar choices.

The past was the past.

"How about you start at that point right after we talked?"

Liberty let her mind drift to places she tried to avoid. "Okay. You remember the Kincades and how they planned to adopt me?" He nodded beside her, his face a mask of discomfort. "I wanted that.

I wanted a family." She nudged up her chin. "When they found out about the pregnancy, and I couldn't keep the secret from them—I was sick every day—they said something about how I'd be a bad influence on their biological teens. They told me I'd have to go live where I 'could get the care I needed at this challenging time.'" She used finger quotes to set those words apart. "A fancy way of saying, 'You're no good to us anymore. We don't want you. We can't be proud of you now. You made an unforgivable choice.' Nothing about how *God Himself* had given me the gift of a life." Hadn't He? If God wasn't in charge of life, then who was? As much as Liberty preferred to keep Him at a distance because of all the pain He allowed, she knew he was the Author of life.

The Kincades' rejection still stung, and she waited out the wave of emotion before continuing. Mom and Dad had chosen the Kincades to take her in if anything ever happened to them. They'd been family friends forever. But as soon as her life got complicated, they'd given up on her. "They preached God to me so often—unconditional love. Wanted me in that church, bragged about me doing outreaches with the youth group."

Clay was quiet beside her, listening, toying with the lid to his bottle.

"Did I do everything God wanted? No. Am I imperfect? Of course. But aren't they? What would they rather I do? Get an abortion?"

At that word, Clay flinched. But she carried on. "That would go over well in their churchy mindset, wouldn't it? So, I didn't follow the Bible. Does that mean God didn't give me the gift of a life? The gift of my own family?" Her voice rose on that last phrase, and she fought the tremble around her mouth. She'd imagined this conversation a thousand times, had thought she'd been prepared. But the pain boiled up, together with her questions about God's character.

"They did not set an example of God's unconditional love to you." He formed a fist and rested it on the tabletop.

Wishing she could discuss this without a deep ache, she yanked another tissue free. "Who knows? God could be like that, like them." Familiar bitterness rose inside, like acid eating at the edges of her rebuilt life.

Clay reached over and touched her forearm, and she let him. Sharing this part of their daughter's story with him brought a taste of relief, and she relished it. "He's not." Clay sounded certain.

When she didn't agree with him, he pulled his hand back. But she sensed he did so to encourage her to keep talking.

"So, I was sent to social services. Funny how the pastors at church who could easily accept me when I wasn't pregnant decided to abandon me when I was." Enough. She'd stewed over that too often. From now on, she'd be brave. Without letting all of it go, she'd never move forward. "The authorities placed me with older foster parents who tolerated—and resented—me for about ten months, during which time I had our daughter." To their credit, Will and Dora had let her stay a few months beyond the birth, though she'd aged out of the system by then. She'd never felt so lonely in her life, coming home from the hospital without her baby.

"So... you had her alone?"

"Yes."

His expression went soft. "You are courageous and strong."

"Ha." She grunted before she could stop herself. She had rarely felt courageous *or* strong. "Sure."

"Were you okay? Was she?" He didn't blink as he waited for her answer.

"Yes." Memories flooded back of those early hours. Liberty could still picture her. "She was beautiful. Red hair, lots of it. Wide awake sometimes. Green eyes, like yours."

A short moan came out of him. "What happened to her?"

So far, Liberty's story had been about herself. Now, she had to get into the part that could have involved Clay, if he'd stepped up. Not that she'd shame him today. But what if, after all this time, he objected to how she'd handled the decisions forced on her? "First, you need to know that as far as I know, she's still alive and well somewhere."

"Okay..." He rested his elbows on the table. This was the part he might feel he needed to fix.

"During the pregnancy, my foster parents put me in touch with an attorney who discussed options with me. The state covered the attorney's fees, and I needed all the help I could get." In the darkening greenhouse, a moth flew over from the live plants and aimed for the chandelier overhead. "The lawyer explained that since you were absent and didn't want to help me or the baby, and you had denied that the baby was yours and hadn't supported me the entire pregnancy..." Her words rushed out. "That I didn't need to name the father on the birth certificate and that I could make decisions around the infant myself."

"Wait..." His brow furrowed. "If I'd been involved, I could have had a say about what happened to her?"

Was that disappointment or irritation in his voice? "That's right." She wouldn't stoop to mentioning how his reactions had made her feel cornered. If he'd wanted to be involved, why hadn't he been? Nine months was enough time for him to change his mind and offer support.

"Why didn't the attorney contact me?" His voice sounded rough.

"I told him you had 'denied paternity.'"

He pushed back in his chair. "I didn't get it. I didn't fully understand." He paused for a moment, and this time, she waited him out. "I was scared of the responsibility and of what everyone would say."

So relatable. She bit her upper lip.

"But I would have liked one more chance to help. I had no way of contacting you."

For the first time since they'd sat down, anger rose inside her. "You're saying you would have... what? Proposed marriage? Offered to support us?"

"We talked about marriage."

"Someday. Not at seventeen. Are you forgetting my scholarship?" The plan had been college first, then see where things stood.

"Still, I would have appreciated having a choice."

"You had one."

They faced off, and Liberty crossed her arms. Let him try to convince her he even attempted contact with the Kincades to see if they could reach her. She'd bet on him never having tried.

He nudged his chair back farther from the table, putting a bit more distance between them. Fine. She'd done what she'd had to.

He crossed a leg over his thigh and gripped his ankle. "What about now?"

"What do you mean? Nothing has changed. It's too late." And the sooner he accepted that, the better.

"Do you know where she is now?"

"I have no idea. The adoption was closed." Her tight shoulders begged for a stretch, and she rolled them to ease the stiffness.

"Did you get to pick the parents?"

"No." And right now, she was glad because she had the sense that if he learned their names, he'd go find their daughter and turn her life upside down in an attempt to "fix" things.

"I thought birth parents—uh, mothers—got to choose."

"The attorney felt it best to let an adoption agency handle everything. I was young, scared, doubting my own decisions. I knew I couldn't handle all of that myself. And without support..." She shrugged. "I was still a follower. I went along with what the adults around me were saying, from the hospital staff to the attorney to the foster parents, who all said I couldn't handle raising her on my own. Her only hope for a good life would be for me to give her away. I'd already messed up my life, why mess up hers?"

Clay's chin dropped toward his collar bone. When he lifted his face, his eyes were sad. "That's what everyone was telling you?"

"Pretty much." Dwelling on this brought up too much pain. Time to move on. But what did Clay want? Or need? She'd cared about him once, and he hadn't had almost a decade to get used to the news she'd dumped into the room tonight.

His head tipped toward the ceiling where he stared for a long moment.

"I'm afraid to ask, but what are you thinking?"

He zeroed back in on her. "That I would like to see her. Do you have a photo?"

"I do." She'd come to their meeting expecting to show him their baby's picture. But sharing their daughter felt risky, like exposing her secrets. Reaching into her bag, she felt around for the small wooden frame. Her hand closed over the edge, and the glass felt cool to her fingertips.

Clay leaned in, and Liberty handed him the frame. He blinked several times, eyes riveted. "Wow. So much red hair."

Liberty pointed. "She cooperated and opened her eyes for the camera. See? Green."

He didn't speak, or perhaps he couldn't. Then, "What's her name?"

Seeing the photo again brought back the heartache of losing her. Most of the time, Liberty kept the image out of sight. But sometimes, she'd pull it out, hold it, and cry herself to sleep. "I don't know. The adoptive parents named her."

Clay peered at her with tortured eyes.

"But I gave her a nickname. Daisy." Mom grew daisies before she died. She had bouquets of gerbera daisies on her table as often as possible. That memory tied Liberty back to her mother. Using the nickname for her daughter bound the generations together in a profound way. If Liberty dwelt on those thoughts too long, she'd end up weeping. She refocused on the present.

"It fits," he whispered, looking back down. "How old is she now?"

"She'll be nine this June." Liberty already had a gift in mind, not that Daisy would ever see it.

He stroked the glass as if he could touch her baby-soft cheek. "I wish I'd been there."

This conversation had drained her. Since she didn't have the resources to rehash his regrets, she reached for the straps of her bag. "I should head out." Standing, she gave him one more moment with the photograph.

"Can I snap a shot of this with my phone?"

"Of course." She waited while he tried to angle his phone and the glass of the frame just right. "We can have a copy made, if you want."

At the door, Clay handed the frame back to her. "Thank you for telling me the story, for sharing her with me."

The room felt too warm, the memories much too fresh in her heart. Clutching Daisy's picture, Liberty said good night and darted toward her car.

Halfway home, she remembered she hadn't brought up her biggest worry. Now that Clay knew, what would he do next? She'd have to find a time to convince him it was best to leave things as they were.

CHAPTER TWELVE

"I have an idea for the greenhouse meeting room, Liberty, and I'd love your input." Elizabeth set her teacup down on the coffee table in the florist shop's fireplace room. She wore a coral sweater over slacks, and her silver necklace shone, as did her green eyes.

The greenhouse room. Where Liberty and Clay had chatted a few weeks ago, spilling secrets and facing regrets. Hopefully, she'd find a chance to talk to him soon, make sure he didn't plan to try and track down their daughter. Cowardice kept her from seeking him out earlier.

The shop would open in half an hour, and Liberty enjoyed the quiet. She had to present competence, even if her stomach churned with memories. She smoothed her sleeves, relishing the fireplace's heat on this rainy April morning as they sat together on the sofa. "How can I help?"

"How are you at design?" Elizabeth pulled sketches from a folder. "I'm toying with updating both the space and the website. But I need new ideas. Clay's on his way now, to brainstorm with us." She checked her watch. "If he ever gets here."

"I'd be happy to offer suggestions. Let's see what you have."

Elizabeth spread the pages before them, and Liberty tried to focus.

Clay. She hoped his dad had sent him on a delivery off-island. Then he and his mother could discuss it after hours. Elizabeth had mentioned he lived on their property in a garage apartment. That meant they could talk anytime.

He'd been working out at the Archers' property on weekends—her days off. She'd found herself holed up in her camper, hiding. If she were brave, she'd ask Roy for a corner of space in his RV garage and get back to creating. That's when she felt most at peace. And now that she'd had an income for a few weeks, her bank account could support her buying supplies to build her fairy houses.

Shea would urge her to indulge her artsy side, saying it was therapeutic. She'd also recently suggested Liberty find a local therapist. But Liberty hadn't followed through with that advice. Why keep dredging things up?

No, her immediate concern was keeping this job, which meant not upsetting Elizabeth. If they discovered her secrets, would she and Jonathan judge her? Would they be angry they'd never known about their other granddaughter? Or fire her out of spite? Elizabeth didn't seem like that type of person, but Liberty would rather not test her.

The bell on the store's front door jingled. "That's probably Clay." Elizabeth rose to check, then turned back. "I was still hoping you'd come to dinner. I'm sorry that didn't work out before." Without waiting for an answer, she strolled out of the fireplace room.

He'd made up excuses for why the dinner idea wouldn't work. Since then, Elizabeth had left it alone. Surely she didn't plan to nudge them together romantically. Anyone could see it was too late.

Except... as he joined them in the overly warm fireplace room, the walls seemed to close in. His ruddy face and green eyes, with that scruffy chin and short brown, wind-blown hair, arrested her awareness. She had to look away and collect herself. He'd only gotten more handsome with age. Taller. Stronger. And she couldn't put the image of him, grieved over learning about Daisy, out of her mind. His regret touched her. They had something in common. A huge loss.

Over the years, to cope with his rejection, she'd judged him as cold and selfish, perhaps heartless—not admirable qualities. Why miss someone like that? But if he wasn't the man she remembered, the one she'd designed in her imagination—if instead he was kind, compassionate, responsible, someone who owned up to his mistakes and apologized—that unnerved her.

"Hey, ladies. How are things this morning?" He stripped off his jacket and accepting the bottled water his mother handed him, he met Liberty's eyes and gave her a smile.

She nodded at him, then turned away, pushing down her inner reaction. The wisest choice was to ignore how his positive traits rallied in a line and waved flags to get her attention. He cared for and respected his mother, going out of his way to help her whenever she asked anything of him, even when she teased him. He cared about what had happened to Daisy. He seemed genuinely concerned about how Liberty was doing. He worked hard at the Archers' property, clearing old patches of dying shrubs and overgrown vines. Sincerity covered him when he worshiped God now.

That list threatened her. Too many positives. What protected her was keeping people at a distance. She was moving as soon as she could afford it. Away from Clay and his family.

Elizabeth patted the sofa beside her, and Liberty rejoined her.

"Thanks for coming, Son. Here's what we're working on." She pointed at the papers out on the coffee table and waved him over. "Come see."

Clay sat beside her, and suddenly the Garrisons had Liberty sandwiched in. His jean-clad leg brushed hers, and his shoulder kept nudging her as he leaned forward to study the sketches. He smelled good, like a mixture of soap and fresh air. The collar of his long-sleeved black Henley rested against his neck.

Stop noticing his neck, Liberty!

Her attention shifted to his fingers as he shuffled the pages on the coffee table. She'd forgotten how long his fingers were. She missed holding his hand.

Girl!

"I thought if we could add more seating to the greenhouse," Elizabeth was saying, "we could expand the meeting area. If we hosted larger groups, we could charge more. Thoughts, either of you?"

The space came to mind easily, and she worked to imagine it without the emotion and history she shared with Clay.

Clay's subtle fragrance washed over her when he stirred again to point at the sketches. "I like this one. Having two smaller tables makes sense." He paused. "What do you think, Libby?"

They had so much to say to each other, this discussion of changing a meeting room seemed ludicrous. But she'd play along. "I agree. And it's *Liberty*, please."

"Sure thing. Sorry." He sounded sincere, unoffended. Honoring.

Elizabeth remained silent as they found their professional footing. She lifted her teacup and sipped, waiting.

Refocusing on the drawings, Liberty angled her body away from Clay and faced Elizabeth. "It is still a lovely space."

"Oh, you can thank Clay for most of the changes over the past several years. He would never admit it, but he's the romantic in the family. Even more than Kourtney." She gave a soft laugh while Clay fidgeted. "But you probably remember that about him."

Liberty wished she didn't. The flowers, poems, kayaking trips, hikes. Clay had a thoughtful side that planned alone time together with her in mind. Sometimes she missed that too.

They discussed options for another fifteen minutes. Then Clay stood. "Okay, if that's everything, I need to get back. Dad has five delivery orders waiting for me."

"You never did find a replacement, huh?" his mother asked him. "Too bad. I think it'd be great if you could help the Archers full time. Finish their project. Take on others."

"Thanks for that, Mom." Clay snagged his jacket from the leather chair across the room and thrust his arms into the sleeves. "I don't think Dad wants to hire someone else, pay them."

"Makes sense. Things are tight out there."

They spoke so freely about their business concerns, Liberty squirmed. No need to hear all the financial woes of the farm, unless there was a way she could help. "Should I go get the first bouquet delivery ready?"

"No, it's fine, hon," Elizabeth said. "I know you'll be discreet, or I wouldn't have hired you. Keeping secrets is part of the business."

And part of our lives. The phrase ran through Liberty's mind, and she peered over at Clay. Understanding flowed between them. Yup. Secrets.

"Could I speak to Clay for a second, alone?" Where the courage came from to make that request, Liberty didn't know, but she had to follow through.

Elizabeth looked between them. "Of course." She stepped out of the room and pulled the gridded French doors together. They wouldn't have visual privacy, but they could talk without being overheard.

"What's up, Liberty?" Clay asked, using her real name. It sounded odd coming from him. But she was glad he'd honored her request. The lighting overhead gave his mussy brown hair a golden gleam.

She took a couple of steps closer to him. She'd analyze why later. "I'm guessing you haven't talked with your parents about Daisy, right?"

Clay shifted on his feet and peeked behind Liberty toward the shop. "Yeah. I haven't found a good time to bring it up. I hope you don't mind. I know it's important to you. I will, soon. I don't want us to be ashamed of our daughter."

"No. I mean, please don't tell them. Let's keep this between us. I think it will cause less tension if they don't know." When he only studied her, she added, "Ignorance is bliss, right?"

"I can understand why you wouldn't want any conflict between you and Mom. I get that. You work here. But I don't think she'll react the way you fear." He'd read her concerns without her voicing them. Shoot, but that familiarity felt good.

"And your dad?"

"Hard to say how he'd react."

"What? You have a great relationship with him."

His shoulders rounded. "I wish I still did. Nah, when you back into your father with farm equipment, he tends to change his opinion of you."

She squinted up at him, her heart pinching. They'd always been a tight family, and Clay adored his father. "What?"

"And they tend to call you all kinds of things." He counted items off with those fingers. "Irresponsible, cocky. Immature."

"Oh no."

"I was reckless in high school."

She couldn't deny that.

"The accident happened right after—after you left."

Interesting word choice, because she'd been *sent* away. Without much of a say in anything that happened for a while.

He took a step closer. "But, if you want, sure I can keep our secret. What they don't know can't hurt them. Or you."

She sagged with relief and reached for his forearm. "Thank you, Clay."

He noticed her hand, and she felt a slight movement beneath the sleeve as his muscles twitched under her fingertips. His warm smile reappeared. When had he learned that expression? He'd never looked at her like that when they'd dated. Such tenderness and... affection? Nah. They were over. Long over. So why was her heart willing to skip toward Clay's kind eyes and take a stroll? She yanked her fingers back.

"I'm happy to do anything I can to help you. Which is why I'd love your input on the Archers' yard too. Mom reminded me you have a visual mind. Could I drop by and discuss the landscaping plans with you and the Archers one evening? I know they'd welcome your input. They think very highly of you."

She took a few steps away. "I won't be living there forever. It's best to leave the decisions to them."

Disappointment creased his brow this time. "They might disagree. And I didn't know you were leaving."

"As I'm sure you saw, that camper has seen better days." She kept her tone even, though her stomach tripped at the disappointment in his voice. "I'm planning to upgrade and move on."

His Adam's apple shifted up and down. "Where will you go?"

"I have no idea." She paused. Even if she knew, she wouldn't share the info with Clay. "Away from Birch Harbor." *And all the memories.* She didn't add the phrase, but the words seemed to hang between them. She moved closer to the fireplace room's door. "I heard the bell out front. I'd better get to work." First, though, she turned to face him. "Thanks for honoring my request."

"Of course." *Anything for you.* His eyes finished the thought, though she didn't fully trust her interpretation. She gave him a weak smile and excused herself to the main part of the shop.

He'd keep their secret. Now she could once more work toward leaving the Garrison family in the past.

CHAPTER THIRTEEN

En route to a delivery address across town, Clay slowed for a school zone. A cluster of probably fourth- or fifth-grade girls filled the crosswalk in front of his stopped truck. Among the group, a few girls had black hair, three were blonde, and two were redheads. He wished he could see their eyes. Now that he'd learned of Daisy's existence, he wondered if she lived nearby. Did she go to this elementary school? Did she shop with her adoptive parents at the local grocery stores? Did Libby constantly search for Daisy everywhere? How painful.

He might have a way to help her after all. An idea filled his mind again, one that Libby probably wouldn't like, since she seemed determined to leave things as they were. But, in the end, it might be exactly what they needed.

He turned toward the church for a quick convo with Pastor Gabe, if the man had an opening in his schedule.

In Gabe's office a few minutes later, Clay settled in a chair across from his mentor.

"How are things going with Liberty? I like seeing her at church."

"Okay. I can tell she's still grieving our past. I want to help."

Gabe threaded his fingers together on his desk. "Sometimes women hate it when we try to fix things."

"True." But what if things worked out well? Wouldn't that make it worth it? "I need your advice. I'd like to search for our daughter's family, but I don't know where to start."

"Closed adoption?"

A bee buzzed against the sunny window as if trying to get in. Similar to Clay who'd like to get access to a family he couldn't find. Then, giving up, it flew off toward the camellias along the outside church walls. "Yes."

Gabe shook his head. "You can't do much with a closed

adoption."

"You're telling me. No advice, then?"

Gabe studied Clay. "You seem determined about this."

Did his mentor have to see through him? Clay fidgeted. Then he pushed to his feet. "Yeah." Though Clay could feel Gabe's doubts from across the room. "You don't think I should search?"

"Ask yourself—who are you doing this for? Your daughter? Liberty? Yourself?"

He was doing this for Libby. No question. Without addressing Gabe's statement, Clay moved toward the door. Gabe followed. He shook his mentor's hand. "Thanks. I'll see you Thursday."

Back on the road, Clay's phone buzzed, and he hit his earpiece. "This is Clay."

"Hey, brother of mine. How's it going?" Kourtney sounded as if she'd downed four cups of coffee this morning—hyperactive.

"Hey, Kourt. What's up?" The crossing guard finished protecting the latest group of kids and stepped back. Clay eased through the empty intersection and aimed for the address on his GPS. He had four ornamental pear trees waiting for a new home.

"Remember Fletcher?"

Her nerdy boyfriend. "Of course." They'd been dating two years now, and Mom kept hinting they needed to "get to the next level, already." Was this headed where he thought?

"We're engaged!"

Her shriek made Clay want to fling the earpiece across the cab, but he didn't. Wincing, he shushed her.

"Oh, sorry. You're driving, huh?"

"Yes, and congrats, little sister. I'm happy for you guys." He made a right-hand turn and headed down a residential street.

"We've got a date picked out, and we want to have the rehearsal dinner in the greenhouse room—you know, family and wedding party only. We're thinking this October."

Fall wedding. "Good choice. Have you told Mom and Dad?"

"Here's the thing. I want to have a family get-together this weekend. I'll bring Fletcher. We can tell them in person. Can you be there? Saturday night. Fletch is a great fisherman. I'll have him bring wild-caught salmon for grilling. Kason already agreed to come."

"Yeah, I can make that." He'd finish up at the Archers' early enough that afternoon.

"And feel free to bring a date. Perhaps someone from church? Or have you given up on Jill and the others?"

Was it possible Mom hadn't told Kourtney that Libby was back in town?

"Or you could bring Liberty."

He grunted a laugh. "You are still a pain in my neck."

"That's what little sisters are for." She paused for a second. "Now, tell me everything. How is she? What's it like seeing her again? Did you two pick up where you left off? Give me the whole scoop."

"First, if I did have news to 'dish,' I wouldn't trust you with it. You're as bad as Mom. But no, we're not dating." As for picking up where they'd left off? That wasn't possible. And it was better for everyone if his nosy little sister didn't know anything about it.

"Are there still sparks?"

He closed his mouth, knowing he couldn't answer.

"I knew it! So bring her. Saturday night. No excuses."

"Kourt, I—"

"I'll set things up with Mom and not tell her why we're coming."

"What's Kason think?"

"He's got strong opinions about Fletch, but I'm sure we can win him over. Tell me you're on board with us getting married."

Another question Clay couldn't answer right away.

"Clay, c'mon. We could use your support."

"Kourt, he's a little too trendy for the rest of us. We're simple farmers compared to Mr. Hipster." But the guy seemed solid enough. He'd probably take good care of Kourtney.

"Har-har. Listen, you'd better get over it. Make him feel welcome. He's about to be your brother."

Clay pulled into Mr. Peterman's driveway. "Gotta go, Sis. See you soon."

"Bye."

How was Fletcher Squire, with his glasses and ties and dressy shoes, going to fit in to their earthy family? Good thing Kason had taken over the farm. Kourtney's tech-wizard fiancé wouldn't like all that dirt.

Dinner with the family this Saturday. Even if he invited Libby to come, and he wasn't sure he wanted her anywhere near his sister, she'd probably beg off.

Mindlessly, he placed the trees where the owners had directed and considered Kourtney's question. Sparks? You bet. Not that they mattered when Libby was determined to keep her distance *and* leave as soon as she could afford to, from what she'd said.

All these years of pining and suddenly she'd dropped back into his world. Was this his second and final chance? Was he too casual about it?

An image flashed of his life without her—going back to the familiar and mundane. And lonely. He needed to change course. See if he could influence her plans. Show her cared about her—still.

Perhaps then he could convince her to stay.

A rapping sound on her camper door startled Liberty that evening. "Hang on," she called. She'd just taken a lukewarm shower and was now wrapped in a blanket wearing cozy socks, sweatpants, and an old thermal waffle long-sleeved T-shirt. She planned to curl up in her convertible bed and read before falling asleep. The florist job kept her on her feet all day. The role was much more physically demanding than she'd have believed, with lots of carrying and lifting.

"It's me, dear. Gloria."

Liberty opened the door, nudging it slowly outward so she didn't accidentally hit her hostess. "Hi."

"Goodness, it's chilly in there," Gloria said, barely putting her face into the camper. "C'mon over to the house. I have cocoa and candles going. A lovely evening. Plus, I need your involvement on something so the guys don't outnumber me in votes."

Liberty peeked toward the driveway. Sure enough, Clay's truck. She'd forgotten his plan to drop by and get her input. Still sporting wet hair, she shivered.

"See, you're freezing. C'mon!" Gloria took her hand after she'd donned her jacket and boots. That's when Liberty remembered she'd barely moisturized her face. No makeup. Hair in a loose braid, damp shirt. But it didn't matter. She didn't need to impress anyone.

Gloria hooked an arm with hers as they tromped across the muddy driveway to the garage entrance. "Roy will be glad to see you. You've been keeping to yourself a little too well lately."

They stepped into the house, and Liberty immediately relaxed into the warm atmosphere. Chocolate scented the air. Heated hardwood floors and cozy slippers, compliments of her hostess, provided creature comforts. Gloria reached for a shawl hanging in the mudroom and handed it to Liberty. "This will help, if you don't mind the bulk."

Liberty never worried much about fashion. She only wanted to feel warm, all the way to her bones. For once. She exchanged her coat for the shawl and followed Gloria into the kitchen. Men's voices carried from the table, and Liberty meandered in their direction. She'd missed Roy lately. She looked forward to offering her input and potentially helping them out. And seeing Clay might not be torture.

"Come join us for cocoa." Gloria waved her forward.

"She's got marshmallows." Clay lifted a mug piled high with miniature white cubes.

Roy laughed. "That's his second cup."

"Sounds yummy." Liberty could already feel her mood lighten as she approached the table.

Gloria placed a mug in her hands. "You can help me sell my gazebo idea to Roy and Clay."

A gazebo? She loved those. She scooped a few marshmallows from the bowl and plopped them into her cup, then inhaled the chocolatey steam before taking a long sip. "Hmm. This is heavenly."

Roy eyed her shawl. "You look cozy."

"Very." The yarn felt soft against her skin. "Did you make this, Gloria?"

"Yes, I did. I've been knitting and crocheting a lot since we retired. In fact, Roy has three new sweaters upstairs already."

Roy's shoulders shook when he chuckled. "Not that I need them." Even now, he wore a sleeveless vest over a long-sleeved shirt. "I tend to run warm. But don't let Gloria fool you. *She* wears them."

Having moved close to him, Gloria playfully slapped his shoulder. "Hush, you." She scooted back to the kitchen counter, where she refilled a platter of peanut butter cookies before returning. Liberty's stomach growled. She reached for one.

"You won't be able to see from all the way over there, Liberty. Here, come sit by me." Roy beckoned her to his left side. Clay sat to his right.

Gloria wiped down the kitchen's granite countertop. "Show her the gazebo."

Liberty settled beside Roy. He'd been like a father to her, and she'd be grateful all her life for how he'd helped her from the first time they'd met. He plunked down a magazine, which he'd folded open.

"It wouldn't look exactly like that," he said, his index finger thumping the page. "But it is the type she wants." He winked at his wife.

"It's charming." The gazebo's pillars were made of stained logs, holding up the pointed roof. Slats created the octagon flooring. If they painted the building in glossy white, the blues of the Sound and sky would contrast well.

"What do you think?" Clay appeared at her other side and sat down. Her attention shot to his face. She let her guard down, and here he came, getting close to her.

He pointed at the chair. "Do you mind?"

Yes. "No." Did she mind that he'd moved into her personal space? Heaven help her, but part of her didn't object at all.

"Then, it's a question of placement." He hooked a thumb

toward the dusky yard outside. "I recommend they position it near the waterside of the property, so they can take advantage of the view. What do you think?"

She considered the expansive lawn leading to the bluff. "What about that group of poplars?" Trying to ignore Clay's nearness, she addressed her questions to the Archers. "Would this be the right size to fit in there? The trees wouldn't obscure the view, and they'd add a hint of seclusion."

"I hadn't thought of that." Gloria clapped. "I love it."

"Good suggestion," Clay said. "If we use that grove, we can add a touch of privacy."

Gloria reached for her husband's hand. "How romantic."

"Yes, dear," Roy said, humoring her. But Liberty could see the love in his eyes. They genuinely cared for each other, setting a high standard in the way they spoke to and about each other.

She raised her attention from them and caught Clay's gaze.

"You've got me thinking." He grabbed the sketch pad and flipped to a fresh page. Within moments, he'd rendered the lawn where the poplars stood sixty feet back from the bluff's edge and positioned a hand-drawn gazebo among the trees. Using quick strokes, he penciled in shrubs and a stone path leading there from the back of the house.

"I think a dry creek bed would be better." Liberty barely recognized her own boldness as she shared freely. She stood and went to the window where she could see the view they planned to change in the waning daylight. "What about using different types of grasses, like you see in landscaping at ocean properties? You know how rentals in Westport or Long Beach have red river rock and swaying grasses in clumps? You could use whatever color stone you liked—red, blue, gray. And down the center, pavers for walking."

Everyone went still, and all of them looked at her. Then Gloria cheered. "Perfect."

"A dry creek bed." Clay used a large eraser to remove his pathway, then drew in a new path with rocks and ornamental plants dotted sporadically along the way. "Like this?"

Liberty moved behind him and studied the sheet. "Yes. And then, a few added groupings here and there. Consider adding a firepit somewhere, if you don't mind the smoke." She could never handle all that pollution. Her throat would burn, accompanied by sneezing, a headache, and choking. But some people loved it.

"You're good at visualizing," Gloria said. The others agreed.

"Of course, you could always add a second walking path. How about over here?" She leaned toward Clay. The yard stretched out between the house and cliff. Reaching past Clay's shoulder, she pointed to the patio's edge and drew a line to the bluff from there. "You wouldn't want to worry about stray stones, especially if you were carrying anything to the gazebo." Clay smelled good. She straightened before ambling to the other side of the table where she'd left her cocoa. Distance.

"That's going to look so grand." Gloria's expression turned dreamy. "The best place to watch sunsets, or people could get married out there. The lawn's big enough for a host of chairs."

Liberty could feel Clay's concentration pinned on her as if he wondered about her thoughts. Perhaps it was time to excuse herself. "If that's everything, I have stuff to finish up before tomorrow morning." Like reading a book and ignoring thoughts of Clay. She poured the last of her cocoa in the sink.

Gloria joined her in the mudroom as she slipped into her boots. "Keep the shawl. I can make another one. And it opens here." She pointed at hidden buttons. "So, it's either a poncho or a shawl. Please wear it." Her mothering reached scarred places in Liberty's heart, areas that soaked up her nurturing like a balm.

Throat tight, Liberty rewrapped herself. "Thank you."

Gloria's hand landed on her shoulder. "You know, don't you, that you're welcome to change your mind at any time. We won't tease you. Please reconsider living with us."

How many times had she entertained that thought in the past few weeks? But getting close would only hurt more. Liberty hugged herself. "Thanks again."

"I hate to think of you alone in your trailer."

Liberty gave her a smile, trying to lighten the atmosphere. "It's not that far from your house. I know where to find you if anything comes up." Of course, she wouldn't bother them. She would handle it herself. Opening the door, she stepped out. "Good night."

Back in her cold living space moments later, Liberty made a mug of hot water to help warm herself up. Ever since the propane line broke on her camper's built-in heater, she'd used an old space heater, but at times that didn't feel safe. To ease her worries, she didn't use it often. She'd sleep wrapped in Gloria's gift tonight.

She took her book to bed. The quiet in her home blared after the welcoming atmosphere of the house. But getting close to others meant losing them. When hadn't she? Her parents. Her guardians, right as she'd begun to trust them. Clay. Daisy, though she'd never had a chance to bond with her.

Normally, she'd refocus her thoughts to something cheerful. But tonight, loneliness drowned her attempts. She fell asleep to the soft glow of light from next door.

CHAPTER FOURTEEN

A few nights later, Clay's truck bounced down his family's driveway, while Liberty held on in the passenger seat. How had she gotten dragged into this? Here she was, attending a family dinner at the Garrisons after all. Soon, she'd meet Kason's wife and kids, see Kourtney again. They'd been friendly over a decade ago, though Kourtney was five years younger.

"If this is too awful for you, let me know. We'll go get a burger or something." Bless him, Clay was trying to ease Liberty's discomfort.

"How'd you know?"

"A hunch." He put the truck in Park, faced her. "I keep wondering what life would have been like if we'd stayed together. Or gotten married back then." *Kept Daisy.* He didn't add the words, but she heard them.

Unclicking her seat belt, she angled herself toward him. "The past is over. Let's get through this—make your mom happy, check 'family dinner' off the list so she'll let it be. Okay?"

He was silent a moment, watching her. "Is that really what you want?"

What was he saying? Could he know she questioned her own resolve, repeatedly? "Of course. Now, don't worry about me. I'll be fine." She started to climb out, but he snagged her arm with a gentle hold.

"Okay, but if you need help, let me know. Deal?" He let go of her arm. "I know you like to be independent, but sometimes there's a wave of loneliness that comes off you and it makes me want to—"

"Fix it?" She gave him a grin so he'd know she wasn't upset. Seriously, though, where was he going with this? Was he trying to give her hints of renewed attraction? And what was she supposed to do about how much she liked seeing those clues?

"Truth is, we've been through a lot together, and I want you to know you're not alone. Unless you choose to be. But I hope you'll choose not to."

He couldn't mean anything romantic, even if that's how it sounded. Her imagination needed reining in. She shouldn't lean on him. The last time she'd trusted him, he'd betrayed her.

But as they crossed the driveway to the door, her thoughts drifted to their shared pain over losing Daisy. He was right. They had a history, a type of emotional bond. And it wasn't completely behind them.

The Garrisons had moved since Liberty last visited them during high school. Their new home overlooked the water, rather than being landlocked by acres of trees at the farm. She loved the wraparound porch and hanging flower baskets.

Elizabeth greeted her in the kitchen after Clay let them into the house. Large windows offered a bright view of the Sound. Two little kids raced through the house, running up the stairs and back down into the sunken living room.

"Kids! Don't crash into anyone." Elizabeth seemed rather comfortable in her role as grandmother, and Liberty felt the sting of that realization. Someone was missing from their gathering.

"Those two are my niece and nephew," Clay said. "Muriel is the youngest. Mitchell the oldest. And this is their mom, Brynn."

A lovely blonde woman sporting a down-to-earth harried mother look, came up and shook Liberty's hand. "Great to meet you. I've heard tales of high school from these two." She jerked a thumb between the brothers. "Glad to not be outnumbered in my age group for once."

"Good to meet you. Looks like you have your hands full with the kiddos." Envy tried to steal in, but Liberty pushed it away.

"Sure do. But they adore their local grandparents, and Elizabeth and Jonathan feel the same way."

"Where is Dad?" Clay asked quickly as if wanting to speak over his sister-in-law's words.

Kason reached for a branch full of grapes from the bowl on the counter. "Outside, firing up the grill. Kourtney and Fletcher are due any minute."

Liberty turned to Elizabeth. "How can I help?"

While the two of them worked in the kitchen, Clay and Kason carried things out to the picnic table and Brynn chased the kids into the yard.

"Ah, family. Delightful chaos." Elizabeth scooped fingerling potatoes into a bowl. "I'm glad you're here today, hon."

"Thanks for having me."

Kourtney and Fletcher pulled in, and Clay appeared at Liberty's side. Did he expect this to be difficult for her?

"Dad says hi," he murmured into her ear, and she checked a shiver. But she didn't move away.

Kourtney breezed into the house, tugging her boyfriend behind her. He smiled at everyone as introductions were made. Jonathan limped inside, greeting Liberty and the newcomers.

"Join me at the grill, Fletch. I hear you've got salmon." Jonathan led the way, and Fletcher waved a bag in his hand.

He already seemed to fit in. He'd likely been dating Kourtney a while.

Muriel darted through the slider before they'd shut it, barreling into Clay. "I need gwapes."

He swung her into his arms and offered her a couple of grapes. "Here you go, Puddin'."

Liberty busied herself cutting up a cantaloupe, trying to ignore what seeing Clay with a little girl was doing to her heart. He'd been right in the truck. This family get-together hurt. Liberty dumped a pile of melon cubes into a bowl and caught the tender expression Clay aimed at her while Muriel squirmed to be let down.

"Take those outside," Elizabeth called after her. "She'll make a mess yet." Elizabeth hoisted a bowl in each hand and, marching outdoors, left Clay and Liberty alone in the kitchen.

"Are you doing okay?" He toyed with the utensils on the counter, but she knew he fidgeted out of concern for her.

Something about that care touched a deep corner of her heart. Her resolve to ignore the pain drained away, and she drooped against the cabinets. "You were right. You're oh for two tonight."

He stepped closer, pretense gone. "It's going to get a little more complicated."

"What do you mean?"

He peeked over his shoulder, then back. "My little sis is now engaged. They're here to make the announcement at dinner."

Why should that bother Liberty? Except... years ago, they'd hoped to make a similar declaration themselves. After college. After starting jobs in their career fields.

"I'm sorry we never worked out." He read her thoughts as if she'd spoken them, which meant he must have been thinking similar things.

"Me too." As a teen, she'd thought they would always be together.

"But," he said, taking her hand and leaning even closer. "I want you to know I don't blame you. Let's leave all that in the past, okay?"

"Of course." That's what she'd been trying to do, though it cost her energy and friendships and peace of mind.

"Start fresh."

"Exactly." She tugged her hand free. Time to shore up her walls. "We're coworkers now."

A flash of hurt crossed his face. "So being here doesn't... I mean, I thought—"

Kourtney strode into the room from the waterside deck. "Liberty, we didn't have a chance to catch up yet. How have you been?"

Clay pulled back, but Liberty could feel his eyes on her.

"I'm well, thanks. Your family has been welcoming and kind from the first moment I got back." A wave of gratitude washed over her, and she gave Clay a smile. "Sounds like things are going well for you," she said to Kourtney, nodding toward the deck where Fletcher played with Mitchell and Muriel.

A big grin overtook Kourtney's face. "I've never been happier." She switched gears and gave her brother a mock punch. He sucked in his stomach, playing along. "How are *you* doing?"

His playful scowl brought a smile to Liberty's face. "Oh, you know, just trying to tolerate my baby sister."

"Har-har." Wearing a mischievous expression, she tracked between Clay and Liberty, perhaps deducing more than anyone had said aloud. "Coworkers?" Kourtney must have heard Liberty use that label moments before she'd joined them.

Clay gave his sister a look that he probably assumed Liberty didn't see. In her head, she heard phrases like *That's rather cozy. But is it enough?* And *I'm guessing you're spending more time at the shop and less time at the farm these days.* Liberty pretended not to notice. She'd head outside and let the siblings work it out. Hefting the bowl of muskmelon, she turned toward the slider. "I'll take this out to the table."

Dinner was a loud meal, with two outdoor heaters keeping them warm this April evening. Clay's attention kept tracking to Liberty. Was she okay? That pasted-on smile seemed tired. He should devise a way to get her excused from the rest of the party.

Across the table, Dad hugged a grandchild on each side of him, laughing at their antics. *Laughing.* Something he only did with them. Had Clay and Liberty robbed Dad and Mom by not finding a way to be a family? Worse, had they robbed Daisy of getting to know this crazy bunch, of living with people who looked like her, and having these cousins to chase?

"Hey, everyone. Could we quiet down a bit?" Kourtney clutched Fletcher's hand. Clay had to admit, the guy fit in better tonight, between grilling with Dad and dressing less fancy. "Fletch and I have an announcement."

Dad smiled as if he already knew. Had Fletcher talked with him ahead of time to seek Dad's blessing? Clay would have gone to Mr. Kincade ten years ago if he and Libby had gotten that far.

"We're getting married!" Kourtney beamed. Mom gasped and jumped up to rush her for a big hug.

The chaos lasted for several minutes, with congratulations and handshakes, while Libby offered good wishes and hung back.

This evening's events were killing her.

Time to escape.

"Hey, guys, it's getting late. I think I'll get Liberty home."

She didn't object, but instead stood to thank his parents for hosting. He'd guessed right again.

"Wait." Kourtney stood in the circle of Fletcher's arms, each of them facing the crowd. "I was hoping you'd both stick around. I wanted to start planning tonight. Maybe talk flowers and décor." She faced Liberty. "I'd love your input."

From behind Liberty, Clay made neck-slicing gestures to stop his sister, trying to deter her. But she didn't seem to notice.

"Sure," Liberty said. "But perhaps another time. You said October, right? We have a few months to bat ideas around."

"True." Kourtney's expression fell. She wasn't used to being refused.

"It's been a long day. Let's chat soon." With a final thanks, Liberty headed back into the house and Clay followed her after waving at his family.

In the truck, Liberty melted into the seat. "Thank you."

"You bet." He pulled onto the street and headed north. Toying with his idea, he considered the consequences. If he told her his plan, she'd probably decide to never trust him again. Better to keep it to himself for now. Besides, the past few hours had obviously taken a toll.

"Sometimes I go into denial about all those losses." She spoke quietly, and Clay wished the truck didn't run so loud. Finally, he pulled off the road and parked a short distance from Roy and Gloria's. "You know, losing Mom and Dad. Being sent away." She stared through the windshield, almost as if she was talking to herself. "Shea said that denial was a coping mechanism so I could do what had to be done. Survive. Bring a baby into the world. But then something happens—like dinner tonight. And the grief returns."

He took her hand. "What can I do?"

"You don't have to do anything. I'm not..." She must have noticed his expression, because she stopped talking and instead squeezed his fingers between hers. "What you did tonight. I've been on my own a long time. Having someone not only look out for me, but anticipate my needs and then meet them?" Pale blue eyes searched his. "I don't even know what to make of it. I'd forgotten what that's like."

Something about her drew that reaction out of him. "My pleasure." If she let him, he'd find more ways to help.

CHAPTER FIFTEEN

Sunshine filtered through the hundred-foot tall conifers in Roy's yard when Clay pulled in with his delivery. Gloria had asked for some ornamental trees for the front, and he'd brought a Japanese maple and a dwarf willow. Roy met him in the drive.

"Gloria's going to love these." He pointed at the garden spot. "They'll look great with her summer flowers."

Clay set down the second tree and brushed his covered hands together before pulling off his gloves. "Is she here?" He'd like to get her personal approval. Liberty was at work at the shop.

"No, she's out shopping. C'mon inside. I've got a scheme to hash over with you."

A scheme? Clay chuckled as he followed him indoors.

Ten minutes later, they hovered at the kitchen's granite island over cookies and coffee.

"What's this about a scheme?"

Mischief glinted in Roy's eyes as he took a huge bite, in no hurry to answer.

"I have a feeling you're a fun dad."

"Ask any of my boys, they'll tell you. I'm a nut. But I love my family." His demeanor went serious. "As you know, we haven't been able to convince Liberty to move in with us. But there must be a way. You've known her a long time, right? How can we prove to her that we care about her?"

Coffee scalded Clay's throat as he gulped to cover a cough. Did he mean to include Clay in his "we"? Perhaps he hadn't hidden his feelings as well as he thought. "Come again?"

"I was thinking perhaps we hide her camper."

Laughter echoed off the walls. They'd only recently met, but if Clay could, he'd adopt Roy. "You know we can't do that right? Police officers, jail time—for you, for theft."

"Might be worth it." Roy's face took on a good-natured grin.

"Tuck that thing into the depths of the outbuilding, tell her someone made off with it... Okay, I get what you're saying."

Clay uncrossed his arms as Roy caved. "Showing that you care for her should not involve scaring her."

Roy clapped a hand on Clay's shoulder. "Good point. So tell me, why haven't I met your dad yet? I mean, your delightful mother has visited several times, but no sign of your father. How come?"

"He prefers to keep to himself." Sometimes Clay felt responsible for his dad's grouchiness, and he was certainly tired of making excuses for him. Other times, he wished he could take himself off the hook. Yes, he'd messed up. Did that condemn him forever?

"What's your old man like?"

Words like *angry, unforgiving, injured,* and *belligerent,* flashed through his mind, but he pushed those terms away. "Hardworking. He built the family farm and nursery into a thriving business."

Roy dipped a cookie in his coffee. "But he isn't willing to support you in growing your landscaping start-up."

"You noticed that?"

"He wouldn't give you the hours, or let you hire someone else for the nursery. I'm surprised he let you drop by today."

"You placed an order. But you're right. I think he knows I can get the work done. And he doesn't want to hire someone else. Money's tight until we see how the season's going to go."

Roy sighed deep. "You're a good man, Clay. Defending him." Did Roy know more than Clay thought he did? Maybe, like with his guesses about him and Liberty, Roy had discerned what no one had spoken. "I mean, you show him respect, even when he isn't here. You defend him. You're a good son. I'd be proud of you, if you were mine."

The words sunk into an empty place inside Clay, and it was a couple of moments before he could speak. "Gloria said you have five sons. That's probably enough." He couldn't meet Roy's eyes.

Roy selected another cookie. "Now, we must come up with a plan to show Liberty we care."

Back to this? Okay. "Honestly?"

"You betcha."

"I want to protect her, even if she doesn't want me to."

"Ditto," Roy said, leaning forward. "Which is why we want her out of the cold. What can we do to make her life easier? She's got a job with your mom, and she's got us. Are there other resources? What about family? We could reach out to them."

This might be the sign Clay had been waiting for. He'd all but promised not to tell the Archers or his family about Daisy, but was Roy someone he could trust? Could he partner with Clay to search? Given his life experience, he might have connections. Would Libby forgive either of them for meddling if she ever found out—*when* she found out?

"Question for you," Clay began.

"Okay."

"If you were going to try to find someone's long-lost family member, how would you go about it?"

"Do you mean her guardians? Liberty told us about them. Sounds like it didn't end well. I don't recommend we contact them."

"You're right. Not them exactly, but like them." He'd try not to get too personal, not divulge too much. "In a situation like that, how would you begin your search?"

Roy crossed an arm over his ribs and rested his chin against a crooked finger, all business. "Let's see. I've noticed posts on social media that lead to people being reconnected. But that's only if you don't mind it going public. Seems to me, Liberty would rather keep her distance from those folks."

"True."

"So, this is about someone else in Liberty's life, if my guess is correct."

Clay squirmed. He shouldn't have brought this up, but Roy had a good tip. Without posting, Clay could check out various groups on social media and see if he could find other ideas for conducting his search. "Listen, please don't mention anything to Libby, okay?"

"*Libby?*" Roy gave him a knowing grin. "Okay, son. Don't worry. But you be careful."

"Wasn't I just giving you that same advice?"

Roy winked. "Aren't you glad I listened?"

Liberty turned off the car's engine and put her parking permit in clear view under the windshield. Sitting here at Deception Pass, she stared into the forest of tall evergreens directly in front of her. She'd snagged the end spot and the channel was visible through the trees, reflecting the almost-white sky. To her right, a stairway led to the trails where she could hike down to the beach. Or she could opt to cross the bridge on foot.

The views were among her favorites—a nearly two-hundred-foot drop from the bridges into the jade green water. A small island dotted the wide channel as it opened into Puget Sound—Deception Island, if she remembered correctly. The Kincades had brought the family here during high school, camping at Cranberry Lake not far away, kayaking, picnicking.

Elizabeth had given Liberty the afternoon off since she'd worked so much overtime lately with weddings. The weather had turned sunny, and tourists were out. Wind gusts rattled her car as she dialed Shea.

"Hi, friend." Shea's welcoming tone wrapped Liberty in a virtual hug. Too bad she didn't live closer. "How are you?"

"Tonight we get to plan Clay's sister's wedding. Yippee." She groaned to let Shea know how she felt, in case the sarcasm wasn't obvious enough.

"Oh, boy."

"Other than that, mostly okay." Liberty lowered her car's windows a bit to let in the fresh forest air.

"Eating well?"

"Trying."

"I thought the Archers were looking out for you." Shea seemed to hear more than Liberty shared. "I wonder if I should call them next."

Liberty laughed. "Making threats to check up on me? You're talking to me like a friend, and not like a counselor."

"I'm not that far away, you know."

"Ha. Come on up. You'll find much the same as last time. The only difference is I'm saving up to move on."

"Wait, you're moving? But you have friends there. I'm guessing, in the next place, you might not. At least not right away."

"True." She wouldn't dwell on the sadness that weighed her down when she considered her plan, but neither would she promise to stay on Whidbey.

"How's Clay?" Shea's voice came out a bit too singsongy for Liberty.

"There's no avoiding him."

"He seems like a nice guy now, compared to how you described the old version. Liam liked him. Has he changed much from high school?"

"Outwardly? Sure. He's taller. Inwardly, I can only guess." Not that she hadn't made her own deductions lately, but she felt like keeping those to herself. "He smells different."

Shea snorted. "What? He's been near enough for you to sniff him?"

"For a moment." Liberty paused, remembering the few times she'd been in range. "Big news—I told him."

"And... how did it go?"

"Pretty rough."

"It can hit someone hard to learn they're a parent when they weren't expecting it. Was he upset that he didn't have a say?"

Liberty squeezed the steering wheel with her free hand. "Doesn't matter. He was absentee by choice."

"Of course." Shea paused for a second following Liberty's defensiveness. "Is he fine with leaving things as they are?"

"Yes." She hoped. They'd never talked about leaving things alone. "You should have seen his face when I showed him her baby picture."

"It sounds to me like you both might feel better since your talk. Perhaps you'll each find some closure."

"I hope so."

"Now, about seeing a counselor there in Birch Harbor. I've

been researching, and I found three people who might be good matches for you. I'll text you their information. Okay?" Just because Liberty might need someone local to traipse through the weeds of her past with her didn't mean she was willing.

"Thanks." Not that she'd promise to reach out to them. Her goal now was to cope with all the reminders of her history and interact with the Garrisons without her heart cracking open. Long ago, she'd thought they'd be her family one day.

"Meanwhile, please take good care of yourself."

"I will. You too."

They disconnected the call, and Liberty locked her car and strode toward the longer of the two bridges. Her phone buzzed in her pocket as she reached the middle, but she'd wait to check it when she wasn't dangling over a thousand-foot span with traffic noise. Perhaps Shea had forgotten to mention something and had sent a text.

Liberty paused mid-span and gazed out at the water. A gust pushed against her, and she gripped the metal railing while the trees bent with the wind. This evening, the Garrisons expected her for dinner. Her phone buzzed again, and she aimed toward the parking lot. Was Elizabeth the one who kept calling? Liberty would get back to solid ground and see who couldn't live without her. Chuckling to herself, she stopped in the shade and pulled out her cell.

A horn interrupted her as Clay swung into the lot and parked next to her car. His expression seemed worried as he waved and jumped out. "Hey, Liberty. We've been trying to reach you."

"What's happening?"

He rushed closer. "Roy said he tried to call and finally he dialed me in case I knew where you were." He pointed back toward the road. "Just finished up a delivery. I'm glad I found you."

Her heart thumped. "You're scaring me."

"Okay, don't worry. Things are fine—mostly." He slowed his frantic words and lightly touched her shoulders. "The wind took down a tree in Roy's yard."

Fighting the urge to race home, she locked her knees so she

could learn more. "Are they okay?"

"Yes. But your trailer isn't. Came right down, crushing the center. Gloria's beside herself. She keeps saying, 'What if Liberty had been in there?'"

"Seriously? A tree?" She couldn't explain it, but humor bubbled up. "Roy did this on purpose."

Clay must have read the laughter in her expression. The corners of his eyes creased with his smile as he released her. "Ya think?"

"I mean, they've wanted me to move into the house since I got here." Her heart slowly returned to normal at the image of Roy directing the tree like the ground crew bringing in planes at SeaTac.

Clay's face went sober. "Will you?"

"What choice do I have now?" Relief replaced surprise in her thoughts because this meant she wouldn't have to be alone.

"Roy's going to laugh when you tell him you think he planned this."

"I'm pretty sure they both did." She pressed their number on her phone's screen and waited for it to ring. "Thanks for finding me, Clay, and letting me know."

"Sure thing. I'll wait for you and follow you back to town."

Roy answered.

"Now, what's this I hear from Clay about you dropping a tree on my camper?"

CHAPTER SIXTEEN

Though she'd been preparing herself as she drove home, the view of the huge evergreen reducing her camper to a crunched *V* startled Liberty. She slowed more than normal and eased into the driveway. Clay turned in behind her. Gloria and Roy were outside, near the garage.

"Oh, I'm so glad you weren't in there." Gloria sounded almost hysterical when Liberty joined them. She wrapped Liberty in a tight hug.

"We both are." Roy rocked on his heels.

When Gloria finally released her, Liberty peered over at the damage. The large cedar had broken off about halfway up, sending a substantial chunk toward the ground.

"This is crazy." Clay circled the camper and jagged trunk.

"I think Someone was watching out for you. Loudest crash we've ever heard." Roy offered his arm, and Liberty took it. They walked a bit closer. "Barely missed the house."

Someone watching out for her? Probably not, but the more she saw, the more relieved she was to have been away. "Did you see it happen?"

"I often check outside when a huge gust blows through. This was a doozy, but I was facing the Sound, not the south," Roy said. "'Course as soon as we heard the crash, we ran out here."

"What if this had happened in the middle of the night?" Gloria jabbed an index finger toward the jutting branches and then shuddered. "We've had several gusts this spring. I don't even want to think about it."

"Doesn't look like I'll be able to get anything out, does it?" The mangled door didn't seem operable from a few yards away.

Gloria approached on her left and took her free arm. "Don't you worry about a thing. We'll get a crew out here and get that tree off. But the camper..."

"Yeah, the camper is a goner." Roy patted her hand as if to ease his proclamation, then he exchanged a look with Clay that Liberty didn't have time to decipher. Except she noted the lack of heartbreak in his voice. Ha. He *had* done this on purpose.

"Please say you'll move inside with us, dear."

Liberty faced Gloria and Roy, taking each of their hands. "Yes, I will. Thank you." She looked forward to evenings of cocoa and conversation and not being alone anymore. "Still," she began, giving them a look of playful accusation, "I think you both have been up to something here."

"Nonsense." Gloria placed her hand over her heart, matching the teasing note in Liberty's voice. "Listen, I'd be happy to take you shopping. Get you the essentials. We could go right now so you'll have what you need for tonight."

Clay joined them. "Mom's expecting us for dinner, but I'm sure she'd understand."

Now Liberty had a chance to get out of the family dinner, but was that the right choice? Or the safest one? Without clothes for tomorrow, or even pajamas or toiletries, how could she avoid a quick trip to a department store? "I could stop on the way. I'll need a few items immediately." And the sooner they got the first wedding planning meeting over with, the sooner she wouldn't have to dread it.

Roy reached for his wallet and pulled out a few bills. "Take this."

Liberty held up a hand in a *stop* motion, but Roy gave her a look. "We want to help. Please."

All their faces showed they hoped she'd comply, and she didn't have the strength to deny them. She offered him an open palm instead, and he placed the money there. "Thank you," she said.

"Let me drive you," Clay said.

"He's right, dear. You've suffered an awful fright. Please, let him give you a ride."

Once more, it was three to one. But there was wisdom in the suggestion. She agreed and went to grab her purse from her car. The stress of the day threatened to unravel her composure. Where was her sense of humor when she needed it?

In the truck, Liberty tried to loosen the tension. "Here we are again, headed to your family's house for dinner."

Clay backed out and aimed his truck toward town. "You don't have to do that." His voice came out quietly.

"Do what?"

"Put on a front with me. I know this is hard."

"You'd rather I be honest with you?"

"Yes."

She wouldn't tell him everything, but his concern for her felt too good to reject. "I hate that a tree fell on my house."

"I know and I'm sorry. And thank you."

"For what?"

He gave her a glimpse of those green eyes. "Trusting me with the truth."

For some reason the moment felt intimate, a thought she entertained all the way to the store.

They pulled into the local Fred Meyer's, and she headed toward women's clothing. This shopping trip was about to get uncomfortable if Clay stuck to her side like he'd done since the produce department. "How about we meet up in, say, twenty minutes?"

"You got it." He took off toward sporting goods as if glad to escape.

Once she'd chosen the essential clothing items, she harvested the beauty aisles for toiletries. Roy's money was more than enough at the checkout, and then, Liberty searched for Clay.

She caught up with him in Floral where he spun from the counter with a bouquet of magenta carnations in his hand. Stopping a few feet from him, she tried to read his face.

He gestured for her heavy bags. "Trade? I can carry those for you."

Was he serious? Absently, she made the exchange, but accepting flowers from Clay? Awkward and confusing.

At the truck, he eyed her. "Oh, I'm sorry." He groaned as if he recognized the message he'd sent. "Those are for Kourtney. And I'm an idiot."

Kourtney. Of course. She was the bride. But something pinched inside that the flowers weren't for her.

"I wanted to pick up a gift for my sister. You know, as a celebration. I didn't stop to think what *you* might think." He placed her bags in the extended cab and stepped close. "Normally, I'd get flowers at Mom's shop, but I ran out of time. I didn't mean to upset you—"

"Oh, it's okay. Of course they're for the bride." She climbed into the cab and laid the bundle of stems and blooms across her lap. Once Clay joined her, she added, "Carnations are fine, but I've always loved—"

"Gerbera daisies. And if I thought you'd accept them, I'd bring you their biggest bouquet."

There was no mistaking his intent that time. Where did her oxygen go? And how had he remembered?

Clay's declaration lingered like a hot air balloon between them, bobbing in the silence for the rest of the drive.

At the house, Kourtney met them outside where Liberty gave her the flowers. The siblings exchanged a look, but neither spoke.

Elizabeth peeked around the corner of the wrap-around porch. "We're meeting outdoors. Join us."

Her acceptance touched Liberty, and she let herself relax on the waterside deck with the family. They made lists over burgers and hot dogs. If Liberty told herself enough times that this situation didn't have to be uncomfortable, maybe it wouldn't be.

Mitchell burst into the waterside yard, Muriel behind him. A second later, Brynn appeared, looking harried. "I could use backup."

Clay reached for Muriel, who crawled into his lap. "How about I take them to the beach for a walk?"

Brynn dropped into a deck chair and blew her hair off her face with a puff of breath. "Good luck." She closed her eyes to the warm sun.

"Why don't you take a break, Liberty?" Kourtney asked from the across the table. "I think we've covered enough for now."

Clay stood in the lawn with the kiddos, making the perfect family picture. "Wanna walk with us? I could use your help."

This setup smelled fishy, but Liberty loved spending time with Muriel. "Sure."

"I will find a way to repay you both," Brynn called as the four of them crossed the yard. "You're a couple of godsends."

"Why don't you hold Miss Liberty's hand, Muriel? I'll keep up with your brother." Clay sought Libby's agreement, then set his niece down near her. Mitchell jogged to the stairs where Clay caught up. This kiddo needed an Off switch. How Kourtney kept up with the kids every minute, he didn't know. No wonder she'd asked for help.

Liberty and Muriel took their time on the steps and then joined the boys on the sand. Muriel sat down, pulling Liberty with her, and Clay liked the picture they made. Of course, Daisy would be older than Muriel. They'd missed nine years of her life. Mitchell darted too close to the incoming waves, and Clay scrambled to keep him from getting doused.

"Let's dig in the sand, okay, buddy?" He coaxed his nephew back toward the ladies and sank down next to them. This far from the surf, they'd stay dry. If needed, Clay could volunteer for tub duty. Better that than swimming in the frigid Sound. "How's it going over here?" His attention zeroed in on Libby, who leaned back as sunshine glinted off her red hair.

Muriel showed him a rock she'd found, and Clay moved closer while keeping a keen eye on his mischievous charge. "Sorry about my sister's questions."

Libby pressed her lips together in an exaggerated way before answering. "You mean, the third degree? It's fine."

He heard humor in her voice and appreciated how she seemed to handle life's waves as they came.

"She hasn't seen me in a decade. Lots of ground to cover—the history of my love life." She opened her eyes, found his. "You may have learned a thing or two as I answered her."

What was this new playful side of Libby? Probably good she couldn't see what it did to him. He didn't want to scare her away. "To even things out, I haven't dated very seriously since we were together, either."

Questions crossed her features. Yes, he was sending messages. What did she think of them? He wouldn't ask. Yet.

"All those women surrounding you at church. Nothing?"

"Mom encourages them. And yeah, nothing."

Libby sat back, closing her eyes into the sunshine like his sister-in-law had done. Must be a female thing. "Elizabeth wants you married. Kason's married. Now, Kourtney."

"Long ago, I was spoiled for anyone else. Mom will just have to understand that."

Mitchell took off running, which meant Clay did too. But he could feel Libby's eyes tracking him down the beach.

CHAPTER SEVENTEEN

The peaceful sound of acoustic guitar chords filled the Archers' outbuilding while Liberty reached for a plastic, miniature bluebird. She enjoyed playing the instrumental music through her mini-speaker whenever she worked. On the bench in front of her, the newest fairy house was coming together. It only needed the finishing touches. What should she do with it when it was finished? No room in her bedroom. Using these weather-proof supplies, she could donate it to decorate a corner of Gloria's garden. Of course, she'd have to seal off the door so no mice or other pests nested inside. The Archers' grandchildren might enjoy it when they visited.

That gave her an idea. Daisy's birthday was coming up in a few weeks. Liberty would make a fairy house for her, though of course, Daisy would never see it.

She pulled a new base from the crate of supplies she'd picked up at the craft store. For her daughter she'd use a palette of colors found in the gerbera daisies her daughter was nicknamed for. Pulling bright green moss from the crate, she knew this fairy house needed the miniature fountain she'd been saving.

Sadness descended on her, full of regrets and pain. This often happened near her daughter's birthday. In her mind, Liberty retraced the steps. Given the same circumstances, there were events she couldn't change, and a few she wouldn't. Clay might feel the same way. If only they could talk about it. After all, she had no one else in town to discuss this with.

But if Liberty brought this up with Clay, he might decide to act, and she couldn't live with that. So, she'd bury the thoughts and pain and keep them to herself. In her teen years, when she'd been surrounded by Christians at church and home, she found herself praying often. After everything she'd suffered, though, there was no way God still listened. He was far from her, and that was probably for the best.

Too bad God's heart wasn't like hers, in her role as a mother. If it were, He'd long to create goodness for people. Goodness and hope. And comfort.

A breeze rustled through the open door with birdsong drifting in. She smiled. This setting boosted her creativity. The garage's original builders had positioned windows above the workbench, and from here, Liberty could see the whitecaps on the Sound far below. She pushed open one of the windows, and a salty breeze from that direction rushed in. She'd never lived in such a beautiful place.

Back to the fairy house. She hummed as she worked, her voice feeling out of practice.

The photo of Liberty holding Daisy filled her mind. If she focused, she could feel her tiny newborn in her arms. Squirming, squealing, and capturing Liberty's heart.

With tears in her eyes, she got to work.

Clay found the garage's side door open when he reached the building. His own clippers were back at the farm, so he wanted to borrow Roy's. Liberty was standing at the workbench when he entered—a welcome surprise. "Hey, Liberty."

"Oh, hey." She brushed a hand against her cheek. "How's the work coming?"

"What's wrong?" On alert, he strode to her. He searched the materials on the table and then scanned her hands and face. Had she hurt herself? "You okay?"

A moment passed before she answered. "You caught me."

"Doing what?"

After a glance behind him, she pointed at the table. "I'm creating a fairy house... for Daisy."

"Come again?" Had she found their daughter somehow?

"I always make her a birthday present." She got back to work, arranging materials on the base before gluing anything down.

"Oh." Now might be a good time to tell her he'd begun his own search. But they were starting to build a new trust, and he didn't want to break it. "Tell me about it." She shared her ideas, and he could see her vision, especially when she pointed to the completed house on a nearby shelf. "I didn't know you made these now. Mom should sell them at the shop."

She faced her project and reached for a tube of paint. "I'm not sure I should mix my art into the business, but thanks." After squirting a dab on her palette, she turned toward him. "But I need to ask you a favor."

"Anything."

"Are you still cool with not telling people about Daisy? And leaving things alone where she's concerned?"

Good thing he hadn't acted on what he'd been learning. He could answer honestly. "I won't tell anyone, unless you decide you want to."

"Thanks. Mentioning our daughter would make things awkward at the shop. I like working for your mom."

"Kourtney inherited her curiosity. Mom's probing questions don't bother you either?"

Libby bit her lip. "She did confess something to me the other day."

"Yeah, what?" His heartrate picked up speed. Mom could embarrass him like no one else.

"We were talking about how she likes having me in the store, then she said she missed me. That she *and* the rest of the family missed me."

"Meaning..." Was Libby fishing here? If so, he'd let her try a little longer. But he couldn't withhold his grin.

"Aw, nothing." She picked up a paintbrush.

She was acting as impish as his niece. "Out with it."

Her chuckle added to the music from that speaker. "She may have mentioned pining."

A rush of adrenaline chased up his spine. "She didn't."

Libby gave a one-shouldered shrug, but Clay could turn this

game around. "You mean, *you've* been pining for someone?"

"Ha-ha." While still smiling at his lighthearted joke, Libby seemed to mentally switch gears. "I wanted to thank you for keeping Roy from a jail sentence."

"Hold on. You can't change the subject now." He moved into her line of sight and waited.

"Roy confessed his original plan to hide my camper and then told me you talked him out of it. Thanks."

"My pleasure. Thanks for letting us care for you."

The air went still as she gripped the counter lightly and rocked back and forth.

Finally, she let him see her face. "You've changed. I can tell you're not the same person. The old Clay wouldn't serve as an usher at church—cleaning up after everyone goes home. The old Clay wouldn't care about other people's feelings like you do. He was never as thoughtful or protective."

He liked how she talked about him as if that version had died. She seemed to shrink back after her speech as if afraid she'd been too open. Though he'd rather be closer, he backed up a step and leaned against the workbench beside her, giving her space.

"Do I get a turn?" When she nodded, he continued. "You're strong and capable. You've rebuilt your life from a new beginning. You don't let hard knocks keep you down. I admire that."

"Thanks."

"But if you don't mind me saying it, I hate seeing you so alone."

"I have the Archers."

"And you barely let them get close. It took a tree falling on your camper for you to accept their invitation."

"You don't have to let people get close in order to avoid loneliness."

"Don't you?" Did she believe that? Such a sad thought. That belief came with its own sentence. She didn't answer, and he wouldn't push her. An idea hit. Clay lowered his voice. "When's her birthday? I know you mentioned June, but not the actual day."

"The seventh." The words were barely audible over the music in the garage.

"Come to my house that night."

"I've had enough meals with your parents. Thanks."

"No, not their house. Mine. This is something we should celebrate together. Alone." He barely moved, waiting for her to respond. "I'll grill dinner. You still eat steak?"

"Yes." Her expression brightened. Maybe she didn't like aloneness as much as she implied. "Okay. I'd like that."

CHAPTER EIGHTEEN

"Since you're here, Clay, how about lunch with Liberty and me? I have an idea to pitch to both of you," Elizabeth said. Working closely with Clay's mom had taught Liberty she had a mischievous side, and today, she was up to something. Liberty peered out from behind the shelf she dusted. Elizabeth faced her son. "What do you say? Or does your father need you back at the farm?"

"Nah, Dad's in a mood. I should steer clear for a bit." Clay sounded resigned, but Liberty could feel how much he hated it.

They'd connected lately. She'd prefer to think herself immune to him, but denial wasn't serving her like it used to. Which was why she'd decided to job hunt off-island. She had her resume circulating in Port Townsend, Mt. Vernon, Bellingham, even a lead back on Bainbridge.

"Then you're free for lunch."

"Sure."

"Liberty, what do you say?" Elizabeth's voice carried toward her.

She stepped away from the display case, about six feet from Clay. "Sounds fine."

Clay's brows rose. "Hey."

"Hi." Could he see she wasn't invulnerable to his interest, all those moments lately when he hadn't disguised what his mother called pining? "Lunch works for me."

Could she help it if she liked his attention?

But she couldn't act on it. That would be playing with his feelings, and she wouldn't do that. He brought out her flirty side occasionally. She'd have to watch that. Feeling insecure, she hugged herself.

Elizabeth came to stand beside her. "Are you chilled again? I swear, you need more meat on your bones, so you can keep yourself warm in our damp region."

"It's not damp today." Clay pointed at the front windows where sunlight shimmered off the parked cars along the street.

"I thank the good Lord for that." Elizabeth flipped the Closed sign into place. Generally, they didn't close for lunch. Whatever she had to pitch to Clay and Liberty must be unusually important.

"Mm-hmm," Clay said, holding the door as Liberty and his mother passed him. He locked up, and Elizabeth volunteered him to drive them to Skye Café, using her SUV.

Liberty climbed into the back passenger seat, as far from Clay as she could get, but still feeling too close to him and his subtle cologne, which always reminded her of Earl Grey tea. Oh, the view from here—he was all strength and competence undisguised by jeans and another dark Henley. He put the car in Reverse and placed a long-fingered hand on the seat rest behind his mother, so he could pivot and check the street traffic. They caught each other's eyes for a sec, and Liberty forced herself to look away, studying pedestrians or other cars, or anything besides him.

At the eatery, which was new to the island from what she remembered, Clay once more held the door as Liberty stepped in behind Elizabeth. The space had a modern loft feel, with cement floors, hanging light pendants high overhead, metal posts, brick walls, and plenty of hard seating.

Tables filled the floor space, with nothing to dampen noise between them, or provide privacy. Shouldn't be a problem. So far, Clay had honored Liberty's request not to mention Daisy to his family. Her secrets felt safe.

"I know the atmosphere is rather cold here," Clay said beside her. "But you'll like the food, I think." The man knew her too well.

Elizabeth led the way to an open back table and draped her jacket over a chair. "Let's leave our stuff and go order at the counter. They'll bring us our food."

Several minutes later, they returned to the table with their drinks. Liberty set down her ice water, and then she sat in the chair next to Elizabeth. Clay chose the seat directly across from Liberty. She could think of worse views. Shoot, but he made himself difficult to ignore.

He fiddled with his tumbler of soda. "Okay, Mom, want to share why we're here?" He perched his elbows on the table, shrinking its size by his presence.

Elizabeth tucked her hair behind her ear so that a silver teardrop earring came into view. "First," she said, studying each of them. "Tell me, what's going on between you two? Everything all right?"

Liberty's focus shot to Clay's face, and he shifted in his seat. "We're fine. Aren't we?" His open expression spoke of sincerity.

"Yes." Liberty bathed her dry vocal cords with ice water. *No secrets here. Totally fine. Three cheers for this coworker gig.*

Elizabeth perched a fist under her chin and leaned in as if watching an interaction she relished. "If you say so. Now, as to why I wanted to meet with you. We need to overhaul the website, and Kourtney has volunteered to help. She suggested we design new brochures. But since she lives down in Langley, we only have her on occasional weekends. Rather than use stock photos, I prefer live models."

Clay's brow creased as he listened. "Meaning..."

Elizabeth's eyes went bright like her smile as the server arrived with their food. "I've hired a photographer. You and Liberty, if you agree, will be the subjects, and we'll stage events for you to enact."

The server placed a BLT in front of Liberty, giving her a chance to pretend to miss how Clay's attention zipped to her at his mother's words as if he were checking on her. But she didn't know what to think yet.

"I understand it might be uncomfortable, given your history. Which is why I wanted to make sure things were fine between you." She flicked open her napkin and spread it on her lap.

"I'm curious why you'd need a couple," Clay said with a glimpse in Liberty's direction. She busied herself with straightening the layers of her sandwich. "But if you do, how about Kason and Brynn or Kourt and Fletch?" he asked.

"Simplicity. The three of us, with my photographer, can schedule the shoots during the workweek. What do you say?" She looked between them.

Clay dumped ketchup near the pile of fries on his plate. "Sure. Business meetings, corporate retreats? Might need new clothes to sell it."

That didn't sound threatening to Liberty. Nothing romantic or personal about it. She sprinkled a bit of salt over her fries before picking one up and nibbling on the end. Of course, he looked more the model than she ever had, but for Elizabeth, and for the sake of her job, she could endure it.

"Or formal dates, wedding receptions, anniversaries." Elizabeth forked up a bite of grilled chicken. "I'm glad that's settled. The photographer is coming next week."

CHAPTER NINETEEN

Dates? *Wedding receptions?* Liberty dropped the fry. Elizabeth couldn't mean what she implied. Something held Liberty back from jumping into the conversation. Perhaps self-preservation, or job preservation. Clay kept checking on her, but he didn't push her to speak.

"Hold on." Clay's raised burger stalled in his hands. "You want Liberty and me to dress up like a bride and a groom? Why not wait until October when you'll have a real bride and groom around? Kourtney loves hamming it up for the camera."

"And lose all the summer revenue a timely redesign would bring?" Elizabeth seemed giddy about her suggestion, while Liberty's appetite fled. "We'll rent clothes for the shoot. Don't worry. Business expense. I'm hopeful it'll pay for itself." She munched on her lettuce as if she hadn't given them an impossible and awkward task.

Clay set down his sandwich. "Kason and Brynn are right here. Liberty and I could babysit, right?" he asked her.

Liberty nodded, her mind spinning. If she refused, would that mean her job?

"I've already asked Brynn, and she'd rather stay behind the scenes. So, that leaves you." Elizabeth looked at each of them.

"Mom, I feel like you've asked a lot of us here," Clay said in a lowered voice. "Doesn't seem fair to Liberty, especially."

"Oh, I'm sorry." Elizabeth wiped her lips with the napkin from her lap. "Of course, you can say no. Don't feel pressured in any way to—"

"I'll do it." Liberty could not lose this job. She forced her voice to sound upbeat. "I can be a model for a day." Pretending there was no raging war inside, she lifted half of her BLT and took a small bite.

"You don't mind?" Clay's expression of surprise almost made

Liberty choke. Now, he was cornered. But she couldn't help that. If she didn't keep this job, how was she ever going to save enough to buy another camper and move on? Unless he meant he'd prefer to fake a relationship with a different woman. "If you'd rather pose with someone else. . ."

Elizabeth picked up her drink. "Oh, now look what's happened, Clay. You've made Liberty feel as if you don't want to include her. Shall I ask if Jill would like to pick out a wedding dre—"

"Mom, for the love of Pete. Stop." His voice cracked in an exaggerated way, and he pressed his lips together. Moments later, he gave his mom a loving—and slightly accusing—smile.

Liberty coughed to cover a laugh.

With a glint in his eye, Clay stared down his mother, perhaps hoping she wouldn't make a bigger scene in the café as others turned to see what the fuss was about. "I would be happy to appear to date and marry Liberty," he said to his mother, with his eyes on Liberty, "if she'll have me."

"Well, ask her, Son." Elizabeth waved in Liberty's direction.

He growled at his mom. Liberty pursed her lips, trying to hide any sign of humor as she waited for his next words.

Clay took on a formal posture, and she imagined he'd stand and bow if he had the space in the crowded café. "May I have the pleasure of a fake date and fake wedding reception for the purpose of humoring my mom and her fill-in-the-blank-with-whatever-words-you'd-like scheme?" He ended with exaggerated blinks and a smirk at his mother. Then his expression sobered when he met Liberty's eyes again.

Liberty chuckled, and Elizabeth broke into giggles too, before swatting her son's arm. But Clay's face bore an intoxicating expression.

One she couldn't resist. She gave Clay a grin. "Sure."

His matching smile said he might not appreciate her encouraging his mother and her antics, but he'd liked her response. She bit her bottom lip and tried not to relish those crinkles at the corners of his eyes.

"Great!" Elizabeth cheered. "Liberty, would you have a few

hours this Saturday? We can shop for clothes." She faced her son. "You'll need to join us."

"Whatever you need, Mom." He held his burger up again. "I should get back to work soon. Oh, and I only have an hour or two Saturday. I'm working at the Archers that day." He took a large bite.

They discussed the photographer's work and how Kourtney could help with decorations.

Toying with her meal, she caught glimpses of Clay as he wolfed down his lunch and humored his mom. How awkward would this be, posing with him? Surely Elizabeth wouldn't demand anything too intimate. Even if she didn't know what had broken them up all those years ago, she knew they weren't perfectly comfortable with one another. Which meant she wouldn't ask for anything more than a hug or hand-holding, right?

Liberty had led a solitary life after giving up Daisy, not wanting to risk her heart in another relationship. But pretending to date Clay again—this version of him? She'd have to shore up her guards.

That night the Archers invited her to play dominoes with them, and they laughed as Roy teased Gloria about her knitting obsession and the pile of shawls in a rainbow of colors. Liberty had feared that letting them get closer would risk their relationship, especially when they saw her flaws. But acceptance flowed from them, and she could relax when they were together.

When Liberty followed Shea's advice and let others in, her life seemed less cold. Like today at lunch. Elizabeth's assignment aside—she'd worry about that later—she'd enjoyed her time with Clay and his mom.

Sometimes there's a wave of loneliness that comes off you... Clay's words came to mind. Had her life gotten too lonely? He'd picked up on it. So had Gloria. And Shea. These were the people who cared about her. Did that mean their opinions should weigh more than others'?

In her en suite, Liberty readied for bed while her mind wandered. She could trace her decision to isolate herself back to those betrayals during her pregnancy. But she was trying to let the past go, like with Clay. They'd decided to leave the past alone, and their relationship was less and less strained.

Was her isolation based in something else?

Dressed in jammies, she found her phone on her nightstand.

Shea picked up on the second ring. "Hey, Liberty. How's it going? Are you all moved in?"

"Yeah, they finally won." She laughed and flopped onto the plush duvet covering the queen-size bed. Gloria's guest room décor was beachy and homey, with creature comforts everywhere. "Sorry, I know it's late."

"No problem. I'm looking forward to an update. You sound like you're doing well."

"I feel pretty good, but I'm analyzing myself tonight, and I could use your input."

Rustling followed on Shea's end, and Liberty pictured her settling into an overstuffed chair in her living room. "Okay, shoot."

"Why do I keep people at a distance?"

"You're afraid of being hurt again."

"True. But is there any chance this is tied to toxic shame?" Shame was feeling badly about something you'd done, but toxic shame was feeling badly about who you were. A mental light bulb lit up when Shea said that months ago. "How much of my life is affected by it?"

"Since it's a lie, you're right. It could affect your life in many ways."

"I'm tired of feeling ashamed of who I am. I mean, why should I?" She fiddled with the piping around the blue pillow sham.

"Indeed. Everyone has the same value, no matter what." Shea went quiet and then added, "If you're convinced you're worth less than those around you, you might pull back, as a way of protecting others from yourself."

The intuition clicked, and Liberty laid back on the bed. "Bingo." She'd assumed others were better off without her, though she'd tried to add to her relationships—she gave her best at the florist shop, helped with chores in her new home. Volunteered to gaze lovingly at Clay for picture day.

"So, this could be both—you're afraid, and you're stuck in toxic shame's prison."

"I want out."

"Living with Roy and Gloria has been very good for you, I think." Shea's smile came through with her words.

Liberty deserved enjoyment, like anyone, right? She might even be valuable enough to merit comfort, like hot showers before bed. Luxuries like the synthetic down pillows Gloria had put on her guest bed.

"Did I tolerate that broken, dirty camper because that's all I felt I deserved?"

"What do you think?"

"It was all I could afford."

"Okay. Except, Gloria offered you a room before you even moved to Whidbey."

They chatted a bit more about Shea's life, and then Liberty signed off and climbed into the memory-foam bed. Melting in, she closed her eyes to relish the simple pleasure. Had toxic shame sentenced her to isolation and suffering? Even when life handed her ice cream, she rarely let herself taste it.

It was time to uproot those toxic beliefs, starting with discovering its lies. Then, she could face them. She had to fight this personal war for herself. No one else would.

CHAPTER TWENTY

Saturday morning, Clay joined his mom in her SUV. They'd stop by the Archers' to pick up Libby and then find a clothing rental shop. They were going through with this crazy scheme.

He still couldn't believe Libby had jumped in so quickly. What motivated her? He'd done more than hint lately about how he felt. Was she starting to feel the same? Or was she only doing this because her employer had asked?

"If we can't find what we need, I'll see if we can borrow something," Mom said. "We won't have time to place orders."

Did she have to be so excited about this? Clay wasn't concerned for himself, but for Liberty. He hated seeing her uneasy, compelled to participate when she may not want to. He'd try to make today as comfortable as possible for her.

Riding shotgun while his mother drove seemed odd after years of independence. He wouldn't feel right about sitting up front while Liberty rode along behind them. That didn't seem honoring, especially given her sacrifice to carry out this plan. When she joined them, he'd move to the back seat.

At the Archers' house, he climbed out before his mom could prompt him and tapped on the kitchen door. Liberty appeared and strode toward the SUV while he checked in with Roy, giving him the update for the day's work schedule. Clay had a few church friends joining him this afternoon to finish the dry creek bed and plant the ornamental grasses. Roy almost had the gazebo finished. A crew had built and installed it, but Gloria hadn't liked the paint job, so Roy was repainting it for her because, as he put it, a happy spouse equaled a happy house.

At the SUV, Libby had climbed into the back seat. Clay opened the opposite back door. "I thought you'd like to sit up front, talk clothes with Mom."

"Thanks. I'm fine here." Her voice shook a little, and she looked small, sitting there. Yeah, she was nervous. He respected her courage.

"Get in, Son. Daylight's burning."

He climbed in behind his mother, next to Liberty. She smelled good, like that lotion she'd just shoved back into her bag. For the sake of letting her off the hook, he should've found someone to stand in. Except she might take that as rejection, which he wouldn't do. As she stared out the window, avoiding his direction, he wished he could take her hand and reassure her that they were in this together, and he'd make the playacting as painless as he could. "Thanks for doing this."

She gave him a glance. "Sure."

"How do you like living in Gloria's delightful home?" Mom asked Liberty.

"It's temporary, but you're right, it's lovely."

He leaned toward Libby, and Mom flicked the radio volume a little higher as if she didn't intend to eavesdrop. "You're still leaving?" Now that she was back, he hated to think of her leaving again. She needed a stable family life. And the Archers had gladly stepped into the position of honorary parents. She needed a home in a town where people didn't judge her. And where those who said they loved her, didn't reject her. Why the plan to move?

Her nod seemed uncertain.

Mom pulled into a bridal shop's lot and parked. Apparently, they were going to begin with the big event. "You two ready?" She grabbed her purse and opened her door, then climbed out.

Clay unbuckled. "Sure thing." He turned to Liberty. "It's not too late for me to ask Mom to stand down."

"Please don't. The more we protest, the worse she'll be, don't you think?"

"Can't argue with that."

She stared at the sign with its depiction of a wedding gown and bit her lip.

"We're in this together," he said.

She faced him with a weak smile. Then she grabbed her bag and opened her door. "All in a day's work." She gave him a look that said she was teasing. Somewhere in the last few seconds she'd found courage for this assignment.

An hour later, when Clay returned from the men's store next door, Libby was in a changing room while Mom paced outside. A preview of the shop told him there were plenty of white wedding gowns, of course, but there were other types of dresses too.

When Libby shared her news over a decade ago, his mind hadn't gone to marriage, but to denial. And he'd never asked if God wanted them to marry. But had He? For decades or perhaps centuries, couples had responded to an unplanned pregnancy with immediate wedding plans—even if a life-long commitment wasn't wise.

Should Clay have responded with a proposal? Would Mom ask them to fake an engagement for one of the shoots?

"Clay?" Hands on her hips, Mom eyed him as if she'd been trying to get his attention for a while.

He held out the suit he'd bought with the company card for her inspection. He'd pay it back. This suit was one he could use again. "This color okay?"

"Doesn't look like a tux."

"True. I can go back for that."

The ensemble was a charcoal gray, and the salesman had thrown in a tie of his choice. If Mom hated it, she could choose a different one. He'd spied a rack near the registers.

"Perfect for the date shoot. Liberty's dressing for that now." She pointed toward a changing room three down from Libby's. "Model that for us?"

"Those rooms are for women," he said.

"Then we'll get permission." She spun to find someone.

The knob on Libby's door rattled before it swept open. "I think this one might work," she said as if Clay wasn't standing there with his jaw hanging open. She looked up and caught him staring. He snapped his mouth shut.

The sleeveless purple dress showed off her slender shoulders. The hem fell in layers right above her perfect knees. His eyes traced back toward her face and all those red wavy curls hanging down, which reflected in the mirrors everywhere. She was a vision, though she did seem a little thin.

"I think Clay's expression says it all," Mom said, and Clay emerged from the mesmerizing effect. "That may be the one. How about you try on the black dress next? That way we can compare. If we like them, we could rent both."

Clay had the suit pants on and was fastening the white button-up shirt when his mom oohed and aahed over whatever Liberty was wearing now. At six-two, he could see over the top of this door, catch a glimpse, but he wanted to be respectful.

"Clay, where are you? How's the suit?"

"Almost ready." He tugged the jacket from the hanger and slipped his arms in. The fit was comfortable. He knotted the navy-blue tie at his neck and eyed himself in the mirror. Close enough. He opened his dressing room door.

Liberty stood on a pedestal with mirrors on three sides. An attendant worked on her hem. Liberty offered Clay a slow smile.

"Nice!" Mom cheered. "Yes, that's the one."

Good thing, since he'd already bought it.

Mom fussed, brushing the lapel while he tried to shoo her away. "Look at those green eyes. Don't you think this suit brings out the color of his eyes, Liberty? My goodness." She mocked fanning herself, and his skin went hot.

His focus tracked back to Liberty. She wore a black dress, which highlighted *her* eyes. He refused to look her up and down this time, but he loved the view of her face—slightly shy, a few visible freckles, and the bluest eyes.

Showing her his admiration for a shoot? No problem.

"I'm thinking a different tie. Something with a hint of green, perhaps?" She faced Liberty. "Preference for tie color, hon?"

"Green," she said, laying a hand over her heart before reaching up to adjust an earring. "Definitely."

"See? There we have it."

Was it his imagination, or was Libby flirting? Or was that for his mother's benefit? He didn't care. He liked it. "I can see I'm outnumbered." He approached the tie display, unknotting the navy blue one he wore. "You know, Mom, I probably have green at home." Something from a wedding he'd attended in the past.

She appeared at his side. "Nope. Let's find something here. Liberty," she called across the room, "come pick out accessories. You'll want a lovely necklace and a pair of earrings."

Barefoot, she approached, the dress swaying around her legs. He looked back to the table. Green, green, green. He found stripes, polka dots, swirls. He held up a checkered sage option. "What do you think?" he asked his mother.

"That doesn't match your eyes. This one!" She reached for the green and gray paisley and held it up next to his face. "Oh, it's perfect. Don't you think so, Liberty?"

It was a little feminine, but he didn't have to look at it. At least she hadn't chosen the peacock one. Feeling choked, he undid a couple of buttons. All this formal wear. Give him a V-neck T-shirt and jeans and let him plant a tree any day.

Moments earlier, Liberty had vanished behind a display of jewelry. She reappeared on command, which impressed Clay. She was being such a good sport. Her attention went to the tie, his collar where the shirt lay open under the suit jacket, then to his face, a spark in her eyes. She studied him for a few moments before she spoke. "It matches well."

"I agree." Mom held it out to him and he placed it around the back of his neck, fitting it under his collar. Mom faced Libby. "Any luck with a necklace?"

Liberty disappeared again. "Still looking," she called.

Using the mirror on the counter, Clay worked on the tie. "Mom, give her space." But his mother was already gone, still clueless to how this adventure might make her feel.

They gathered at the tall mirrors. A salesperson had arrived to take notes and offer suggestions. She darted around, exclaiming over the choices. Mom's hands overflowed with chains and earring cards. And Libby endured the circus with grace.

Finally, Liberty put on a shiny silver-toned necklace with small green stones. She wore dangling earrings and had somehow pulled her hair back with only a few red tendrils hanging down.

"Now, stand together, you two," Mom directed, passing her handful of costume jewelry to the attendant.

Clay and Liberty studied each other, and the room went quiet, as if awaiting a verdict.

"The tie is nice," Liberty said, her necklace shimmering against her skin.

She took his breath away and he couldn't comment back, except to offer, "Thanks. You're ..."

"We'll take it!" Mom exclaimed. "This is perfect. Now, to the wedding apparel."

CHAPTER TWENTY-ONE

This charade shouldn't get to Liberty, right? She was merely acting like Clay's love interest. It'd be easier to remember they were pretending if Clay would stop looking at her like she'd invented sunlight. In high school, he'd given her expressions full of longing. Today, in place of lust there was almost a sense of reverence. What had changed him?

A bit ago, Elizabeth had sent him back to the men's store to find a black tux for the wedding reception shoot. Mother and son had whispered ideas back and forth. But Liberty loved the suit he'd chosen for the fake date. The man had good taste. And she and Elizabeth had found the perfect dress for their fake reception.

As a seventeen-year-old, she'd dreamed of his proposal. That he'd agree to make them a family—the three of them. Sure, they'd have to lean on others for a while in the beginning, but somehow, they'd make a future for themselves. And if too many months had passed, Liberty might have chosen a champagne-colored gown as a wedding dress. Now, while Clay waited in a local coffee shop under strict orders to let them finish up alone, Elizabeth had chosen white for her. The dress fit perfectly, which meant no time-consuming alterations.

Gazing at herself in the beautiful, lacy gown, Liberty wanted to believe Elizabeth's assessment—*you are a vision.* She didn't feel like a vision. She felt like a failure. How had she gotten into this situation where she had to enact this heartbreaking scenario?

Wait. Her new determination to combat toxic thoughts urged her to fight back. *I matter. I'm valuable.*

They'd spent too many hours shopping. Liberty's feet hurt on the drive back, so she rubbed them one after the other. Clay complained that his landscaping crew would be half done with the work by the time he returned, but they'd found what Elizabeth wanted. She had the idea to keep them from seeing each other in their wedding dress and tux until the photo shoot. That way, the photographer could capture their genuine reactions.

Liberty had told herself she'd fake her reactions because her job depended on playing the role, but she hadn't been pretending today. He seemed genuine too. His expression made the day easier to handle somehow.

He didn't say much on the trip back to the Archers', where he would spend the afternoon, thanks to his mom convincing his dad to spare him. Maybe he was too tired to entertain his exuberant mother. Elizabeth pulled into the driveway, and Liberty gathered her things.

"Oh, Clay," Elizabeth said, "I almost forgot. Dad wants to chat with you tonight after you're finished here. Say, after dinner sometime?"

"Okay. Would you mind dropping those off?" He pointed to his garment bags.

"Of course."

He closed his door and moved toward the yard, and something crazy in Liberty wanted to follow him.

Several of the guys had already taken off when Clay joined Gabe near the dry creek bed. "Thanks for doing this." The crew had laid the pavers and planted many of the grasses.

Gabe wiped sweat from his forehead. His jeans bore mud stains at the knees, and his T-shirt was smudged with dirt. "Sure thing. Feels good to work outside." He studied Clay. "How's it going?"

"I meant to get here sooner. Mom's got us working hard to bring in more business." He slipped off his jacket and tossed it on a chair on the patio.

"How are things with Liberty?" Gabe kept his voice low, his back toward the house.

Clay peered over his shoulder. They were alone.

"Complicated." He pictured her in those gowns today. Black or purple looked great on her. "She's not the same person who left here."

"You still feel something for her."

The man was too discerning. Clay grabbed a shovel. "We should get to it."

They worked together to transplant the next potted clump of tall, ornamental grass into its spot.

Gabe gave himself to the task for several minutes. Then he looked around before leaning toward Clay. "What's this I hear about a wedding reception?" He wasn't one to joke, but his voice held a hint of teasing.

"How did you hear?"

"My wife was shopping this morning and texted me a couple of photos."

"Huh. She's a detective." Maybe he should confide in Gabe. Who else was he going to discuss this with? "Remember Mom's plan? It involves photo shoots that portray Libby and me on a date and then at our own wedding reception."

Gabe hiked an eyebrow. "Kidding aside, that sounds like a tough job."

"Yeah, she's not meddling at all."

"Does Liberty know you've fallen for her again?"

Clay shot a glance at the house. "It's that obvious?" Yes, Clay had let Libby see a few hints, but if Gabe and Roy caught them, that meant others probably did too. This was getting more complicated because it could scare Libby away.

"To me. I've known you for a while. My wife thought you looked good together."

"Your wife is full of news today."

Across the yard, sprinklers came on, watering the new lawn. "I'm saying, it might be time to settle down."

He needed to help Gabe understand. "I don't think she's on board with God these days."

"Oh."

They dug a hole and grunted another root ball into the ground.

Maybe Gabe could help him with something else. But how much should he say? The man was too good at deducing meaning. "Changing the subject. If you were trying to reconnect with someone, and social media didn't have anything, where would you start?"

Gabe's expression said it was a strange question, but he'd play along. "Maybe track down the last place you saw him or her. If it's an organization, like a school, for example, you could reach out to them. Find their website. When folks are planning high school reunions, they gather all kinds of information."

"Great idea. Thanks." They finished planting the ornamental grasses and looked at their work.

Gabe passed his shovel over. "So, when do these photo shoots happen?"

"Next week." He squeezed the handle with gloved hands.

"If you get a chance, tell her how you feel."

When Liberty reappeared in the kitchen after dropping off her garment bags, Roy was there, munching on strawberries from a flat on the counter. "Gloria's out buying groceries." He bent toward the sink with one hand on the faucet. The fingers of his other hand dripped watery juice. "Hey, Liberty, what do you say we go direct our favorite landscaper?" He grabbed a towel and wore a grin that said he wanted to make mischief.

She peered through the kitchen window as she rinsed a shiny, fat berry and nibbled on it. Clay worked alone now that his crew had all left. "He might need more help. Let me change." Without analyzing her eagerness for long, she moved toward her room.

Minutes later Roy and Liberty headed outside. Clay worked at planting a tree near the gazebo.

"How's it going out here?" Roy tucked his fists into his vest pockets.

"Hi." He gave Liberty a warm smile, then answered. "Look at

this creek bed." The rocky path, flanked in grasses, led back to the patio from the bluff. The blue stone set off the bright grasses and deep green of the lawn, which gleamed with health since Clay had doctored it.

"That's exactly what I pictured." She felt Clay's eyes on her and faced him. "What can we do to help? I noticed your crew left."

He gave her a good-humored expression that said they'd shopped too long this morning. "I'm planting these two Summer Gold dogwoods. One here." He pointed to this side of the gazebo. "And the other over there for balance. When they've grown a bit, they'll add to the setting. Their flowers are white, but the leaves turn red in the fall."

Glancing around, Roy nodded his approval. "I think you've done a fine job. I wondered if you could add a firepit down on the beach. There's that area near the stairs where you could gather rocks into a circle. High tide shouldn't be able to reach it." Roy's back condition limited him to making requests and giving input.

His fathering affirmation always seemed to make Clay stand taller. "Sure. Be happy to." Clay turned to Liberty. "You up for that?"

She agreed, and Roy excused himself to putter in the garage.

Sunlight shone off the cobalt blue water over the bluff, calling Liberty toward the wooden steps. After they'd planted the second dogwood, Liberty led the way down the switchback staircase. Someone had done a good job building this. The stain seemed fresh and the wood solid—no creaking or peeling.

She stopped at one landing and let herself take in the view. From here, she could see both up and down the gray sandy beach. A few motorboats passed in the Sound, creating wakes that would send waves up the shore. Salty air reached her on the breeze, and for a moment she lifted her face to the sky and took it in.

"I love that smell too." She opened her eyes as Clay joined her on the landing. "Hey, sorry about this whole dress-up-old-family-friends-and-make-them-pose thing." He winced. "Not that I think of you that way."

"Easy, Clay. I knew what you meant." She watched the incoming tide as it pushed the seaweed higher up the beach. "It's fine." *Mostly.* So long as she didn't let herself get pulled too deeply into his world again. "I don't mind humoring your mom. I'd forgotten how playful she could be."

"Sometimes I wonder how she and Dad get along. She doesn't seem to let his sour moods bother her."

His confiding in her felt good—beyond coworkers, beyond "old family friends." The type of intimacy they used to share, only with more humility. Would he tell her more if she asked? "You haven't explained what happened."

Clay rubbed the back of his neck, shoulders rounding. "I ran over him with farm equipment because I thought I knew it all." Old Clay would've painted a picture that made himself look good. Nothing about that sentence propped him up.

"You what?"

"It was right after you left. I was so cocky." He faced the water, hands gripping the landing's wooden railing, elbows locked. "I was still fighting my conscience over what had happened with you."

His jaw muscles danced, and she let herself study him. "You know, I always figured you never regretted any of it."

"Even before God and I had a knock-down, drag-out fight, which ended in my surrender," he said with a self-deprecating grin, "I knew, deep down, that I was wrong."

"What changed?" She had been avoiding God for years, ever since learning He wasn't who the Kincades preached He was. They'd rejected her so completely, wearing smiling faces and mock concern, eager as they created a loophole in their commitment to her late parents.

This will be best for everyone, you'll see.

But you were planning to adopt me.

What type of message would that send to our children?

"Our children." As in, "You've never been a true part of our family. All of that fuss about inviting you in and saying we were going to adopt you was all for show, so we'd look good at church and could brag to our friends about doing our Christian duty." They'd forgotten their loyalty to her late parents, and nothing would change their minds.

What type of message? How about one of unconditional acceptance, or even—hello!—love? Loyalty? Perseverance?

"Libby?" Clay's voice broke into her thoughts as he leaned into her line of sight. "Where'd you go?"

Her face felt wet. Was that the spray of the surf? She reached up. Tears.

"Was it something I said?" His face wore genuine concern.

"I'm fine." She hugged herself, trying to ward off a chill that came from inside. "I guess I got caught up in a memory."

He frowned, pocketing his fists.

"Not about you. The Kincades. Do you remember how they were always bragging about taking me in? How they'd honored my parents, like loyal friends?"

He nodded, compassion etched in his eyes. "I'm sorry."

Wanting to pretend it didn't hurt, she forced a strong posture. "Doesn't matter. I learned a lot. I learned I could make it alone, eventually. I learned God wasn't Someone I wanted to know. I mean," she quickly added, "I'm happy you found what you wanted in Him, but a God who could turn His back on a pregnant mom? Reject her for her humanness? I don't want a God like that."

"That's not what He's like." He leaned against the railing, his brow furrowed with tenderness. "Who do you think gave you—us—a baby?"

"That's simple biology." She crossed her arms. "Plus, He didn't *give* us a daughter. He *took* my daughter." Tears fell again, and she brushed them away, angry that she couldn't stop them.

"I believe God decides if there's a life or not, and I believe life is a gift from Him."

Was he saying God wasn't like the Kincades?

"I didn't always think that, but I do now. And if people judge you or reject you, God will handle them. You keep working to make your life better. Did we do things God says aren't the best for us? Of course we did. Who hasn't? I mean, look where it got us. There's a reason He says to do things His way, as hard as that is. But does He love us less or wish us harm? No." Clay faced the water. "I wish Dad could see that. He's acting like the Kincades with me, ever since the skid loader accident, even though I've apologized again and again."

"You're talking about forgiveness."

"Absolutely."

There was that message again. Would forgiveness help her feel less rejected, help her move beyond the past? Had the Kincades been waiting for her to apologize, all those years ago, as if she'd harmed them and needed their pardon? They acted like they were God's instrument of judgment in her life after they heard the news. As if He approved of how they treated her. As if they'd never done anything God might not like.

Didn't matter. She'd given up on Him like He'd given up on her. He obviously disliked her—why else would He take away her only family?

She shook off the heavy thoughts. "We should find rocks and build that firepit."

"You're right. But," he said, reaching for her arm, "is it possible God isn't the way you think He is?"

Freeing her elbow from his light touch, she pushed curls from her face, redoing the ponytail the wind kept trying to undo. But she didn't take the bait and answer Clay's question.

"You could ask Him to show you what He's like."

She nodded toward the stairs. "Let's get to work."

"Yup." He jogged down the remaining steps and pointed to a level, sandy spot nearby. "How about you clear that space over there for the circle? I'll collect rocks."

Using a stick, she removed seaweed from the space. And though she'd prefer his words not sift through her thoughts, they did. *Ask God to show you what He's like.*

During those church services all those years ago, she'd sometimes felt God's presence. At least, she hoped she had. Like that first Thursday night service this spring—warm and welcoming. She'd left those services feeling uplifted and loved— that was the strongest element. Love.

While Clay searched the lower beach for suitable rocks, she

dragged over a couple from near the staircase. If the Archers wanted to, they could add a pair of Adirondack chairs and create a spot for chatting. This hundred or so feet of frontage gave them plenty of privacy.

The firepit circle was nearly closed when Clay pointed. "Hey, look." Out in the Sound a few sea otters bobbed, rolling and watching Clay and Liberty. "I haven't seen those in a while."

"Aw…" She wanted to hug them, like the stuffed otter Dad Kincade had bought for her at the Seattle Aquarium. She'd slept with it every night. One more thing she'd had to leave behind when the Kincades kicked her out. A memory surfaced of clutching that toy, though she'd been almost a grownup, while praying for help. At the time, she had just learned she was pregnant.

Yeah, and those prayers bounced off the ceiling because God didn't care, He wasn't listening, and He hadn't helped. Not one bit.

The otters swam closer and reappeared, staring at Clay and Liberty as if craving social interaction. Clay wore a big grin. "They're looking for new friends."

She met the nearest otter's stare. She hadn't thought of that prayer for a long time.

But God hadn't sent otters as a sign today.

The creatures swam away, disappearing under the water.

"Tell me something?" Liberty asked.

"Shoot."

"How did God convince you—I mean, how did He win you over?" She'd rather hold on to her accusations, protecting herself, but she hadn't found peace on her own.

At the firepit, Clay hollowed out the center of the circle. His face creased into a chagrinned smile. "It's not a pretty story." Something about his grin said he didn't mind, that whatever it was, it'd been worth it.

"No worries if you'd rather not tell me."

"I'm fine talking about it." He glanced at his watch and pointed up the stairs. "Let's go get dinner."

"You know the Archers will hover." She chuckled, picturing

Gloria and Roy homing in.

"We could find a restaurant that you might like better than the Skye Café. Or grab dinner and hang out at the beach."

She surveyed their work. "This looks like a good spot. All we need are chairs and food. Maybe a blanket since I'd rather we not have a fire."

"I remember—you hate smoke." He gave a decisive nod. "Done."

CHAPTER TWENTY-TWO

Western sun warmed the sheltered firepit spot, setting Libby's red hair aflame. She munched on an apple slice next to him, and he relished the peace between them. Somehow, they'd gotten back to a place of being at ease together.

His news would wreck that.

But not tonight.

Neither would he tell her how he felt. Not yet. If he could show her he cared before he confessed what he'd done, she might trust him more when the news came out. Because he would have to tell her.

"You're sure you don't want a fire?" She gestured toward the sandy pit.

And smoke her out? Nope. "Positive." He finished the last of his sandwich. "I wouldn't change anything."

Seagulls cried, and the tide pushed in. Now and then a crab skittered to a new hiding place among the rocks several feet away. Clay wadded the aluminum foil from his sandwich and tucked it into a bag, which he pinned under the leg of his chair to keep the wind from snatching it away.

She handed him her trash, and he stashed that too. "So, are you going to tell me, or not?" she asked him.

Had she learned his secret? "About...?"

"What happened between you and God? I remember you and I were pretty good at faking the Christian thing as teens."

The words scraped an old wound. "We weren't always faking." Or at least he wasn't. "Were we?"

"Honestly? Probably not. But you lose your parents, and you question everything—including, maybe especially, God."

"Makes sense." They'd replace these camp chairs with Adirondacks later. For now, Clay could lean toward her. "I'm sorry."

She stared in the direction of the waves. "Thanks for being

there for me back then."

"Still wish I'd been less selfish."

"I don't want to rehash all that." Her expression was warm, unoffended.

He'd like to hear her say she'd forgiven him, but maybe her actions demonstrated it. "Okay." He'd let her decide what they discussed next—her parents' car accident, or his salvation, or whatever.

"Missing Mom and Dad made everything else harder." She wrapped her arms in front of herself in that self-hug that he'd seen her do several times since she'd returned. "Made me needier."

"I remember." His thoughts spun, images of how he'd—

She reached for his hand. "Stop."

Her touch brought him back to this moment. She knew him well.

"Talk to me." Her invitation disarmed him, and the story of his salvation floated up. She didn't release his hand.

"Remember Pastor Charlie?" Their youth pastor.

"Sure."

"He knew something had gone down, and he kept calling to find out what. Everything happened at once. Your news." He squeezed her hand, anchoring himself in the present while acknowledging her. "Then, the skid loader accident with Dad a couple of weeks later. I think after you left, I got cockier—put up more of a front with people. Dad was in the hospital, not talking to me. I avoided youth group. Charlie left fifteen voice mails. 'Hey, checking in. Remember, God is close to the brokenhearted.' Only, I wasn't brokenhearted. I was angry."

Picturing Dad, agitation flowed through him now, and he stood. "Walk with me?"

"Sure." She joined him, reaching for his hand again.

A cliff rose on their left as they strolled parallel to the water. "Something hit me, and I got reckless one evening. Decided to swim in the Sound." She gasped. "I know. Really cold." He didn't want to dive into the depths of this story. He'd keep it short. "I didn't get far before I was stung by a jelly. Ended up in the ER, treated for that and hypothermia. Stupid. When Charlie came in, he didn't judge me." Clay stopped. "I hope when you were going through your medical stuff with Daisy's birth that you were surrounded by people who didn't judge you."

"At times, I was." Her expression turned thoughtful. "I wish Mom and Dad could've met her. She looked like you and me, of course. But I could see my parents in her smile."

Her words felt like an opening. "Would you like to see her again?"

She disengaged and strode a couple of paces down the beach. He followed. "I wish you could have seen her," she said.

He caught up. "Me too." She hadn't answered his question, so he'd leave it. He still needed to finish his story. "When Charlie acted cool, I wondered if maybe it wasn't too late for God to help me." He couldn't believe what it had taken to realize that. "After he left, I prayed—got real."

"But things are still strained with your dad. He uses a cane. That was ten years ago."

"Yup. And he hasn't let me off the hook since. But hey, I'm fi—"

"Don't do that."

"Fair enough." He'd said the same thing to her about being real with him. "Answer something for me? What's next?" That was either the bravest or most foolish thing he could ask. "Are you still planning to move?"

She stopped. Faced the water, breathed in the mist that surrounded them as the sun sank lower. "Maybe."

"Your job's here. You have the Archers." *Me.*

"Memories. Everywhere."

"Which you're coping with fine. You have friends here."

"Friends?" Was she fishing? Couldn't she see it?

He reached for her hand. "One friend, in particular."

She let him thread his fingers through hers, but she didn't respond.

"Unless I'm someone you're coping with. Like Mom and photo shoots and playing dress-up." Now he was fishing.

An impish grin formed on her face, and he relished it. "You mean 'just another day on the job'? It's not so bad. Certain coworkers make it easier."

"You had fun today."

She covered her lips with the tip of her index finger. "Don't tell."

Clay's phone buzzed once in his pocket, reminding him Dad wanted to talk to him. "I gotta head home."

They returned to the picnic spot, and Clay grabbed their trash bag while Liberty toted the empty water bottles for recycling. "I hope things get better with your dad."

"Thanks." He stopped her on the bottom step. Now she met him eye to eye while he stood on the sand. "Suddenly I have hope for old relationships getting back on track."

She gave him a weak smile. "I remember how close you and your dad were. Maybe one day you can have that again." She moved up the stairs.

No question, she sometimes flirted. Then, when he tried to be direct, she redirected. Why was she still planning to move away?

Somewhere inside her a battle waged. And inside him, a desire to fix things for good between them.

She hadn't kept her status with God a secret, not that Clay could fix that. He couldn't overlook it, either.

Inside the house, Liberty headed to her bedroom. Roy and Gloria were out. After a while, a text came through from Clay that all was well with his dad, for now. She sent back a smiley face emoji.

Then, she texted Shea: I'M POSING FOR WEDDING RECEPTION PHOTOS WITH CLAY NEXT WEEK. Her phone rang moments later.

"What's this?"

Liberty curled into her window seat where the sun rested right above the horizon. She hugged a pillow with one arm. "He's been so... attentive. Affectionate." *That* didn't get to her at all. "And I can't help it. I've been flirting back."

"Sounds like you're still attracted to him."

"I am." There, she'd admitted it. "It doesn't feel like a compromise to be drawn toward him now that he's changed. I'm never falling for the old Clay again."

"Good for you. That leaves the question of falling for the new Clay."

"Posing for formal date and wedding reception photos probably won't confuse things at all, then."

Shea's laughter burst into the phone. "How did they talk you into that?"

"I can't lose this job." A Steller's jay landed in the grass outside, her brilliant blue contrasting with her black coloring.

"Are they coercing you?"

"No. Both Clay and Elizabeth have given me an out."

"But you haven't taken it."

"Nope." Liberty squeezed her pillow, still smelling Clay, feeling his fingers entwined with hers. "I've never met anyone like him."

"You said he's been affectionate."

"Yes, *and* I've told him I'm moving."

"This is complicated." Bless her. Shea didn't mention her concerns about the move.

"I'm starting to trust him again. He's cool with leaving Daisy alone, which was a must. He doesn't mind not telling his family about her. That makes both our lives easier." Her fingers cramped from clutching the pillow so hard. She unfurled them. "But I'm afraid something will happen—like last time. Not another baby. We're keeping our distance. But if he betrays me again, I don't know if I could take it."

Of course, there were other reasons they weren't compatible. The new version of him might glisten. Her new state? Wounded. Scarred. Wary.

"Sounds like you're focusing more on where he's at than where you are."

"I'm afraid of my own feelings. Zero consistency. I promise myself I'll keep my distance, and then, bam. I'm reaching out to hold his hand."

Shea was quiet for a few moments. "I say go through with the photo shoots. You've already promised. And try to enjoy yourself. Be cautious, sure. But I have a feeling it won't hurt as much as you fear it will. You deserve to be happy."

CHAPTER TWENTY-THREE

Thursday evening, Liberty couldn't quell the butterflies. You'd think she was actually getting married this weekend.

Elizabeth had asked that Liberty arrive at the greenhouse with her garment bags an hour early. They'd do the date shoot first, then the wedding reception photos the following morning. After work, she had seen Clay at the Archers', splattered in mud in the front yard. But when she arrived at the greenhouse forty minutes later, he'd just gotten there. He climbed from his truck, looking showered and freshly shaved.

"Hey, Liberty." He wasn't wearing his suit yet, but he still arrested her attention.

"Hi." She held back any flirty words, though being near him prompted those thoughts often lately.

After reaching into his truck for a garment bag of his own, he joined her outside the greenhouse entrance. "I wish we could do this all in one session. Less of an imposition on you. But Mom wants evening light for the date and daylight for the wedding shots. I hope you don't mind two shoots in a row."

"I'm glad to help your family business." If Clay was going to feel uncomfortable or coerced, this assignment would be all about endurance. They'd talked repeatedly about Liberty feeling obligated, but never Clay. She bit her lip. "Do *you* mind?"

His face broke into a tender smile. "Are you kidding? Pretending to romance you? Not a problem."

Her lungs hitched at the genuine expression of interest and warmth in his green eyes.

"Shall we?" He nodded toward the building.

"O-okay." For the next two days, she'd let her guard down—a little. She wouldn't think about moving on, or how lonely her life would then be. She wouldn't rehearse what she'd say next week when she returned calls to the hiring reps off-island. She'd simply tackle this crazy task and please her boss. And perhaps enjoy herself a little. *You deserve to be happy.* Shea's words. Liberty wanted to believe it.

Garment bags in hand, they strode toward the entrance. Given the puddles in the parking area, Liberty was glad she hadn't changed into the rented dress or her new shoes.

The greenhouse had an unusual design, since they'd chosen to use part of the space for a meeting area. The office and bathrooms were located near the front door, with the meeting area not far away. The rest of the greenhouse served its nursery purpose with rows of seedlings and flats of flowers and other plants. Elizabeth met them near the bathrooms and the office.

"Hi, you two. You can change in there." She pointed to the restrooms. "The photographer and her assistant got caught in a long ferry line, but they're on their way. They'll stay on the island overnight, and we'll get an early start tomorrow. I have two gals covering the flower shop. Oh, why am I chattering on? I'd better let you get to it."

Liberty dressed and checked the full-length mirror after slipping on her shoes. She'd pinned up her hair and let red curls hang beside her face. Perhaps she should save this hairstyle for the wedding reception photos.

Since their shopping trip, she hadn't let herself dwell on how hard these shoots would be. Almost like a cruel joke—*here's what you will never have.*

Maybe that's why she didn't want anyone to find Daisy. Another opportunity to look her loss in the face and try not to crack in half.

She unpinned her hair, letting the soft curls fall in waves around her shoulders. Stepping out into the greenhouse, and feeling vulnerable in her black gown, she peeked around for Clay. The sun fell in the western sky, slanting golden light through the windows. Voices carried from the meeting area, and she followed the sound.

Candles flickered on the countertop against one wall. The chandelier was lit to a soft glow. The aroma of peaches filled the air.

Were the candles fruit-scented? She met Clay's eyes. Had he chosen them? How much had Kourtney influenced the décor, and how much was Clay's handiwork? A bouquet of cranberry gerbera daisies decorated the table. *Daisies.* Her favorite. Her attention shot back to Clay.

"Oh, my," Elizabeth said, spotting her and breaking the spell of their gaze. "What a vision."

They'd seen her in the dress the previous weekend, but she basked in Elizabeth's words. "Thanks."

"Wow." Clay walked closer, and somehow the cut of the suit looked better today than when she'd seen it before. Clicks went off nearby, which meant the photographer must have arrived. The shoot had begun.

Clay took Liberty's hands. "You look breathtaking." A genuine smile lit his eyes.

She ducked her head, overcome by his sincerity. "Thank you," she whispered.

He nodded toward the counter where sparkling cider waited in tall champagne flutes. "Mom said we should interact like we're on a real date. Talk. Laugh, whatever. She'll adjust the chandelier and the photographer will take her shots, only interrupting to ask for specific poses—you know, images she didn't get."

He handed her a flute, two-thirds full of apple cider, sparkling like yellow topaz. The photographer stalked around them, crouching, stretching, and clicking away. Liberty couldn't imagine where they'd use all these images, but she was here to work.

"Got it." Raising her flute, she smiled up at him. "What shall we toast?"

"Second chances?" He kept his voice low. Was he serious? Maybe he meant with his dad.

"To healed relationships." She clinked her glass with his.

Clay's open expression showed he agreed. He took her free hand. "I'm glad you're here. And I might even owe Mom a thanks for setting this up."

He leaned in, putting his lips near her ear. "You're beautiful in black," he whispered.

She went still, but her body betrayed her, shuddering. Every moment they seemed to fall deeper into this pseudo performance.

He pulled back. "Are you cold?"

"No, but thanks." She needed to set down her glass. He followed suit. As if on cue, soft music kicked on. "Methinks your mother is up to something."

"I agree." Clay laughed. Then, he gave a half-bow and reached for her. "Shall we?"

Mindful of the photographer and her assistant shifting reflectors and madly shooting pictures, Liberty gave them a moment to capture Clay's gesture and then accepted.

He tugged her away from the counter, into the wider space. If they weren't careful, they'd have rows of pansies and violas in the shots. The team moved to that side of the greenhouse, and Clay pivoted with Liberty for the best angle.

Pulling her closer, he curled their joined hands together against his chest. Once she found her footing, she leaned into him and he bowed his head next to her face. His lashes brushed her cheek when he closed his eyes, and she heard a small sound. "I was hoping," he said, so quietly she was sure the others couldn't hear, "to have a chance to tell you how I feel."

She startled and tried to pull back, but his arm held her gently, firmly in place. She was glad the others in the room couldn't possibly hear them. Elizabeth would be unbearable if they confirmed her guesses.

"Do you mind?"

"You surprised me. I wish I could see your eyes. I mean, how much of this is for the camera?"

He squeezed her hand at his chest. "None of it. They can't hear me." His murmured words almost took her knees from under her. "Do *you* want to hear?"

She yearned to pull back, watch his face as he spoke. But here they were, posing. Maybe hiding from her gave him the courage to say what he wanted to. This moment, with the sun setting behind the row of trees, and Elizabeth fading the chandelier lighting overhead, well, Liberty could get caught up in the spell. The camera clicks faded with the lighting.

"Yes," she breathed. "I do."

"I've never stopped caring about you, hoping to see you again."

They swayed to the music, and she let the words settle inside.

His thumb caressed her hand between them. "I know we've both changed. I think I care more now than I ever did."

Her first instinct was to raise her guards, deny. Redirect. But what if she tried honesty? "I like the man you've become." That sounded lame. Formal. She didn't understand her own heart. No use complicating this with more words.

He leaned in close again. Was he smiling against her face, giving himself over to her words? "Do you think we could try 'us' again? Take it slow?"

He must have gotten a cue from the photographer, because he spun them. Now she could see the table decoration. "Were the daisies your idea, or Kourtney's?"

He pulled back, but he didn't mention her redirect. "Mine."

"Thank you."

He drew her close again. "You're welcome." Maybe he was content letting her think about his suggestion to try again.

"Okay, guys," Zoe said, camera lowered. "One more pose and we're ready to finish for tonight."

They eased apart to take direction, and the room felt colder.

"Elizabeth asked for a proposal shot." Zoe pointed toward a spot with daisies in the foreground and candles in the background. "How about right here?"

Liberty's palms sweated. They'd almost managed to get through this task without an incredibly awkward moment.

Elizabeth rushed over, pinching a ring between her thumb and index finger. A three-stone display shimmered, set in platinum, if Liberty guessed correctly. She loved the imagery—past, present, and future. "Use this. It's mine, but it'll make a great prop."

Clay seemed to accept the ring more from reflex than agreement. "Mom..."

"You don't mind, do you? I mean, this will work well with tomorrow's shoot." Elizabeth mimed opening a brochure. "Proposal on one panel, wedding reception on another." She met Liberty's eyes. "What do you say, hon?"

Wordless, Liberty nodded. They were acting. No reason for grief or regret or nerves. The longer she spent getting to know Clay this spring, the less she regretted their years apart. They were right not to get married back then. Time and experience had reshaped them.

What was real? Past, present, future? Confusion pushed in. Her emotions went numb, silencing her questions. Now, she could cooperate with her boss. She gave Clay a reassuring nod, but his expression said he didn't buy it. Would he play along?

Zoe and Elizabeth waited. Clay stepped close. "One sec." He held up a finger toward the women. Into Liberty's ear, he said, "Are you sure?"

She nudged her shoulders up and down quickly, and he stepped back. "I'm fine. Let's finish up and call it a night." Regret chased into her chest following her flippant words. This assignment had drained her.

He knelt before her, gave her a speech she didn't hear. Hopefully the glazed feeling in her eyes came off as emotion. When he held out the ring and went still, she noted how the camera zero in on the spark of hope in his gaze.

After a few moments, she nodded. Smiled. Posed.

The camera clicked several times as Clay stood to slip the oversized ring onto her left ring finger. Then he hugged her, not even trying for a kiss.

On her drive home, that restraint expressed more than any words he'd said all evening.

Before dawn Friday morning, Clay sat in his kitchen watching the sky turn orange over the Sound. He'd gotten maybe an hour or two of sleep overnight.

He hadn't meant to confess everything, but the setting

demanded a reaction. They'd both been bound to Mom's scheme. And maybe part of the evening was pretend, but as the day got nearer, Clay had planned certain candles and flowers for the table. And she'd liked them. She'd noticed.

He had put his heart out there for her to toss over a cliff. Of course, he'd hidden from her while doing it. But she hadn't laughed.

She hadn't answered him, either. Which meant, she was probably still determined to leave. If he wasn't reason enough for her to stay, was Daisy?

They still had one shoot to do. She'd shut down during the fake proposal. Would she even show up at the greenhouse? The photos required certain poses. He'd prefer to let her choose how they interacted. If he got there early, he could chat with her. Check in.

Or he could call her. But what would he say? The same thing he'd been saying. "You don't have to do this." "If this makes you uncomfortable, I'll get us out of it." "You know how Mom is."

Liberty had asked him not to ask his mom to tone down her meddling, and he wanted to honor that. But what a toll this was taking—especially on her.

CHAPTER TWENTY-FOUR

At the farm, Clay pulled his truck in beside Liberty's car. The place was quiet. Dad had said he'd be over, but later since his wife was up to, in his word, tomfoolery. Clay shook away thoughts of his father. He had a tux to throw on. Mom had insisted he go with classic black because "it would work best with Liberty's gown."

His heart pounded as he walked inside. No sign of Libby, but Mom was waiting for him. "Hey, Son, head on in and get changed. Then, please wait in the meeting area for Liberty. Zoe and Jared are setting up." Mom seemed giddy. Honoring his agreement with Liberty to not confront Mom challenged his resolve, while humoring his mother challenged his patience.

"Where is she?"

Mom pointed at the doorway. "Shoo!"

Fifteen minutes later, he emerged into the greenhouse's meeting space, searching for Liberty. Still no sign of her. Mom rushed up. "I'm going to leave you with Zoe. She wants to get a few solo shots."

"Okay."

In the meeting area, he found Zoe and Jared checking their equipment. "Good morning," she said, her short black hair glistening in the sunlight streaming in the windows. "Let's get a few with the forest in the background."

"Sure thing."

Kourtney had suggested a simple white theme, so white roses and baby's breath decorated the surfaces today. He'd stayed out of it this time. A date was logical. Possible. A wedding was presumptive.

Letting Zoe pose him, he cooperated with her redirections and smile coaxing, but his thoughts drifted to Libby.

"You're very photogenic, if you don't mind me saying so." She looked to Jared as if he'd agree.

The assistant gave her a snort. "Don't ask me."

Movement from the other side of the room caught Clay's eye, but Jared blocked his view. Zoe readied her camera while Jared cleared out of Clay's line of sight.

A white, flowing dress with sparkling beadwork. Flashing red hair. Bright, pale blue eyes. Jared grabbed a separate camera and focused on catching Liberty as she walked up, but Zoe zeroed in on Clay. His heart thumped as Libby joined him.

He reached for her hand. "You are so beautiful."

She dipped her head. "Thanks." Then, she raised her eyes, studying him. "That's a nice tux."

"This old thing?"

Their interactions from the previous night rolled through his mind. "Are you okay this morning?"

"Sure." Her casual answer seemed out of place with her formal gown. And her cheer—forced. She was hiding again.

Sometime overnight, she'd decided to cover her real emotions. To make this shoot less uncomfortable, he'd keep any personal revelations to a minimum this morning. He'd already followed through on Gabe's advice to tell her how he felt, which left her response as the deciding factor for whether they could have a second chance. As long as she didn't move right away, there was still time.

But seeing her in that gown? Beautiful and heart-breaking at once. Here she was, near him and yet distanced. His second chance, but out of reach. Like now, with her pasted-on smile and the sense of persevering. He'd seen her genuineness when they'd talked lately. And last night, she hadn't shut him down when he told her he still cared—outright. No more guesswork, but she didn't admit to anything mutual. She gave signals but acted like she regretted them right after. She'd take his hand and then pull away.

Mom cued up music and they danced again, like last night. He pushed the thoughts aside and focused on her. Cameras clicked around them, but they didn't talk.

A cake waited, and they cut it. Liberty's grin went mischievous before she shoved a slice into his mouth. He was far more careful with her piece.

They clinked glasses for a fake toast, and Clay wondered if Zoe would photoshop guests in later.

He wanted to talk with Libby but couldn't find a chance. She seemed fine, playful even. But today's shoot drained him. Finally, Mom called off the team and dismissed everyone. Libby disappeared before he could speak with her.

Dad was waiting near the office when Clay left the meeting space, and he didn't look happy.

Liberty changed out of her rented wedding dress, trying not to tear the satin in her hurry. This week confused her, which meant she needed distance. She'd busy herself at the shop the rest of the day while Clay was elsewhere.

Yet, she couldn't ignore those vases full of daisies from last night or Clay. The fact he'd gone to the trouble. His mother had reminded Liberty of his romantic side, then he'd shown her by bringing peach-scented candles and her favorite flowers to the greenhouse. How uncomfortable had these shoots been for him? He put on a good show, perhaps for his mother.

And his confession. He'd hinted, but having him tell her in words... That could change everything. Especially since he'd asked her for a second chance. And she still hadn't answered.

The events of last night replayed in her mind. Honestly, she'd enjoyed parts of their evening—the way they'd slow-danced. The lack of directions from Zoe, as if the event were natural. Clay's confession of how his feelings for her had returned. The way that knowledge knocked on a bolted door in her heart.

Then, the fake proposal.

Elizabeth had pushed too far, but Liberty was grateful for the wake-up call. They'd portrayed romance, but reality unraveled the fairy tale. Their history sabotaged it, didn't it? How could they have any type of ongoing relationship with a loaded past like theirs?

Arms weighed down, she emerged from the bathroom to the sound of loud voices—two men, one of them Clay—arguing. Was he arguing with his dad? She caught snippets from the other man's accusations, like, "When are you going to grow up?" and "You don't care about this business."

Why would he accuse Clay of either of those things? Even Liberty could see they were unfounded. Her heart ached for Clay.

"I just spent two days posing like a Ken doll so we can keep the business going. Don't give me—"

"Boys, please!" Elizabeth interrupted them as Liberty stepped closer. There stood Clay in a T-shirt and jeans with his father, who leaned heavily on his cane, his face a mask of anger and perhaps pain.

Posing like a Ken doll? Is that all those moments meant to him? Nothing more than a show to him either? Doubts multiplied. Except, now he'd confirmed her instinct. Too much baggage.

He strode over to her. "Hey." His eyes said how sorry he was. He reached for her hand, and she pulled away—angry at herself for her neediness. Neediness made her vulnerable. Independence made her strong.

Jonathan's glare could make ice. But when he turned Liberty's way, his expression softened. He gave her a nod. "Good morning, Miss Liberty." He'd often called her that since they'd met. "Thanks for putting up with my son. Then, and now." He stalked off. What did that mean?

"Sure, it's all part of the job," she said to his retreating back.

Clay's expression said he didn't understand, but neither did Liberty.

Elizabeth gathered her jacket and purse. "I'll be over at the store. Take the rest of the day off, hon. You've both been very helpful. Thank you." She squeezed Liberty's forearm, giving her a nod. "I'm so glad you're back in Birch Harbor. You looked stunning today and last night. Thanks again." She spun for the door, seeming undampened by her husband's cloudy mood.

Alone in this part of the greenhouse, Clay faced Liberty, his face a mask of regret. "I didn't mean that how it sounded."

"Forget it." She needed to resign herself to the fact that there was never a guarantee that he wouldn't reject her, no matter how many tender moments they shared. She draped the bag over her arm, smoothing the vinyl covering the satin dress. On the way home, she'd detour to the rental counter at the bridal shop.

He dipped his head, made eye contact. "Please listen to me."

Something about the pleading tone made her hang her garment bag on the office door. Somewhere inside, she did care for him. "I have a couple of minutes."

"I didn't mean it how it sounded," he repeated. "Dad wants me to give up my plans for my own business. He has no time for my landscaping jobs, and he doesn't want me heading off to hang out with you—like grabbing an early lunch today." Clay stared in the direction of the barn. "I've tried to be patient, but he keeps pushing. Please don't take all that"—he gestured toward where his father had stood—"personally."

Her choices lined up—she could keep her distance, or she could rethink this situation. Maybe give Clay the benefit of the doubt before giving up on him. He reached over and carefully freed her from every burden in her hands, placing them on the nearby table one by one. Then he opened his arms.

What would it feel like to fully let go of the past? Forgiveness, right? God, church. She stayed where she was and lightly shook her head. He dropped his arms.

He seemed resigned, but the tender glint in his eyes returned. "Please tell me we're still on for the seventh."

June 7. Daisy's birthday.

That was something she could share with him. "Okay." After spending the last eight of them alone, it might be less painful sharing Daisy's ninth with her father.

CHAPTER TWENTY-FIVE

Clay laid the steaks on the grill one after the other, enjoying the loud sizzle, followed by the savory aroma of searing meat. His apartment's balcony was just big enough for the grill and a small table with chairs. From this side of the building, he couldn't see the driveway down below, but he heard a car pull in. Unless his parents were expecting someone, Libby was here.

There was so much left unsaid between them, but he guessed she'd prefer to keep tonight about Daisy. He'd act on that assumption.

What had Dad meant last week when he said to Libby, "Thanks for putting up with him, then and now"? And if Dad had such a problem with the shoots, why not try to stop them?

Clay strode into the apartment and crossed the living area to the front door, which he yanked open. Sure enough, Libby climbed from her car. He waved, then trotted down the steps. Meeting him at the trunk, she pointed to the cake that lay inside next to a wrapped package.

"Was I supposed to get a gift?" That seemed illogical, but what did he know about celebrating an absentee daughter's birthday? In a way, celebrating her birthday without her almost felt like a funeral. He'd put away those morbid thoughts and try to figure out what Libby needed tonight.

She lifted the present. "Nope. Whatever you want to do."

Her willingness to share this event with him was a gift of its own. Maybe she'd like how he'd decorated upstairs.

Since their photo shoots had thrown them together before she was ready, he knew it was time to back off. He'd treat her more like a friend—a bit closer than coworkers.

"You seem deep in thought." She smiled up at Clay.

He focused on her. "Welcome." She wore a sundress covered in flowers—of course, and sandals. "You look nice."

"Thanks." She carried what looked like carrot cake, and he toted the gift while they crossed the driveway.

"I appreciate your having me over." She preceded him up the tall exterior staircase. When they hit the top step, he reached around her and pushed open the door. She stepped inside and toward the right, but then paused to take in his home. "Oh, wow. Look at this place."

Her attention locked on the purple balloon bouquet he'd tied to the back of a chair. Then she must have noticed the gerbera daisies on the island because she went still. He held his breath, waiting, hoping he hadn't overstepped and guessed wrong.

She turned and hugged him, and he closed his eyes. "Thank you," she whispered.

"My pleasure."

She sniffed and pulled back, running a finger under her eye. He gave her time to collect herself.

He hadn't hung streamers or anything else, just picked up balloons and that bouquet as a way to honor Daisy and Libby too. She set her gift on the nearby table. "Those are perfect."

He closed the door and watched her scurry to the slider. "The view." She spun, her dress swirling. Mesmerizing. "And I love this open space, how your kitchen is on that wall, but the view is visible straight through from the door to the balcony. And a gas fireplace? No mess, no odor."

They moved to the balcony. Standing outside with her, taking in the sounds of the birds and the waves, Clay inhaled a hint of her peach scent. Having her here felt right, as though she belonged here, and he belonged with her.

"That smells amazing."

A wind gust threatened to blow the smoke back into the apartment, and she pushed the slider closed and moved away from the plume. He'd thrown two baked potatoes on the grill with a couple of ears of corn. He adjusted the cobs but left the steaks to sear a few more minutes on this side.

"I'm glad you're still talking to me after Mom's stunt." They hadn't seen each other all week, and he'd wondered how she was but didn't want to hover. He'd sent her a text and gotten "fine" when he asked after her.

She hugged herself, and he wished she'd let him do that. "We have a few more minutes of grilling. Want to tell me about previous birthdays?"

Sunshine warmed the balcony on this rare sunny evening in June. She pulled up a chair. "Usually, I create something as a gift. I spend a few hours letting myself remember the day of her birth. Normally, dwelling on those memories isn't practical. I try not to focus too long on the pain of that day—physical, mental, emotional. Instead, I remember how she looked. I sing her 'Happy Birthday,' eat a cupcake, and study her picture."

"You miss her."

"Every minute of every day." Her voice wobbled. She put a hand to her neck, and a wave of emotion came over him watching her.

Perhaps he could rescue her for a moment. Would she like a drink? "I have juice—lemonade, orange, apple." He tipped his tongs toward the cooler full of ice and individual bottles. "Want one?"

"Sure." She reached in and selected a lemonade, but her face still bore the pain of missing their daughter.

"I'm sorry you've had to face all of them alone."

After sipping her drink, she met his eyes for the first time since beginning her story. "I'm glad we're doing this tonight. It's nice to share this with you."

He wanted to thank her for letting him into this part of her world, but if he stated that outright she might spook. She tended to skate along unless doubts tripped her up. "Feels like I've missed too many." He flipped the steaks. They were about ready. "I have a lot of time to make up for." And he would, if she'd let him. He gestured toward the serving dish on the table, and she handed it over.

"I don't see it that way. I mean, what would you do?"

He couldn't answer that, so he scooped potatoes and corn onto the tray. Then, they exchanged platters so he could plate the meat. "Here's hoping this birthday isn't as hard as the earlier ones."

She stilled his busyness with a hand on his forearm, and he froze. He worked faster when he felt uncomfortable, and she'd picked up on it. "Relax, Clay. I get it. And this is already better. Your effort means a lot."

At the table, he dished up their food.

"The only person who knew about her back on Bainbridge was Shea, and we had a therapist-patient relationship until recently, so we didn't cross that line. Not spending tonight alone is rather nice."

"I didn't know if purple was the way to go." He referred to the balloons inside as he took his seat across the bistro table.

"And I have no idea about the carrot cake. It's fine."

"It doesn't bother you that she'll never know?"

She buttered her corn. "I don't have a choice. No use camping on the negatives."

Seals entertained them in the Sound while they ate, and Clay debated divulging his secret. Their rapport seemed fragile again, which meant her level of trust might not withstand his interference.

Perhaps, though, he could test the waters. "Do you still want to keep Daisy a secret from my family?"

Her gaze snapped to his, her brows furrowing. "I do. Why?"

"Everything's fine." His reflex said to take her hand, but he squelched it. "I haven't said anything to them. Let me know if you change your mind, okay?"

"I won't." She set her juice down, her meal finished.

"I didn't mean to upset you."

Her expression softened. "I'm good. Should I grab the cake?"

"I'll get it." He collected their dishes and carted them to the kitchen. His guess was correct. No news about Daisy seemed best. He'd keep his secret for now.

A few minutes later, he returned with small plates, the gift, the balloons, and the cake box all in hand.

She grinned at him as she removed the items and set them on the table. Next, she untied the balloon strings from his wrist, her fingers grazing his skin. "I could've helped."

"No problem." He wanted to bring out the daisies too, and he'd forgotten a knife. "One sec." A few steps carried him back to the kitchen.

Over their short lives, he'd celebrated his niece's and nephew's birthdays, seen the delight on their faces. Watched his brother and sister-in-law enjoy their kids. In person.

As he rejoined Libby outside, the soberness of the moment

overwhelmed him. She accepted the bouquet and set it on the table, giving him a small smile. Then, she pulled a candle from the pocket of her sundress. The number nine, in pink. How was she not crying while cutting their daughter's cake? Had years of performing this ritual given her a strength he hadn't found?

When she'd placed a piece in front of each of them, and one in the center of the table with a lit candle, she sang the birthday song and he joined in. His throat felt dry. They quietly used their daughter's nickname, and Clay peeked toward the house in case his parents were out in the yard. No sign of them.

Right then, Mom appeared from around the waterside of the house. She waved up at them. "Hi there."

Clay jumped up and stood in front of the cake. He moved toward the railing. Libby hurried to blow out the candle and remove it. They couldn't hide the balloons. They should have done this inside.

His mother crossed the yard to stand under their balcony. "I thought your birthday was later in the year, Liberty. Forgive me! We'll have to celebra—"

"Oh, it's not my—"

"We're . . . honoring someone who's not here with us," Clay said, shifting so he didn't block Libby's view. That was honest enough, right?

Libby nodded at him as if she appreciated his explanation. With a dazed look, she spun the plate holding the candle-indented slice.

Mom's face dimmed. "Oh. How sweet. I'll leave you be. Sad to hear about your friend, and I sure didn't mean to interrupt." She skittered away.

Clay resettled at the table, taking Libby's hand in his despite the decision to keep his distance. "Sorry about that."

She turned her wrist, threaded her fingers between his. "Thanks for covering for Daisy."

"Of course."

"You've been cool about all this—the secrets, the birthday. I know I've said it before but thank you."

"My pleasure."

CHAPTER TWENTY-SIX

"I don't know where that leaves us. It's making me crazy." Sunday afternoon, two days after Daisy's birthday, Liberty walked the beach below Roy and Gloria's bluff. Clouds blocked the sun off and on, chilling the air and threatening rain. But Liberty needed the privacy of the beach for this chat.

"Understandably." Shea's voice huffed from her end of the connection as if her walk demanded more oxygen. Maybe she'd found an even outdoor surface there on Bainbridge.

Due to the rocks here, Liberty kept her own pace slow. Waves splashed to her right, but she was a good distance from the tide. "I feel like I'm bouncing back and forth. He keeps doing these honorable things. Like trying to protect me from his mother's meddling."

"Go, Clay."

"Or, celebrating Daisy's birthday by inviting me to his house."

"Oh, shoot. That was this last week, wasn't it?"

"It's okay. Yes, Friday. But here's what happened. His mom interrupted our singing to Daisy. Clay came up with the perfect cover, without lying."

"He's trying to honor your decision to not tell the family about her."

"Yes." Liberty tipped her head back to take in the sun's rays when it reappeared.

"All that could be a friend helping a friend."

"Except he's told me how he feels." Sometimes at night, Liberty replayed his words in her mind. The slow dance, the murmured confession. "He seems all in. I'm half out and wholly confused."

Shea laughed over the line.

"I have a phone conference about the job leads tomorrow."

"Oh."

Liberty settled on a huge log that had washed up. "There may be a chance I could go back to school if the university job is a good fit."

"You've always wanted that."

Wind rushed in from the water, and Liberty pulled her jacket tighter across herself. "I know."

"Do you want that more than what you have on Whidbey? The Archers, Clay, your job there?"

"My living situation is temporary. I don't know how I'll afford local housing on my income. The places that seem halfway safe are out of my budget, and I'm not being picky about countertops or other finishes."

"So, moving on means a job that lets you afford your own housing, take art classes."

"Maybe earn my degree." Patches of blue sky reflected in gray Puget Sound, lending hope.

"Okay."

Liberty kicked the pebbles and shell fragments near her foot. "It's not like I wouldn't make new friends. I know I'll be an older college student, but better now than never."

"I agree. Now is a good time. You aren't tied down. But one thing confuses me."

"Shoot."

"You've always wanted a family, and you've found that on Whidbey." Shea's voice was gentle. "Why go somewhere else?"

"I hear you. But what is the alternative? Settle down with Clay, forget everything that's happened? Put aside my college ambition?"

"Not necessarily."

Anxiety slithered through her middle, but she pushed it away. No one was making her do anything. "Haven't I already given up nearly everything in my life, more than once?"

"If you move, you'll be doing it again."

"If I don't, I'll never know." She searched her mind to rack up more reasons. "Not to mention, Clay isn't the one for me." Was he?

"That's part of your decision. You have to decide where you are with him." Once again, Shea had heard what Liberty hadn't said. "Could you ever trust him again—fully? Could you love him again?"

"I care about him. And I admire a lot of things about him."

"That's not the same as trusting him."

As they disconnected a few minutes later, Liberty's mind drifted to two words—*home* and *Clay*.

Being with him, returning here to this island and having him in her life again, felt like home. Caution demanded she protect herself. What if she ended up relying on him, and he let her down again? She couldn't let that happen.

The following day during her morning break at work, Liberty sat in her car outside the florist shop. Pressing her cold phone to her ear, she waited for it to ring. The job placement specialist that Gloria had recommended months ago finally had a list of leads.

"Ah, Liberty. Good to hear from you." Alan always sounded upbeat, as if he'd never faced a job crisis. "I have a list of opportunities that have recently opened up. That's how it goes— feast or famine. Two are located on Bainbridge, one in Langley. But the Bellingham one might be ideal. There's nearby housing, not too expensive. Working as a receptionist on a university campus during the day would leave evenings free for classes. Employee tuition is at a very reduced rate, but I might be able to negotiate that down to free."

Liberty's heart thrummed. Free tuition. Almost as if she'd been able to follow through on her original scholarship. Guilt tried to harass her, but why should she feel uncomfortable about seeing to her own future? She hadn't promised Clay anything.

She hadn't been clear with him either.

Alan gave her more details of the job for several minutes, directing her to send a customized cover letter and tweaked resumé. He'd attach them to the Archers' recommendation letter. Then, Alan would nudge the decision-makers toward an interview.

Another reason for Liberty to feel guilty. If Gloria or Roy knew that she was using their names and their letter to secure a job elsewhere, they might feel betrayed. She'd spent a lot of her life worrying about what others thought or might want. Was it wrong to finally consider what she wanted? And if not, why this ache inside?

At lunch, she called Alan back. They discussed the cover letter and then the resumé, tweaking both to match the job's requirements with her applicable experience.

"Ready?" Alan asked after he'd made the changes. She pictured him with his finger poised over the Send button.

"Thanks for doing this. Without a laptop, it's challenging." Months ago, she'd used the computer at the optometry office to send him her resumé and the Archers' glowing letter.

"No problem." He paused. "Are we ready for the next phase?"

Was she? Everything on Whidbey seemed temporary. "Yes. And thank you." A keyboard click sounded from his side. She wasn't completely clear on how Alan got paid or from whom. Perhaps he was doing this as a personal favor. *She* couldn't afford to pay him. "Tell me, do you get a commission or something if you land me a job?"

"Don't worry about me." He used his schmooze voice as if he were selling cars rather than placing her for a job. "I'll follow-up today with them. See if there's anything else we need to do to secure that interview. From what I remember, they prefer a video call. A smart phone would work."

"Except I don't have one."

"Can you get access to a computer?"

The Archers had a laptop, which she might be able to take to her room. Anyplace in the main parts of the house risked interruption or someone seeing her. She'd hate for Gloria or Roy to hear her. "I'll work on that." She'd rather drive the hour-plus to Bellingham for a face-to-face, but even for that she'd need time off.

They disconnected, and doubts chased Liberty through her duties as Elizabeth's assistant.

CHAPTER TWENTY-SEVEN

Sunday evening, Clay pulled into the farm and climbed from his truck. His father had mentioned moving equipment around, saying, "We best do it before Monday's workload buries us." The place smelled familiar—like musty straw. This wasn't an animal farm, but they kept hay bales on hand for wicking up moisture as needed.

Clay heard him near the tractors by the rear barn doors, muttering ugly words. They kept the machines back here, out of the way. Overhead lighting cast shadows and emphasized floating dust. Clay inspected the barn for other family members. No sign of them, thankfully. Dad's summons tonight felt confrontational, especially since there were no witnesses.

"You finally here, Clay?" Dad called over his shoulder, standing near the skid loader—a machine Clay rarely used, and then only when he was certain everyone else was far away. Merely seeing the loader sent him into flashbacks. Their last exchange hadn't been too bad. What had happened between then and now to get Dad so agitated?

Clay had come right over, but he clenched his jaws against a tirade. If Dad wanted a confrontation, he'd give him one. But he'd keep his tone civil, as long as he could. "What can I do?"

Pivoting on his cane, Dad faced Clay. "You may as well know, I didn't call you here for help with the tractors." Dad's hunched shoulders said he'd had a rough day trying to get around. He'd probably spent too much time on his feet. He wasn't the type to sit, no matter what the doctors said.

Clay waited him out, dreading his next words.

"I can't believe you. Always trying to act so righteous. And that poor woman, back for more of your nonsense." Dad waved in the direction of the greenhouse. "Photo shoots. All those pictures of you guys dressed for a wedding? What a joke."

Clay's blood buzzed through his veins. "Okay, Dad, what's this about? We did that"—he copied his father's hand motion—"for the sake of the business, at Mom's request. Liberty didn't have to, though she may have felt like she did. I tried to let her off the hook several times, and she refused."

"A gentleman would have gotten Kason and Brynn to do it."

"They're busy with their kids and the rest of the farm." Clay couldn't keep his voice down, but he worked to resettle his anger. "This is bigger. You've been barking at me for years. What's eating you?"

Dad scowled but didn't answer.

Sure, Clay had messed up, as a seventeen-year-old. Granted Dad still had to use a cane, a fact that grieved Clay. But would he never let it go? Never see past Clay's mistakes? He pointed at the skid loader, parked in the shadows. "When are you going to forgive me for that?"

Instead of muttered curses or angry accusations, Dad lasered a serious, unblinking stare in Clay's direction. "When you ask for it."

Clay stepped back, struck. Had he never done that? In all these years? Had pride stopped him? What prevented him now? He closed his mouth, unable to form the request. Begging for forgiveness would make him vulnerable. After all, Dad could still deny him.

"Since she got back, you've been acting innocent, like you did back then. But you had secrets. Then she disappeared, and you brushed it off. But I knew." He thumped his own chest with a forefinger. "I knew."

Clay blinked at his father, almost dizzy with the words hitting him. What was he talking about? "You knew... what?"

"About the baby, you selfish—"

Sucker punched, though Dad hadn't touched him. "You knew about her?" *All these years?*

"Her?" Dad went still as he repeated the word in a hoarse voice. Clay paced, his thoughts tumbling. His father knew about Daisy? How? And what did it say about Dad that his voice went hoarse after hearing the news that his first grandchild was a girl?

"What's her name?"

Dad was so argumentative, so cold most of the time, and Clay didn't trust him with this secret, even though his voice and demeanor showed brokenness. Libby had asked him not to tell his parents about Daisy. Too late. Dad already knew. Did Mom? To honor Libby, Clay wouldn't share their daughter's name. "We have a nickname for her."

"Where is she now?"

"We don't know." He flashed back to that moment in this barn a decade ago when he'd thought he and Liberty were alone. "How did you find out?"

"I was over there." He pointed to the corner. "Kept waiting for you to come tell your old man in the following hours, days, weeks. *Years.* Your mother and I would have helped. Next thing I knew, Liberty's gone and you're strutting around like nothing ever happened. Cocksure and ridiculous." He spat the final words—a judgment.

The names cut. But Clay hadn't been the same person for a long time. A battle waged inside between confessing and asking forgiveness, and wanting to deny his mistakes, defend himself. Run. Pride again.

Dad studied Clay for a long moment. "I thought I'd raised you to be a better man than that." He limped away, out through the front.

Clay replayed his father's expression over and over— accusations of betrayal, a sense of disappointment. Disgust. Feeling an inner tug from God, Clay wandered to the back door, out into the yard between the building and the first line of trees.

I blew it, Lord. Pride had won.

God didn't answer, which spoke grace to Clay. Why shame someone who already felt guilty? That wasn't God's way. Clay waited until he'd cleared the lawn behind the barn before looking around. Dad's truck pulled out of the driveway. Still no sign of Kason's family. Probably bedtime in the house across the property. Clay hiked between the rows of Christmas trees to the sound of frogs in the distant pond.

He was waiting for me to come to him, condemning me the

whole time. Especially as months and years passed. A bat swooped between branches overhead, and Clay turned back.

I do not condemn you. Jesus's words felt like a balm. Clay had a sense—a nudge, in fact—that he should apologize and sooner than later. Making himself vulnerable to Dad... He didn't know how he'd do it.

He'd been trying to honor Libby's request, but ever since Gabe had pointed Clay toward a web page, the idea of doing this search had nagged at him, especially after Charlie said nearly the same thing. Liberty obviously ached to learn more about their daughter, but at the same time denied wanting to. Maybe doing more research would help her.

Tonight, he had to check.

Sitting in front of his laptop in his apartment, he navigated to the online directory for Charlie's new church. Folks probably wouldn't allow their family photos to be posted publicly like this now. At least on Facebook, users could choose their audience. But they didn't seem to mind sharing eight-year-old photographs. The photo directory appeared.

Under the tab "Then and Now," he found pics from well over sixty years ago to today, and lots of images from the years in between.

On a whim, he opened a new tab for his childhood church's site, wondering if they'd ever posted pictures of Clay and his family from when they attended. Sure enough, there were stills from his time in the youth group. The shots even captured him with Libby a few times. They seemed happy and young, with a forced look of acting carefree. Today, he could read their guilt. He recalled the fear of having their secrets exposed.

After Libby left, Clay got tired of all the questions. He found excuses to miss church. He started going somewhere else. No more contact with the Kincades. No more questions or reminders.

Multiple families had posed for professional shots, and he scrolled through. Libby's guardians were there. And under *W*, there was Libby, with her own parents. His lungs squeezed seeing the three of them, smiling and unaware that soon after the picture was taken, both her parents would die in a car accident.

With a deep sigh, he clicked another year's link. There were the Kincades again. No sign of Libby's family, of course. This would have been around nine years ago. Daisy was born in June. He couldn't recall what time of year the photographer took the annual pictures.

Heaviness settled on him. She'd suffered so much loss. Clay navigated back to Charlie's "Church Directory" link and found the one from ten years ago. Of course, Clay didn't know anybody. And Charlie hadn't said he would, he'd only said something about finding church directories online, starting with big churches. Just in case social services had placed Daisy with a Christian family. Clay didn't see any redheaded babies appearing with non-redheaded parents—a hunch he followed now that he knew their baby's gender and appearance. He picked up his phone and checked the image he'd taken of Libby's photo. He checked the next year and scrolled through the images. The church had grown, and many more families filled the directory.

His eyes grew tired as he skimmed the smiling families, not recognizing anyone. Maybe he'd search smaller church's sites next. Or give up on this method.

Suddenly, under *N*, a pretty redheaded baby appeared with one of the couples. Her name wasn't Daisy, of course, but she resembled Libby enough that he froze.

He'd found her.

With quick motions, he checked the subsequent years. There she was. Growing up in front of him. Surrounded by her smiling parents as the years progressed.

With another few clicks, he'd collected her images into one file on his laptop. Cropping and expanding the photographs, he isolated Daisy and resaved the JPEGs. Then, he pressed a button and the pictures printed out across the room.

Now he knew where she went to church. The latest directory included her most recent family portrait. He knew her last name.

She was here on the island. That group of girls in the school crosswalk might have included her. She could have shopped at his grocery store, eaten at Skye Café with her adoptive parents.

Right here, all along.

CHAPTER TWENTY-EIGHT

Liberty finished helping a customer Wednesday afternoon and wished her well. She turned to her boss. "Elizabeth, do you mind if I take off a little early this afternoon?"

"Things are pretty calm here. I can close up. What time would you need to leave by?"

Her phone interview was scheduled for four o'clock. "About 3:45, if you don't mind. I can make up the hours."

"Are you kidding? You put in enough overtime to cover it." She waved. "Go ahead."

Thankfully, she'd talked the human resources representative out of doing a video chat.

At 3:45, she excused herself and drove toward home. But she couldn't very well call from her bedroom. Instead of pulling in to the Archers' driveway, she steered farther down Beachside Road until she came to the state park. She pulled in and eyed the rolling waves coming in off the strait.

Nerves rattled her. Nerves and confusion. If the interview went well, they'd ask for an in-person as a next step. If it didn't, she'd be back to searching. Did she still want to leave?

Her pros and cons list lined up in her mind. If she chose to pass on college classes now, when would she take them? The Archers had helped her sell her trailer for scrap metal, which reminded her how homeless she was without their help. She hated freeloading and would only feel better when she was independent again.

But any semblance to a family in her life lived here.

Twenty minutes later, she disconnected the call with the HR rep. Not long after, Alan rang in. "I'm hearing positive things," he said before she could do more than accept his call. "Good for you."

"Thanks for your help on this." She'd proven that she had employable skills and experience. She *could* live independently, mostly.

"You don't sound too enthusiastic. Don't you feel it went okay?"

"It's not that. I'm unsure about the move is all." Clay had asked her over this evening, said he had something for her. But the more time they spent together, the more confused she became.

"This may be a pivotal moment in your life. I'm sure you'll make the right decision. Chin up, okay?"

The man could talk the bark off a madrone tree. "You got it." They ended their call, and Liberty aimed her vehicle toward home. She'd grab a shower and drive down to Clay's.

These days, you could order a book online, but Clay wanted this gift to have a personal touch. He'd hoped to have his project completed before Libby was due to arrive. If he hurried, he might finish in time. He'd bought picnic foods for a meal out on the balcony, if she decided to stay.

He hadn't meant to manipulate her but sharing a meal might help her more easily accept his gift. Especially since the present came with a couple of confessions.

He wouldn't tell her everything today. Without more research, he didn't know as much as he'd like to. But he could begin with what he did know.

When he'd pasted the last piece into place, he closed the cover and slipped it into the box he'd found in Mom's storage room. She saved wrapping supplies, which made this job simpler.

Lord, please help this go well.

Western sunlight warmed his balcony, whenever clouds didn't block the light. He threw together a cooler of ice, bottled juices, and water, then carried paper plates and plasticware outside. A peek at one of his clocks told him Libby was running a little late, but hopefully she'd still come.

A knock on his door brought him back through the slider.

"All right if I come in?" she said, sounding lighthearted as she turned the doorknob. Was that cheerfulness faked? Or had something positive happened?

He loved that she felt comfortable barging in. "Absolutely."

"We have sunshine."

He relished her bright expression. "Sounds like things are going well."

She set her bag on a chair and nodded. "We've got most of the details in place for your sister's wedding." Brushing her hands together, she grinned at him. "Feels good."

"I'm glad. She can be demanding."

"I haven't seen that in her. We're getting along great."

"Is something else going on? I hope you don't mind me saying it, but you seem happier than I've seen you lately."

She gave him an intoxicating expression—part grin, part mystery. "Let's say things are finally looking up." Would she tell him more if he pried? Maybe he'd try over dinner.

"We could have a meal on the balcony, if you wanna stay."

She eyed the gift box on the kitchen counter, then focused on him again. "Let's eat."

He grabbed cartons from the fridge. "Help me carry these?"

"Sure." She held out her hands, and he loaded her up with a container of potato salad and a bowl of washed grapes. He grabbed the plate of fried chicken and the bag of rolls and followed her through the open slider.

They'd celebrated Daisy's birthday only a couple of weeks ago. Was Libby thinking about their daughter as much as he was lately? Over the years, she'd had to adapt to living with all she remembered about Daisy. Now it was his turn. And he suddenly knew more than even she did.

He'd start with the hard news—something he'd had no control over, but information he needed to admit all the same. But first, he'd cherish a few more moments of her joy. He hadn't seen this in her since her return. Until now, he'd forgotten this appealing side of her.

She held her chicken leg midway to her mouth. "What?"

"I've missed you like this."

"You know what? I have too. It's been a while." Still the light didn't dim in her eyes.

Maybe he'd start small. Nonthreatening. "The other day, I found pictures of you and me and the youth group from our first years there."

She set down her chicken. "Before Mom and Dad died?"

"Yeah." He rested his elbows on the table, plate pushed back, chin on his hands. If he didn't occupy them, they'd reach for hers.

"Those outreaches were intense." She rolled her shoulders as if recalling a physical ache.

"Remember the homeless shelter and the backpack drives?"

"Pastor Charlie cheering us all on." Her stomach growled, and he gestured toward the food while she laughed.

"Eat up."

They finished their meal in peaceful companionship. Knowing he had to destroy that with his next two declarations made him want to put it off, but he couldn't. The days were ticking by and the sooner Libby knew, the better.

"I know you've said you don't want to interfere with Daisy's life." When she started to interrupt, he quickly added, "Neither do I."

She resumed leaning back in her chair, arms on the rests, face turned toward the sun. "I'm glad. It's been nice to share her with someone."

"And I've liked learning about her." He grabbed their dishes. "Let me clear these. I'll be right back."

Inside, he scraped the plates and ran water over them, leaving them in the sink. *Enough stalling.* Libby seemed at ease, waiting him out. He gripped her gift and headed outside. Now that he had this in hand, he hoped Mom and Dad would stay at the farm for their dinner with Kason's family a while longer. Well, Mom anyway. Dad... That's what he needed to talk to Libby about.

He settled and found her attention pinned on him. "You mentioned I seem cheerful. You seem worried about something," she said.

"I need to talk to you."

"About Daisy?" Her carefree expression faded.

His slow nod prompted her to sit up in her chair, lean toward the table. "What happened?"

"I've kept my promise not to go meet her."

"Good. But..."

He laid his forearms on the table, the gift waiting in the empty chair next to him. Gripping his hands together, he gave her eye contact. "Dad called me out to the farm one Sunday night. He had plenty to say."

Her expression went from wary to compassionate as both her brow and her mouth softened. "Oh, no. I know things are hard with your dad. But I thought they were getting better. What happened?"

"Lots of fuss about you and me doing the photo shoots—no surprise."

"What is his issue with that? I mean, we did those for him, for the family business."

He reached for her hand, and she let him take it. "Libby, he was there."

"Where?"

"In the barn the night you and I talked. The last time I saw you before you were sent away."

She stared at him. "He heard?"

"Yeah."

"Did he tell you what he knows?"

"He doesn't know her name, but he knows you were pregnant with our daughter."

She sat back, her hand slipping from his. Facing the Sound, she gripped the arms of her chair. "Has he told anyone else?"

"I don't think so. If he had, Mom would not be able to keep it to herself. She'd have brought it up already."

He wanted to tell her more, explain what this meant regarding Clay's relationship with Dad, but this moment was about how the news hit Libby.

"Wait," she said. "If he knew, and you never talked to him about it in the years following, then he has probably wondered why this whole time."

Huh. She got him. He was worried about her, and she was checking in with him. He'd been watching for signs from her, and this one said a lot, though he couldn't decide exactly what. "You're right. It's why he's been so angry. Said I should have told him. But more than that, he feels I should have done the honorable thing and come clean, stayed by your side, and seen you through it." Dad hadn't spelled all that out, but Clay knew the way he thought.

"Which means his anger wasn't based on the farm accident."

"Nope. I think I've known that all along. It's not like him to hold a grudge over a childish mistake, even when there are lasting consequences." Dad had implied that Clay had never sought his forgiveness. Something Clay needed to do, soon.

"Does this mean you two are going to be okay?"

"Eventually. And thanks for caring."

She took his hand again, squeezed. "Of course."

Oh, how he hated to break the spell of this moment. "One more thing."

"Okay. Out with it." Her red hair glistened, a few tendrils sweeping into her face on the salty breeze. If she'd let him, he'd brush them away. Her free hand got there first.

"You're not upset that Dad knew?"

"He's keeping it quiet. That's all I could ask."

"True."

"But it sounds like it might be time for you two to have a heart-to-heart."

"Goodie."

She chuckled, and he let himself grin, though the topic was weighty. "Have you thought about reaching out to the Kincades again?"

Surprising him, she didn't react with anger. Her expression stayed calm. "Mom and Dad trusted them enough to name them as my guardians, and I trusted them at one time too. What could I possibly gain by getting in touch now? They obviously didn't keep their agreement with my folks to see me through high school."

He couldn't argue with that, but he'd take their side for one second to see how she'd respond. "What if they're sorry?"

"Then they should have found me and apologized. Don't you think?" She eyed him. "Why the questions?"

"If they still live in town, I wouldn't be surprised you might run into them someday." Not unlike their daughter. "I wondered if you had a chance to see them, what you'd say."

Irritation clouded her eyes. "I would walk the other way. Let them earn it, if they want to chase me."

"I'm sorry you've had to live in fear of running into people since you've been back."

She pressed her lips together as if that was truer than he knew. "Thanks. Now, when do I get to open my gift?" She gestured toward the chair. "At least I'm assuming that's for me," she added in a playful voice.

"It is." His burden pressed on his shoulders. "But before you open it, I need to tell you something else." He fought to fill his lungs with air. "I found Daisy."

CHAPTER TWENTY-NINE

Surprise and confusion arrested her thoughts. Had she heard him correctly? "What?"

Adrenaline rushed through her veins, with the urge to flee. But she locked her hands around the arm rests. She'd been right not to trust him, and she'd been wrong to think he'd leave it alone. Of course he had to find their daughter.

"Don't worry. I haven't gone to see her. I don't even know where she lives, exactly. Only generally."

"What does that mean?"

"Libby, she's on the island."

Her heartbeat skipped. "She is?" So, Liberty could run into her somewhere? The thought both excited and scared her.

In the moment of calm between them, Clay handed her the gift. "Do you want to see a recent photo of her?"

This box didn't look like it held a single frame, and she'd soon know for sure. She accepted the package and set it before her on the table.

The sense of wellbeing that had followed her job interview, making her think her life was working again, fled. She'd convinced herself she could handle a few more weeks here on Whidbey, even working with Clay's family before walking away. She needed to focus on her long-term goals—get her art degree. Work in that field one day. Suddenly, her world felt upended again.

Absently, she opened the box to find a book. Aqua and lavender swirls made up the cover's pattern, and the multiple pages were made of photo paper. But she wasn't ready to peek inside. Photographs?

"How did you get these?" Clay had mentioned one current photo. She guessed there were several.

"Without telling Gabe anything," Clay began slowly, "I asked how he'd go about searching for someone he wanted to reconnect with if social media didn't help."

"Right. Since we didn't have her new name, we couldn't search for her online." Liberty's heart thumped, knocking, wanting answers, begging her to open the book.

"We know her name now." He gestured toward the album. "Look inside."

Closing her eyes, she raked up her courage. Then, she opened the first page to read: *Jaelyn Emily, our daughter.* No last name, but Liberty didn't care. There, below the title, was the image of Liberty's baby, a year later. It was obvious Clay had cropped the picture to single her out.

Their daughter's green eyes and red hair identified her, drew Liberty in. She stroked the photo. Her one-year-old.

"I could tell, in the months since you've been back, that you've ached for her. It's tragic that you celebrated eight of her birthdays by yourself. I wanted to do this for you. For each of us, I guess."

Unsure what to say, because Clay was right—she had wanted to know more—she stayed silent. Curiosity not only ate at her, it kept her awake. She turned to the next page. The images were grainy at times, depending on how much he'd blown them up after cropping them. No one else occupied the photos, but she saw arms, sweaters. Someone held her.

With each turn of the page, Daisy's hair grew longer. Then, she stood beside her adoptive parents.

"I was prepared to be angry about this, I mean, if I ever discovered you'd gone to find her." Liberty knew her voice sounded wistful as she devoured every detail.

"I haven't. Only online research. But Libby, I want to. We could go together."

"And do what?" She closed the book, without seeing the final shots. "We've been over this. We cannot interfere in her new life. We can't interrupt what they've built. What if she doesn't even know she's adopted? What if we show up, she sees herself in us, and she finds out her parents lied to her about her history?" She gripped Clay's hand. "We can't do that to her. Promise me."

"I feel like you're always asking that of me."

Couldn't he tell how desperate she was to leave things alone? "You know, I debated telling you about her. This is why. You always react by trying to *fix* things. Tell me you understand that this can't be fixed."

Clay didn't answer. He pressed his mouth closed, which he did whenever he couldn't agree with what was said or when he couldn't comply.

She stood. "Who were you really doing this for, Clay? Honestly, it seems more for yourself. Your curiosity got away from you."

"That's not fair." Grief lined his eyes. "I thought you wanted to see her. To know she's okay. Did you notice her smiling face?"

For that, Liberty was grateful, but she couldn't make herself admit it to him. Nor would she tell him she'd spend tonight hugging this photo album and then flipping pages over and over. He had given her something she'd never have had without him.

But the risk... "I need to go." She started to set the book down, which felt like giving up her daughter again.

"Keep it." He stood with her, shoving his hands into his pockets. "Please."

She snagged the album from the table and headed through the open slider.

At her car, she stopped, door ajar. Clay hadn't followed her all the way down, but he watched her with a sad expression. "Goodbye, Clay."

Of course she'd see him at work until she moved away, but she was through entertaining the thought of anything rekindling.

Her world was coming apart. But maybe he'd confirmed her choice to withhold trusting him again.

Yeah, if they offered her the Bellingham position, she'd take it. If she left, Clay would leave their daughter alone.

Hopefully.

CHAPTER THIRTY

A week later, she'd still had no word from Bellingham. Alan avoided her, letting her calls go to voice mail. No news didn't feel like good news to her today as she pulled into the Archers' driveway after work. With a job offer, her questions would be answered. An open door made her decision for her. A closed door...? That either meant keep searching or give up and stay right where she was.

Gloria met her in the mudroom. "Welcome home, dear. Have you had dinner? If not, Roy cooked his beef stroganoff, and I made biscuits to go with it."

She could use a peaceful evening with her surrogate family, though she hated keeping secrets from them. "Yes, thank you. Give me a minute?" She dropped her things in her room and kicked off her shoes in exchange for her comfy slippers.

Her job had worn her down this week, trying to perform for Elizabeth without mentioning her argument with Clay. Whenever he came in, she escaped to the backroom and worked on a delivery or tidied up. Reverting to avoiding him seemed the wisest choice before she moved north. Yet, every passing day without Alan contacting her ate away at her hope. She didn't have a backup plan in place.

She joined her hosts in the kitchen as Gloria slid the biscuits off a baking sheet and into a towel-lined bowl. The house smelled of onions, beef, noodles, and biscuits. They chatted about work, and she tried to keep her responses upbeat. If she could get them talking about their interests, they might not dig around too long in her world.

Roy ladled stroganoff into her bowl and passed it back. "We wanted to chat with you about housing."

That sounded ominous.

Gloria touched her hand. "Oh, don't worry, dear. We're not kicking you out."

She felt her lungs relax as she waited to hear what they had on their minds.

"It's nothing like that." Roy handed a filled bowl to his wife, and then he directed his attention back to Liberty. "We've heard from local agents that rental prices are rather high, especially for someone in your situation. So, we wanted to make you an offer."

Liberty spread butter on the steaming biscuit she'd sliced open. Her camper was long gone. Were they planning to help her find a new one? She'd noticed they hadn't been very urgent about replacing it. Until now.

"What are you doing on the Fourth, dear?"

The abrupt turn in conversation stalled her response. What did the holiday have to do with her living arrangements? "I don't have any plans. Why?"

Roy folded his hands together and leaned forward. "We'd like to take you shopping."

"For a tiny house." Gloria's smile lit her face.

Pointing toward the window, Roy seemed to indicate the vacant, and well-treed, lot next door. "We own that property. We thought a tiny house might look good parked over there."

A tiny house? That was an upgrade from a camper. She'd seen them featured on TV, and she'd daydreamed about owning one, especially if she lived alone.

"It'd be affordable, and you'd have us nearby if anything came up."

"Don't worry. We'll bring out an arborist and clear any unhealthy trees. No more surprises."

Was everyone out to tempt her to stay? Elizabeth had casually brought up a possible raise once she'd been there six months. And September was coming. Now the Archers wanted to help her buy a house and plant her next door? She didn't have money for a down payment. Were tiny houses financed like a camper or other vehicle? Or like a house, with a mortgage? That didn't sound right.

"That is a very kind offer. But we'd be window shopping." Admittedly, it might be a fun way to spend the holiday. "I can't afford to buy yet."

"Oh, we understand that." Gloria tsked as if money wasn't a

concern. She munched on her meal, and her nonchalance almost made Liberty laugh. "Plus, I like window shopping."

"Thank you for suggesting the lot next door. Whoever ends up there will enjoy a grand view, like yours." The thought made her heart tighten. Maybe it was time to tell them about her job hunt.

She dug into her meal, leaving the topic unspoken. Why hurt their feelings if she didn't actually have a job?

"How's Clay?" Roy could act as innocent as he wanted, but with a question like that, Liberty knew his goal. The man didn't need a map to hunt for information.

Gloria leaned toward Liberty as if afraid she'd miss the answer.

"Seems fine. He dropped by the shop this week. Busy with new landscaping clients whenever he can fit them in, according to his mother." She remembered his sorrow around his dad. Another worry—whether Jonathan would divulge their secrets.

Liberty's intention was to protect Daisy from well-meaning folks tracking her down. Had she failed? Had moving back here been her second biggest mistake to date?

Gloria lifted the pitcher from the table and refilled Liberty's water glass. "That's not the type of update I was expecting."

At times, everyone's meddling became overwhelming. Alone in Bellingham, she wouldn't have to worry about Elizabeth, or anyone, conjuring up fake events to push romance. Or Gloria and Roy asking pointed questions. "I guess I'm tired tonight. I think I'll head to bed early." She lifted her dishes and carried them to the sink. The Archers were great hosts, and they genuinely cared for her. She didn't want to hurt or offend them, but neither could she endure their antics. "Thanks for dinner."

As she headed into her room, she heard Roy's voice. "Think about the shopping trip, okay, Liberty? We'll make a day of it."

"Thanks. Good night," she called over her shoulder, not making any promises, and wishing Alan would contact her.

Clay clicked off the phone call. Charlie had helped him more than

Clay thought he could. His former youth pastor had offered solid advice about Clay's search. Sometime in the last decade, he too had changed churches. His lead was the strongest so far. Without saying anything, and compromising his role as the pastor, he'd helped a lot.

Libby had effectively avoided him all week. Mom said she'd been acting odd, and she'd asked him why Libby's car hadn't been in the driveway lately. He worried Libby was planning to move, sooner than later. Even with Mom's promised raise, Libby didn't seem committed to staying.

Sure, the Kincades were here, along with bad memories. But in Birch Harbor, she had people who loved her. Two families who welcomed her. What would she have anywhere else? If she returned to Bainbridge, she'd have Shea and Liam, but what if she decided to go somewhere else out of sheer stubbornness?

He texted her again: TALK TO ME?

Like before, no immediate response. Then, HAVE YOU GONE TO SEE HER?

I DON'T KNOW WHERE SHE IS.

GOOD.

I WAS TRYING TO HELP YOU.

The nautical clock his mom gave him ticked loudly from his kitchen wall, marking the seconds of her avoidance.

What could he do? If Libby didn't want his help, or that of his family or the Archers, what could anyone do? No one could force her to let them accept her—which they'd already done.

Stubbornness. He wanted to punch the wall, but then he'd have a repair his dad would question.

Speaking of Dad, he needed to talk to him soon. Clay had job news, and he needed to clear up the past. Libby would appreciate his assurance he didn't plan to divulge their secrets. He could get that promise from Dad for her and ease her mind.

Lord, we can't make her stay, even if it's the best thing for her. Only You know if it is. Your will be done. The prayer carved his insides like a pumpkin, but what power did Clay have in this situation?

None.

CHAPTER THIRTY-ONE

This wasn't supposed to happen. A quick trip to the drug store for a new shampoo bottle should be simple. Liberty would get what she came for, maybe pick up a few things she'd forgotten she needed, and head home for a shower before bed. Instead, she'd spied Mom Kincade—her old nickname raked Liberty's heart tonight—in the pharmacy line.

Liberty would shop somewhere else. Arms empty, she bolted for the exit.

"Liberty?" Alisa Kincade called from behind her, as if she were chasing her. Liberty didn't slow long enough to find out.

She darted to her car and tore out of the parking lot. She'd felt threatened, but that didn't make sense. She was an adult. No one from her past could hurt her now. And what made Alisa think she'd talk to her after she and Carl had sent her away? What had she wanted?

June rains kept her windshield wipers busy as she found a different drugstore. She parked and sat in her locked car, surrounded by evening light. Gripping the steering wheel, she tried not to replay the hurtful words of rejection. The false concern, barely veiled judgment. All that nodding that said *You should agree with us. This is best for everyone.*

Liberty squirmed. Was she moving north in order to run away from the past?

Perhaps she'd fooled herself, believing she'd overcome. That living here was a victory after everything that had happened. Though she'd lived in fear of running into certain people, she'd made a new life here, despite the past. Didn't that count?

Was she strong? Clay kept saying she was, that he admired that about her. But a strong woman would have faced her former guardian, right? Shown her that all that rejection didn't haunt her this many years later. Maybe acted like everything was fine.

Even people who had God in their lives didn't claim life was perfect. Clay's dad couldn't even talk to him without yelling. Despite his salvation, Clay's life was messy too. Though he seemed upset, he never seemed undone by those situations. Like fighting for his new business. Working with Liberty to keep their secrets, even trying to help her in his own misguided way. His foundation didn't seem to shift with the trials. He seemed secure.

She hadn't felt secure since before Mom and Dad died.

Rain sheeted down, blocking her view outside and cocooning her in her car. What did Clay have that she didn't? His parents were still alive. He had his own place, mostly. He hadn't suffered the type of rejection she had, but that didn't seem to be the answer as to why he came across as secure.

She second-guessed herself all the time, doubtful and unsure of her next steps. Even this possible move to Bellingham. *He* knew he wanted an independent business, and he'd been building clientele to get there. No doubts. No delays.

What could give her security? Or how about confidence? The Archers seemed to have both. Kourtney, Brynn, Kason. They all seemed "normal." Liberty didn't feel normal sometimes.

She darted through the rain into the store and had to brush wet ringlets from her eyes when she got inside. The floor squeaked under her feet at she searched the aisles for her favorite shampoo.

"We're closing in ten minutes, ma'am, just to let you know," a clerk called from the counter.

"Thanks. I'll be quick." She chose her footing carefully, given her wet shoes. In a couple of minutes, she had her purchase at the checkout. Her phone buzzed in her pocket, and she waited until she'd locked herself in her car again before answering. Shea. "How did you know I needed to talk to you?"

"I called for an update. How are you?"

Liberty turned on the ignition and worked the defrost to clear the foggy windshield. "I ran into Alisa Kincade, my one-time guardian."

"Did you talk to her?"

"Nope. Like with Clay, I bolted."

Shea's quiet pause invited Liberty's introspection. "It's a habit, isn't it? Running?" Liberty finally said.

"I'd call it a pattern." There was no hint of judgment in Shea's voice.

"This conversation feels like déjà vu." Would Liberty forever spin her wheels?

"Are you still thinking of moving away for good? Any word on the B-ham job?"

"Yes, I'm still hoping to move, and no, no word. But, here's the thing—for the first time I felt like a coward when I escaped tonight, rather than a... I don't know, victor?" Liberty turned the fan lower to quiet its noise.

"Maybe it's time you faced them. Rehearse what you'll say and then you won't have to live in fear of running into them. You'll be prepared to stand and hear them out or let them hear you out. How did she seem?"

"I don't know. I only saw her from the side. I escaped before she could catch up to me."

"Gotcha. How's Clay?"

"You are the second person to ask me that this week."

"Uh-oh..."

"He made me a photo album of our daughter because he found her online."

"What?"

Liberty spent several minutes catching Shea up, defending her decision to no longer hang out with Clay. "I didn't move back here to make more negative memories, but that's what happened."

"You've also made a few good ones."

"True."

"Do you remember the question I suggested you ask yourself?"

"Of course. 'What would you tell your best friend to do?'"

"And..."

Liberty bit her lip. "I don't know. There are a lot of areas of my life that are uncertain now."

"Sounds like it."

"I want security, like I see in Clay." The man had his good qualities. She smiled. Several good qualities. But he also challenged her.

"Security? Where do you think that comes from?"

"I'm uncertain about that too, my friend."

Shea laughed, but then sobered on the line. "Have you prayed lately?"

Rain thundered on the roof of Liberty's car, and she adjusted the volume of the call. "Not for about ten years."

"Are you guys flooding tonight? That's loud."

Liberty chuckled. "We might."

"It sounds like you could use clarity, and He's the ultimate Counselor."

"I've heard that before." God was light, and God was love, from what she remembered. She could use both in her life. But He'd also caused her pain. A lot of pain.

"I remember you telling me you thought God was like the Kincades—judgmental. But, Lib, what if He's like Roy—kind and even playful at times? What if He's nurturing like Gloria?"

She admired those traits in her hosts. Those qualities drew her. "I don't want God to be like the Kincades." The emotional punch of that statement made her chin tremble.

"Good, cuz He's not."

Brushing away a tear, Liberty chuckled. "You don't usually give me absolute statements."

"I think He wants to show you who He is, and who you are. If you let Him."

Clay's similar words came to mind. "I think He already has been."

After several seconds, a shuffling noise came through from Shea's end of their connection, followed by quiet. "Tell me more about this job lead."

Liberty gave her the details, though she'd pretty much given up on that opening.

"Can I be honest with you?" Shea asked after listening for several minutes.

"Of course."

"I hope you can someday allow yourself to let others care for you, without needing an escape plan."

CHAPTER THIRTY-TWO

When Clay arrived at the farm, he strode to the greenhouse. Dad banged around in the deep recesses of the building, muttering and making crashing noises.

Spending the night rehearsing what he'd say, Clay hadn't slept. He stopped near the meeting area where he and Libby had posed for photos. Stalling, he grabbed the hose and doused the hanging fuchsia baskets. Sunlight poured in, heating the space and conspiring with his stress to raise his temperature.

"I have them!" Mom burst into the building, waving brochures. "They're here." She waited until Clay coiled the hose, then handed him a glossy trifold. He studied the image on the front, and his lungs hitched. Libby, in her black gown. He'd drawn her close, hands on her back. She gazed up at him with a hint of shyness, anticipation. His expression was pure adoration. No need to fake that. Her red hair fell in waves down her back. Even in a photo she was breathtaking.

"Wow." Not bothering to read the wording, he flipped open the page and saw the center image of their "wedding" dance. Could they have that in reality, one day? Libby had dismissed him from her life lately. He had a plan in place to fix that, but it could drive her away for good.

"What is all this?" Dad appeared from the back, huffing. Clay checked the room for customers. For now, no one else lingered.

The internal nudge hit Clay again. *I hear You, Lord, but do You know how hard it is to talk to him?* No doubt He did.

"The brochures arrived," Mom said, waving them toward Dad. "They're gorgeous." Oblivious to Dad's dark mood, Mom kept up her usual jovial manner. She marched over and put one arm around Clay in a side hug. "Well done, Son."

"Let me see," Dad barked. Mom handed him a copy from the stack in her fist. He gave it a peek, flipped it open, scoffed.

"Ridiculous."

"Oh you, hush." She turned to Clay. "I'm hopeful you two can get back together. I knew you should have never let her get away."

Clay cringed. Mom didn't know the latest news. And her words were like an invitation for his dad to ignite in three, two, one—

"You're what?" Dad squared off with him. "You mean to tell me you're together again? After all you did the first time around?" He paused, his expression full of condemnation. "What mind games did you play to convince her to give you another chance?"

"Jonathan!" Mom scolded.

Clay clenched a fist at his side. If Dad said too much, Mom would know their secrets. This dynamic with Dad had to change. "Mom, could I talk with Dad alone?"

His mother glanced between them once more. "Okay, but no more yelling. You never know when a customer will drop by." Then, she pointed at each of them. "Fix this."

Clay waited until she had left. "It wasn't *mind games*," he began, trying to keep anger out of his voice like their last confrontation. "She forgave me." Though never in so many words. Not that his father deserved to know that. In fact, after he said it, Clay wished he could draw the sentence back in. What if Dad mocked him now? What if he threw this attempt to reconcile back in Clay's face?

"Forgiveness, my ankle." Dad snorted. "Foolishness."

As much as Clay wanted to do what he knew God directed, he couldn't make himself shove pride aside, couldn't imagine being that vulnerable with Dad, not when he was this belligerent. Clay could practically see smoke rising from his ears.

Silence swirled between them with the dust flecks, tension tightening with each drip of water falling from the hanging fuchsias.

And the nudge hit again.

Clay had tried everything else. He'd have to leave the outcome to God.

Fine.

Dad turned for the door.

"I'm sorry I let you down." The words came out quiet, and Clay wondered if his father had even heard them. He stilled, waiting for Dad's reaction, fearing he *had* heard.

Finally, he slowly pivoted, facing Clay. "Come again?"

Clay inhaled, counted to five. "I know I let you down back then, and probably a hundred times since, given the way you treat me. But, for what it's worth, I'm sorry."

"Huh." Dad's eyes narrowed as if he couldn't believe what he'd heard.

"I wish I'd never said that to her—denying my part. I shouldn't have kept it from you and Mom. I should have faced it, supported her in every way I could." He paused for a second, knowing he had one more statement before he made his request for continued secrecy. "I'm sorry I wasn't someone you could be proud of, that I'm still not."

Dad didn't respond. His puzzled expression told Clay he hadn't expected such a speech.

"Will you do something for Liberty, though?" He forced the words out.

Dad grunted, eyebrows raised.

Clay stepped closer as he heard a vehicle pull in on the gravel outside. "Please continue to keep this between us. She'd rather not have people judge her for her past."

Dad's faded eyes locked with Clay's. "I've never blabbed, and I don't plan to start now." He didn't address Clay's apology, but what had Clay expected—high-fives and lollipops and a game of catch?

He'd leave Dad to the customers stepping inside and head over to the barn for the day's deliveries. Now wasn't the time to bring up his business news.

A sense of peace covered him as he greeted their customers and left the greenhouse. Dad's response was up to him. Clay had apologized. Years of guilt rolled off him. He'd done his part for now.

Liberty stood at the checkout counter at Seaside Floral. Elizabeth had gone down the street for a coffee run that might include a box of those mini cinnamon rolls she favored. Meanwhile, Liberty oversaw the shop. Today was a light delivery day, which would keep her here more, but she didn't mind. In a bit, she'd grab the glass cleaner and dust the shiny surfaces to keep them sparkling. No customers roamed the shop. Why not start now?

She headed to the back where they kept the spray and paper towels. The front door bell jingled when someone entered the store. "Be right with you," Liberty called, setting the cleaner aside before strolling to the front. "How may I help y—?"

Alisa Kincade stood there, a meek smile on her face. She wore slacks and a jacket over a sweater. She gripped the straps of a large bag slung from one shoulder. "Hi, Liberty."

Two run-ins in a few days? But she'd chided herself last time for not facing Alisa. Today she would. She kept her expression neutral, professional. "Hi. What types of flowers would you like?"

Alisa's face showed surprise, like she'd been expecting a different greeting. "Oh, um, what do you have in summer bouquets?"

Elizabeth should return soon. When she did she could take over. Liberty only had to serve Alisa until then. She pressed the store tablet's screen to bring it to life before scrolling to the gallery of summertime arrangements. Clay's mom wasn't always high tech, but she liked this gadget. Liberty handed the tablet to Alisa. "See if anything there looks good to you. Feel free to scroll through."

Alisa complied, though Liberty felt an invisible timer winding down, as if she would only play along for a few more minutes before saying what she'd come here to say. "I like the one with daisies." She pointed at the screen, turning it to show Liberty. "And that seems like a reasonable price. Could you put that together for me? I don't mind waiting."

Daisies. Did Alisa remember Liberty's favorite flower or did she sincerely like them too? "I'll need a few things from the back. Make yourself comfortable." Liberty ducked into the back room where she'd stay until she heard the front door again. As she tore off paper to wrap the bouquet in, and laid it on the counter, words lined up. Was this her chance to talk to Alisa? Was she squandering it?

The front bell dinged again, and Elizabeth's voice followed. "Oh, hi. Have you been helped?"

"Yes. Your assistant is working on my order."

"Great. One of us will be right back." Elizabeth slipped into the room where Liberty pulled flowers from the fridge. "Looks like you've got a customer. Here's your cocoa and two mini cinnamon rolls." She set the items on a distant counter, then came to stand near Liberty. "Are you all right, hon?"

"I'm fine."

"Do you know her? You seem rattled." Didn't Elizabeth recognize her? Surely, they'd known of each other back when they all went to the same church. But Liberty couldn't recall if they'd all gotten together much.

"I could use some air. Would you mind if I took a short walk?" Liberty would escape through the rear exit and walk the alley behind the stores, wait for Alisa to leave out front.

"What about this order?"

She'd forgotten. "Oh, of course. I'll finish it first."

"And I'll cover the front." Elizabeth laid a hand on her arm. "Take it easy."

Moments later, their voices carried toward where Liberty worked. At any moment, Elizabeth might figure out who Alisa was and then Liberty's secrets might come pouring out.

The front bell dinged, and she sighed in relief. Another customer to distract her boss. "Hey, Mom. I have those dianthus for you."

Clay.

"Put them in the back, Son. Thanks."

This day kept getting better. As Clay pushed into the room with his hands full, Liberty finished wrapping the bouquet and braced herself.

CHAPTER THIRTY-THREE

What was Alisa Kincade doing in the shop? Clay hadn't even greeted her, pretending to be preoccupied with his delivery from the greenhouse. He slipped into the back room and closed the door firmly. "Hey, Libby. You okay?"

"Did you see her?" Libby must not have noticed he'd used her nickname. Something about her wide-eyed, almost panicked expression urged him to drop any pretense, even at the shop.

"Yup. Have you talked to her?"

"Not beyond 'how can I help you?'"

He set the box on the counter, the nutmeg scent of carnations lingering under his nose. "What can I do?"

"Get me out of here?" Her brow wrinkled after she spoke. "Wait. I should go face her."

"Whatever you want to do, I'll back you."

She reached for his hand, surprising him. "Thank you."

He'd save his good news about Dad until they'd tackled this ghost from the past.

She scooped up the bouquet. "Ready?"

"Right behind you."

They entered the main part of the shop, and Mom was busy with another customer. Mrs. Kincade stood in the front corner of the store, far from the others.

Libby held out the bundle of summer flowers. "Here you go. Will that be all?"

Mrs. Kincade gave a sad expression as she accepted the order. "I—I was hoping we could talk."

"I'm at work," Libby said, her voice cool.

"I understand. Hi, Clay." She looked between them. "I guess I thought I might see a child with you, if I ever ran into you both again."

"Seriously?" Steam lifted off Libby, and Clay considered

supporting her with a hand on the middle of her back. But he liked seeing her strength surface. She might not need his help after all. "You came here out of curiosity?" She kept her voice low. "How did you know I worked here?"

"I saw you at the drugstore, then I noticed you in here when I drove by. Finally, I worked up the courage to come in."

"To say what?"

"Is everything all right over there?" Mom called from across the shop. But she had an unspoken point. Perhaps Clay should urge the women to take their conversation someplace more private.

"We're good, Mom," Clay said, pointing to the back room. "Perhaps we could finish this in there?"

Libby swept out a hand, and Mrs. Kincade preceded them. Once inside, Libby crossed her arms over her chest, but not in that self-hug motion. Anger determined her stance today. "Well... Now that you've stalked me here, what did you want to say?"

"I wish I'd brought Carl." She eyed the front of the store as if Mr. Kincade might walk in. "He would like to add to this, I'm sure. But I wanted you to know we've both regretted our words, and our actions, from that day. For years." She clutched the bouquet, squeezing the wrapping until the ribbon loosened enough to slip off. Mrs. Kincade didn't seem to notice. "I'm so sorry we said those things and sent you away."

Libby's face softened. "You are?" Her words a few weeks ago about how she'd always assumed he'd never regretted his actions came back to Clay. Maybe she'd made the same assumption about the Kincades.

"I'm sick inside thinking that your child"—she glanced at each of them, knowing the whole story no doubt—"isn't with you today."

"Why would I bring her to work with me?"

"Her? You had a daughter?"

Libby pressed her lips together, her expression cold again. Clay was glad that look wasn't aimed at him.

"You have no right to know where she is or how she is. You betrayed my parents' trust in you to care for me. You rejected me and abandoned me, complete with plenty of judgment and piety."

Mrs. Kincade blanched even paler than she'd been before. "I agree with your description. We truly failed you and your daughter." She hiked her bag higher on her shoulder. "I hope your anger at us doesn't eat away at you after today. I'm truly sorry. Carl is sorry. We wish you only the best."

Quietly, she slipped from the room and took her bouquet to the counter to pay for it. Liberty sagged against the cabinets, out of view of the front of the store. A silent tear tracked down her cheek.

When Clay moved closer, opening his arms, she stepped in.

Then she pulled back. "Oh, I forgot. I didn't ask her for her discretion. She might assume Elizabeth knows since you walked in, she recognized you, and you called Elizabeth *Mom*."

"You're right." Clay yanked open the door, and the bell dinged on the shop door as Mrs. Kincade disappeared.

"Everything okay, Son?"

He knew if she'd learned anything, his mother would spout it any second, so he reassured her. "Yup. Liberty's going to take a break, if that's all right?"

"Sure. I told her that would work." Mom waved him away. Apparently, she hadn't put it together who Mrs. Kincade was. Good. One less fire.

In the back room, he discovered the rear door open. Libby had already walked out. He found her pacing the alley as if trying to stay between buildings long enough for Mrs. Kincade to drive away out front.

"I finally got to say what I needed to say."

"Yeah. Feel better?"

"A bit. I was probably too harsh." She gave him a watery smile. "Thanks for your support in there. That could have gone even worse."

"No problem."

"You keep coming to the rescue."

"Right place, right time."

She eyed him. "I thought you were going to destroy my world, but you haven't. You've threatened it, but nothing too awful so far."

He laughed, relieved she didn't see him as the enemy. The last thing he wanted was to hurt her.

"I dreaded running into the Kincades because years ago they had the authority to break my life in half."

"It's awful to feel powerless." He watched her think through her next words.

"Is that why you like having God on your side?"

"One of the reasons." Not wanting to push, he gave her a gentle smile. "I long to see you happy."

"Me too." She chuckled. "Sometimes I wonder if happiness isn't for everybody."

"You seemed content lately."

She held up her thumb and index finger an inch apart. "Maybe a little."

Mom appeared out the back door. "Hey, Liberty, I've got six customers. Help?"

Libby's posture changed. "Sure. One sec?"

"Thanks." Mom disappeared while Clay wondered what else Libby needed to say.

"What are you doing on the Fourth?" Her grin was intoxicating. "I know I'm impossible and I keep flip-flopping where you and I are concerned. But the Archers have asked me to go house shopping— can you believe it? Wanna come?"

If anyone else changed courses as often as Libby did, Clay wouldn't cooperate, but because it was her...? "I'm in."

CHAPTER THIRTY-FOUR

Was it possible she might find a couple of God's traits in Clay? Standing at her bathroom mirror, Liberty plaited her long red hair into a side braid and smeared sunscreen on her face. In half an hour, she'd join the Archers and Clay for their day of shopping for tiny houses. Roy knew of a sales lot off-island, and over breakfast Gloria seemed giddy to get started.

Liberty recalled hearing during her church days that no one could match God's character. But she guessed people could have their pure moments. Roy was a gentle father-figure with a dear sense of humor. He didn't seem judgmental, and he genuinely wanted what was best for Liberty.

Lately Clay seemed to accept Liberty unconditionally. She'd been hot and then cold, pushing him away and then needing him again. Like an unstable person. Or someone playing games, which she never meant to do.

She kept up a texting conversation with Shea as she finished preparing for the day.

Still no word on the B-ham job?

Nothing. I'm going to put aside all my worries and have fun today.

What's happening with Clay?

I have no idea.

You invited him to come shopping.

Ha! Yes I did.

I like your plan. Go. Have fun. Relax.

Does God love us unconditionally?

Yes.

Doesn't matter if we're on again, off again?

Nope. Shea's responses came through quickly.

Take your time. Think through your answers, my friend.

A laughing emoji followed Liberty's sarcasm.

She peeked at the clock on her phone. Almost time to go. THANKS, SHEA. I'LL UPDATE YOU LATER.

YOU'D BETTER.

Liberty answered with a smiling emoji and a heart. She never used to send hearts, but over the past few months, she'd decided to show the people who cared about her that she cared about them in return. And Shea was golden.

Was Clay?

His decisions didn't always make her feel secure. He pushed her outside her comfort zone. But his attentiveness... He'd arrived at the perfect moment to rescue her from Alisa Kincade this week, and he'd known what to do—give her space, be there for support, understand what she was facing. Withhold judgment.

All these thoughts carried a sense of shame. Liberty was such a taker. Today, she'd focus on giving to those around her. Someday she had to become strong enough to care for others instead of always being the one others shielded and worried about.

Under no circumstances would she let the Archers buy her a house. She chuckled as she joined them in the living room.

"What's funny, dear?" Gloria tucked bottled waters into a cooler.

"I'm looking forward to our trip." She gave Gloria a hug and looked up to find Roy's eyes on her in a warm expression. "You are not allowed to make any deals or hitch up any homes for transport." She wagged an index finger at them as they moved beside each other in a gesture of solidarity. "Got it?"

Roy cupped his ear and leaned down, pretending to listen closer. "Did you hear that, darling?" he asked Gloria. "Something about transportation?"

Liberty ran her tongue over her teeth. "You are impossible." And lovable and generous. Was God like that?

A truck pulled in outside—Clay's. Liberty darted toward the door. "I'll get it." Okay, she shouldn't be so eager, but she craved his nearness and all those traits that made her world less cold and lonely. Was that selfish? Would it help if she apologized for appearing to play games the past few weeks? She hadn't been, at least not purposely. Sometimes her own motives didn't make sense to her.

Liberty wouldn't hug a coworker, but it seemed natural to hug Clay when he strode toward her in the driveway. "Mornin'," he said. He'd chosen not to shave this morning, and she loved the look.

"Morning." He smelled good when she got close enough for that hug. She let herself relish his arms around her for a few seconds, and he seemed in no hurry to release her. Finally, she said, "Roy wants to drive us all in the SUV. Gloria's got a picnic basket and cooler."

"Sounds like we're all set."

"I'm glad you could come today."

His warm smile melted something inside her. "Me too."

They sat in the back and Liberty's mind flashed to an innocent moment, riding in the backseat of Mom and Dad's van. She'd held hands with Clay, hoping the adults couldn't see them. Electricity zinged between them now as it had back then.

At one point, Clay leaned close on the leather seats. "I need to tell you something—good news. When we get a chance today."

"Okay." Good news? Sweet.

At the lot, Roy pulled in and they parked with several other holiday shoppers. Sunlight shot darts of heat between clouds overhead, ducking away and attacking as if playing cops and robbers. But no sign of rain.

An acre or two of space lay covered in RVs and campers of every size, along with a sprawling section for tiny houses. Selected ones had been parked and set up as models with outdoor décor. Liberty beelined to one with a miniature front porch and scooted inside.

"Wait for us," Roy called with a laugh behind her. "Like a kid in a candy store, that one."

Clay stepped in behind her, ducking his head.

Hands on her hips, she worried she'd bump her elbows on the kitchen cabinets. But did he know how silly he looked, slouching like that? "The ceilings are high."

He glanced up. "Good point. Still, this is small."

"It's cute. Quaint. Perfect for one person."

"It's an upgrade from your camper, for sure. You like it?"

The Archers joined them, though they waited outside the open door.

"It's a little too retro for me. I like a cozier feeling, more contemporary."

"On to the next," Gloria called, and Clay and Liberty followed them through the lot.

After an hour of peeking in and walking through house after house, there were plenty more to see.

"Gloria and I want to find a salesperson. We'll catch up with you, okay?"

Liberty narrowed her eyes, tucking away a persistent smile. "No buying, Roy. I mean it."

He held up Scout's honor fingers. "No buying." Then, he crossed two of those three fingers and Liberty swatted his arm.

She turned to Gloria. "Keep an eye on him?"

"Always, dear. Always."

"That seems more threatening than Roy alone," Clay said beside her as the retired doctors walked away.

"If they bring me a set of keys, you and I will return them to the sales office."

He laughed. "Deal."

They meandered toward the next house. Liberty still hadn't fallen in love with any of them. But she was only here to browse and perhaps let herself dream. "You mentioned you had good news?"

He stopped at a pathway near a tree and benches the owners had no doubt included for tired shoppers. "Sit a second?"

"Sure." She joined him, enjoying the shade overhead and the peace between them.

"I finally talked to Dad."

She liked when he let her into his world, liked how it drew them together. "You did? How'd it go?"

"Nothing is solved, but I said my piece. He said his, I guess."

"Did you ask about Daisy?"

"Yeah. He's going to keep the secret."

She leaned over and hugged him, relief flooding her. "Thank you."

He held on an extra moment, and she closed her eyes.

"That's still what you want?"

She eased back. "Yes." If she stayed in Birch Harbor, her secrets would always threaten her. Yet, so far, the things she thought had been threats—like running into Clay, having his father know, facing off with Alisa Kincade—hadn't been. Maybe there was hope for a future with the people who cared about her. "I think the worst is behind me. Finally."

He touched her upper arm as if he wasn't sure of the best gesture, and he was going for brotherly. "I hope so."

Roy and Gloria reappeared with the picnic basket and cooler. They pointed to a table in another grassy area of the lot.

"Still haven't found one you like?" Roy asked, setting the cooler on the ground and flipping it open.

"Not yet. Maybe I should go back to a camper."

Gloria passed out sandwiches. "Oh, no you don't. It's a tiny house or nothing."

Liberty saluted her. "Yes, ma'am."

"I like Roy's idea." Clay paused to accept his ham and swiss on rye. "Thanks, Gloria." He faced Liberty again. "That spare lot is a nice spot for one of these."

Roy passed out condensating bottled waters. "And maybe a large, permanent home one day."

Liberty needed to distract these precious folks from promising a mansion with a pool. "Let's go see that burgundy house on the end when we're finished. I like the white porch."

Why not dream a little more?

Watching fireworks at Birch Harbor Bay was a family tradition, but Clay was happy to pull Libby away from the Archers and his parents to sit on a blanket on their own. Since the sky didn't get dark until 10:00 p.m., the show would start then. They had a few minutes.

Liberty seemed relaxed beside him, elbows locked, leaning back. "I thought they were going to bring me keys today."

He chuckled. "Me too. They may still do it."

"I don't doubt it."

He nudged her shoulder. "They take good care of you."

"Yes they do."

He may not get another chance like this one. He'd better ask her now. "What's next for you?"

"I thought I knew. Now, I have no idea."

Light faded around the boats in the harbor as he worked up the courage to ask her something. "Why do I have a feeling you're still planning on moving as soon as you can?"

"Because you know me pretty well."

"I was hoping you'd change your mind about that."

She shifted, turning so she rested on one arm instead, legs bent. "I have changed my mind about a few things. Remember our chat on the beach about God, when the otters showed up?"

"Sure."

"I don't think that was a coincidence. And the way Roy treats me like a cherished daughter. The way Gloria nurtures me, even when I'd rather have space. The way you—" She cut off her own words.

He still didn't want to push her. She'd continue if she wanted to. He'd stay quiet, but he'd let her know he was listening. When a few minutes of her fidgeting had passed, he decided to get comfortable. Crossing his ankles, he pulled his knees up and held them, relaxing. The show would begin soon. Her unspoken words hung between them.

"I left God behind me. But maybe He didn't give up that easily." She scooted over and put her head on his shoulder as the first fireworks went off overhead. He wanted to turn and hold her, but would she let him? "Thanks for not giving up on me either."

CHAPTER THIRTY-FIVE

"Once again, I'm sorry this took so long to bring together, but thanks for coming in for the interview. I'll be in touch."

Liberty shook Alan's hand. "It was good to meet you in person." She hadn't expected Alan to be here on campus for her interview. "I'll wait to hear from you." She worked her way across the grounds, back to her car.

The position involved greeting visitors to the school during business hours, which left evenings open for classes. That was her favorite aspect. Her years of experience at the Archers' orthodontists' office gave her an advantage, if she believed Alan. He'd finally gotten in touch with her the second week of July. They needed someone lined up to begin in late August. Of course, they hadn't offered her the job on the spot.

She'd visited Bellingham a few times in her life, but now she imagined living here. One of the employee benefits was a housing option of furnished apartments near campus for less than Liberty had expected to pay elsewhere. Her salary should be enough to afford a studio. Next, she'd drive to the apartment complex and someone named Sally would give her a tour.

The units sat high on a hill. Alan had mentioned the old building was a converted motel. They each boasted a single bedroom, minuscule kitchen with teensy living area, and a bath off the bedroom for both the resident and guests. Sally showed her through, but Liberty's mind wandered. There was a shared laundry. Liberty didn't like the fact that any guests she had over would have to walk through her bedroom to use the bathroom.

The space was larger than her old camper, but not as updated as the tiny homes she'd seen on the Fourth.

When Sally walked her out, Liberty asked, "Any coffee houses nearby?" She didn't drink coffee, but she could use a place to relax. The sky had clouded over, and rain scented the otherwise salty air.

"Sure, down in Fairhaven there are a few. You can't miss them, along the main road through town. I like Bayview Coffee Klatch best." She walked Liberty out to the parking lot. "Have a good afternoon."

Liberty steered her old car in the direction of Fairhaven. People strolled the streets, but as the first raindrops fell, they ducked into galleries or dodged traffic to return to their vehicles. As someone pulled away in front of the coffee house, she pulled in. Rain this far into July was a rare occurrence, but Liberty liked the peacefulness of the summer shower.

Her phone buzzed with a text as she ordered hot water for tea, made her selection, and found a small table near the window. No bay view here, but she didn't care. The street full of galleries inspired her. Art. She could move here and pursue her degree, take those classes.

After setting her Earl Grey tea to steep, she pulled out her phone. Alan sent a text. GREAT JOB! THEY LOVED YOU. MORE SOON.

A snippet of conversation drifted toward her from a nearby table. "... that's why I'm glad for my church family."

It had been a while for her since they'd failed to support her when she'd needed them most. She lifted her teacup, and the familiar scent washed over her. *Clay.*

He'd been supportive lately. Without preaching at her, he calmly lived out his faith. She never felt him judging her or rejecting her. Why? Why would he patiently put up with her instability? Their jobs—and loved ones—threw them together, but he seemed to enjoy those minutes. He'd admitted he still cared for her, and she could feel that when they hung out.

But did he know what type of example he made?

Last month, Gloria had left a Bible on the coffee table with a short note inviting Liberty to accept it as a gift. The turquoise leather cover drew her, and she set it on her night stand. Now and then, she'd pick it up, read passages in the New Testament and the Psalms.

She cupped her tea in both hands and rested her elbows on the table. If the otters hadn't been a coincidence, and if God *had* been showing her His traits this summer, that meant He wasn't distant and unconcerned. Reconciling her losses with this goodness she'd seen lately—that wasn't meshing yet. He'd taken away her family. Thoughts of Daisy haunted her every day.

Had He sent the Archers into her desolate world seven years ago? Had He orchestrated Liberty's return to Birch Harbor, with all its opportunities to face the specters that didn't turn out so threatening after all? During her months on Whidbey, she'd been surrounded by a personal support group—a family. She hadn't needed to face her past alone. That sounded like mercy.

Provision, protection, mercy, generosity, unconditional affection.

Had she made her life harder than it had to be by leaving God out of the past decade? If He truly was that good, how could she resist Him? *I think I want You back in my life.* Not that He'd kept His distance, after all. She smiled. *Thanks for chasing me.*

The long return drive to Whidbey gave her a chance to pray aloud, ask forgiveness, surrender.

She needed to find Clay and tell him what had happened.

"Let's play this cool, okay you guys?" Gloria looked up at Clay and then over at her husband. "We'll save the announcement for the end of dinner. Any idea when she'll be home?"

Clay snagged a carrot stick from the veggie tray, feigning calm. Was Libby still moving away? "No. Mom said she'd taken a personal day. That's all I know."

"Strange. She hasn't been here."

Arriving half an hour ago, Clay had wondered where she'd spent the day. All Mom told him was two nights ago, she'd made the request and his mother had granted a paid day off. Maybe she'd gone to Bainbridge to see Shea. He could hope, but he had a feeling she'd followed up on a job lead. Why would she do that? What drove her to want to leave?

"What if she doesn't come home for dinner?" Roy spoke Clay's concerns.

Gloria adjusted the dip in the center of the veggie tray. "Then we shift things to tomorrow night."

Since the Fourth, when Libby let him hold her while they watched the fireworks, he'd wanted more time with her. More time to convince her to stay. Her words, *Thanks for not giving up on me* ran through his thoughts. Forever, he was trying to discern where she stood. A lot of guys would have given up by now, including himself in his earlier days. But while it might seem foolish to stay, he couldn't walk away.

A car pulled in, and he peeked outside. Libby. She smiled big as she approached. "Hi, everyone," she said. Walking straight into his arms, she held on. "Hey you. I have news."

"Yeah?"

"Can we talk outside?"

"Of course."

She set her bag on the bench in the mudroom and fairly skipped back outdoors. What would put her in such a good mood? A lead on her move? Maybe. But why would she hug him like that if she planned to move away?

He turned to the Archers who eyed the show. "Give us a sec?"

Gloria waved him away. "Go."

Roy grinned. "Good luck, son."

Liberty waited by the willow tree near the driveway. This spot wasn't visible from inside the house because of how the garage was situated. He had a feeling Libby had chosen it for that reason.

She reached for his hand. "I have something to tell you."

That light in her eyes could power his life. "What's happening?" *Please don't say you're moving.*

"First, full disclosure. I had a job interview off-island today."

His gut sank. That's what he'd been afraid of. As long as she lived on Whidbey, there was hope for them. He'd keep wooing her, being available. Hope she might one day reconcile with God. But if she moved away that couldn't happen. He'd finally grown a list of clients here. Nearly ready to launch his own business, he couldn't leave now. His life was here. "You're still moving."

"Not necessarily."

"Wait, I don—"

She put a fingertip to his lips, and he caught his breath but let his grin loose. She lowered her arm. "I had an interview for a job that would allow me to take *free* art classes and earn my degree."

"Oh." She'd always wanted that. In fact, their baby had come right when she could have accepted that scholarship. "You know there are smaller art schools on the island that might—"

She raised her index finger toward his mouth again. He liked this game. He'd have to think of more things to say so she could interrupt him.

Sparks glinted in her playful eyes. "That's not the news. Listen?"

Mutely, he nodded.

"I've been thinking lately about God. I realized today how He has chased me, and contrary to what I believed, He's been with me all along." The light dimmed in her eyes a smidge. "I still have questions. I don't understand why I went through all that pain. I don't have it all worked out." The joy returned. "But I let Him catch me today."

He took both of her hands. Was she saying...?

"I'm His."

He scooped her in a big hug while she laughed. "That's fantastic news." Now she could find peace. Another barrier down. *Lord, let nothing ruin this.*

She tugged him back toward the open garage. "All these good things are happening in my life this summer. Like restoration, I guess. I still can't believe it sometimes." She squeezed his hand.

"Are you going to tell the Archers about the job possibility?"

"You know, I'm not sure on that anymore. I may want to stay right here."

Clay couldn't believe how one afternoon could change his

outlook. They weren't official, but Libby's signals lately seemed to say she enjoyed spending time with him. There might be a future there. Now, she'd surrendered to God again, so that hurdle was behind them.

But this job thing. She didn't sound certain about that.

Maybe Roy and Gloria's announcement could keep her here. For good.

CHAPTER THIRTY-SIX

Liberty and Clay sat across from Roy and Gloria at their dining table. She relished their smiling faces. Her family. Maybe she didn't need an escape plan after all. She didn't know what was next for her. She only knew that joy and peace had replaced her anxiety inside. And the view of her life had become clearer, with her blessings lining up for inspection.

Roy served broiled salmon to everyone at the table, and Gloria passed long grain rice. They'd put out corn on the cob and watermelon slices, along with a tray of veggies. A feast. "Are we celebrating something?" Liberty asked.

Gloria peeked at Roy who wore a small grin. "Yes, we are. You look like you have good news."

"I do." She reached for Clay's hand. "God and I had a long conversation today. He has welcomed me back."

Roy stood and pulled her into a hug. "Congratulations, Liberty. This is the best news."

Gloria hugged her next, and then Clay was there. She laughed and let him have a turn. "Really happy for you," he said, his voice intimate in her ear.

"You should tell them your news," she said, referring to his business. He'd shared a few details over the Fourth.

They spent their meal discussing current happenings. And there was nowhere else for Liberty than here. At least at this moment.

After a dessert of strawberries over vanilla pudding cake, Roy took Gloria's hand. "You've probably noticed we had tree work done next door over the past couple of weeks."

Liberty waited him out, but the last time he'd brought up arborists and trees and the spare lot, he'd been talking about her living next door. "Yeah. Looks good."

Clay reached for her hand as if he knew what was coming. He

wore a smile that matched Gloria's. Roy pulled keys from his pocket. "We have something for you."

"Follow us." Gloria and Roy led the way toward their outbuilding. Clay grabbed her hand, kept pace beside her. The merry band marched toward the large garage. They didn't. They wouldn't, would they?

"What is going on?"

No one answered her, and she let herself get swept up in their joy. Yet, if what waited for her matched her guess, she couldn't accept. Even if she stayed in Birch Harbor, she could never accept such an extravagant gift.

"Here we are." Gloria halted the group. Roy ducked into the oversized building and moments later, the door raised. The previous owners had probably parked an RV here. The workshop in the back was where she'd created her fairy houses.

There, in the once-empty RV spot, stood a tiny house—the one she'd fallen in love with at the end of their shopping trip. Her throat went dry. "You didn't."

Burgundy siding with white trim and a white porch. The inside was comfortable, with a loft bedroom over an efficient bathroom. But the kitchen was her favorite.

Roy appeared at her side. "She's all yours." He dropped the keys into her hand, and she caught them by reflex.

Clay opened the door and swept his hand toward it. "Want to peek inside?"

Feeling almost frozen in place, she faced Roy and then Gloria. They'd gone through with it. Tears blurred her vision. Such kindness, consideration—this was her favorite model at the lot— and generosity. "I thought we had an agreement. I can't repay you." Even if she got the new job, which of course would mean leaving the house here, she couldn't afford to pay them back.

"Liberty, dear, that's what we've been trying to tell you. You never have to pay us back—for anything."

"It would honor us if you'd receive this gift from us," Roy said.

They all looked at her with such hope. How could she turn them down? "It's hard for me to accept such extravagance." But wasn't that what God had given her lately? Did He want her to agree? *Lord...?*

So many positive events in her life the past few months. If she could never have Daisy back, which of course she couldn't, she'd celebrate the people who *were* present in her life. And because it would honor her hosts for her to receive their gift, she would.

"What do you say, dear?"

"Thank you," she said, barely holding back a blubbering snort. "I accept." Another round of hugs followed with tissue passing and cheers from her benefactors.

CHAPTER THIRTY-SEVEN

Clay spent the following Friday at the Archers' all day, helping get the spare lot ready for the tiny house. Today, they'd mowed a large section of land, clearing brush and blackberry bushes. She'd have a good distance from the Archers' home. Utility companies would be out this week. Maybe in seven to ten days, she'd be able to live here. For now, she stayed with her hosts and the tiny house remained in the RV garage.

God had surprised him. He'd brought Libby back to the island, and more importantly, to Himself. He'd given her a family here, a reason to stay, beyond him. Clay had a second chance with her.

She approached, carrying lemonade glasses in each hand. Clay's crew was finishing up. Gloria carried two more glasses while Roy followed with a pitcher.

"Thanks for all this, Clay."

"Of course. My pleasure." He sipped the icy, tart liquid. "Oh, this is good."

"Your dad's cool with you being here?"

"I chatted with him about cutting back my hours. He finally let me hire someone. I guess he realized I'm not backing down on this. I'll phase myself out."

Her compassionate eyes drew him. "Are things still tense between you?"

"Yup. But I did my part."

She clinked glasses with him. "Yes, you did. I hope he comes around."

"Me too. How are you doing with everything?" he asked her, keeping his voice low.

"Good. I still can't believe this." She indicated the spot where they'd park her house. "That view." She pointed toward the Sound, visible between aged conifers.

"I'm guessing this all means you've decided to stay."

"I never heard back, so I'm not putting my life on hold."

He blinked. "Which means if they offered the position to you, you'd take it."

Her shoulders hiked and then dropped again. "I guess I'm still watching for open or closed doors."

"God will show you. And He might ask you to trust Him." He hoped she didn't recall this conversation later and think he was using God for his own purposes. Several weeks ago, Clay made a decision that he'd since doubted. One that could threaten their future.

"Doesn't He work by opening and closing doors?"

"Sure. But sometimes things aren't that easy to figure out."

"Gotcha." She looked around, and he followed her gaze to the Archers before her attention focused on him. "No, I can't imagine leaving here."

"I'm glad. Listen, I need to—"

"Clay, could you help?" Roy waved him over, and Clay followed him across the property line toward the RV garage. Time to move the house into position. Clay needed to find a chance to tell her what he'd done.

He only hoped their world didn't unravel when he did.

Saturday afternoon, Liberty put the finishing touches on the fairy house resting on the work bench—a touch of additional moss to act as grass near the stone path. Next, she'd add fairy tale figures, and soon she'd be ready to show Elizabeth her creation. Maybe they could sell her work in the florist's shop. She had three more lined up on the shelves, including Daisy's, which wasn't for sale. Shea was right—creating allowed her to experience both beauty and a sense of peace.

Her church days came to mind. There she'd heard Jesus referred to as the Prince of Peace. She'd been going to church lately, and in the evenings, she'd spent time reading the Bible Gloria gave her. God was described in lots of ways. At times fearsome, at other times merciful. An occasional passage was familiar from her childhood. She loved discovering a new verse describing God's heart or His ways.

One evening, seeing her interest, Gloria sat with her at the table and handed her a huge concordance. Over a shared pot of tea, she explained how Liberty could search the Bible by word and collect verses on any given topic. Roy passed through and reached toward the bookshelf, where he found a three-by-five card book he'd filled with references. He said the collection gave him peace when he needed it.

One of Liberty's first searches had been on *hope*. The next was on *love*, and the most recent, *freedom*—her name's meaning. She'd learned that if Jesus set her free, she could be free indeed.

At times, though, fear crept in. What if something else hit— something unexpected and painful?

Keep holding on to Me.

God's words clicked. If she was going to learn to trust, she'd have to take the good and the bad and simply cling to Him.

Perhaps that's what trust looked like. Maybe the journey was as messy and unpredictable as that.

Scary.

A strong sense that He longed for her cooperation enveloped her and melted something inside. Wow. God was emotionally invested in this back-and-forth. Emotionally, heart-level invested.

She'd felt a nagging inside lately, though, about something she'd rather avoid. Alisa Kincade had reached out to her again by sending a card to the floral shop. The apologies and request for forgiveness didn't hit Liberty the same as it had before. A dose of sincerity and hopeful wishes for restoration prompted Liberty to reconsider her decision to give up on them, as she had for about a decade. What good did it do her, or them, or anyone, for Liberty to keep holding a grudge?

"I need to forgive them, don't I, Lord?" Her words were quiet in the empty shop. Perhaps letting them off the hook would free her.

"Liberty, you in there?" Clay called from outside.

"Yeah, c'mon in." She looked forward to seeing him. They hadn't labeled their relationship, but she wasn't in a rush, and he didn't seem to be in one either. For the first time in years, her world felt right. Like there was something to live for. A future she didn't have to dread.

"I wanted to tell you something. You got a minute?"

"Yes. You know, I was standing here, thinking about everything going on in my life. Pretty soon, my new house will be ready. You and I are hanging out. The Archers. I checked into that nearby art college. I know it's only a two-year program with a certificate and not a degree, but who cares?"

His expression was sober, maybe even a bit worried, which wasn't like him. "Libby."

"Plus, I've decided to forgive the Kincades. Why not be free of that too?" Okay, part of her kept talking so she didn't have to hear his news. Whatever it was, she feared it would change everything.

He took her hand. "Remember those pictures of Daisy?"

"Of course. Thanks again for that album."

"I think I mentioned those were from a local church's directory and website."

"That makes sense. Of course, now I'll be tempted to get on their page and dig around."

He squeezed her hand. "I found her new last name."

"I figured. Don't tell me." She stilled. "Hold on. What changed?" He'd assured her he wouldn't go see Daisy. Had he broken that promise?

"When you first came back here, you seemed so sad. Depressed, almost. I only wanted to help." He kept saying that. Why?

"We talked about your need to fix things." She pulled her hand away. "What happened?"

"You even admitted you wanted to see her again."

"Of course I want to see her again. I've had friends who've had miscarriages or whose babies died at a young age. Daisy is alive. Seeing her again is a possibility for me, unlike my friends. But that doesn't mean I go searching. I signed papers."

"I didn't."

Afraid to ask, yet needing to know, Liberty braced herself. "Did you go see her?"

"No." He rubbed the back of his neck. "I called her parents. Her dad, actually."

"Why would you do that? And don't say you did it to help me. This wasn't about me. This was about your curiosity." Anger boiled inside. Anger and fear and old accusations. How dare he break their agreement?

His face stayed calm, but she sensed her words hurt him. "Once I found out she lives here, and that we could accidentally see her, I figured why not help things along. Is it against the law if you accidentally see her?"

Her stomach rolled as her new sense of security fled. "Of course not. I have to act in good faith." Her phone rang in her pocket. She yanked it out and checked the screen. Alan. She held up a finger to Clay. "I need to take this." Then she stepped outside and accepted the call.

"Liberty?" Alan sounded excited through the phone. "It looks like you impressed them the most. You got the job. They're asking how soon you can start."

The Bellingham job came through. Perfect timing. She'd have to smooth things over with the Archers. Maybe they could rent out the new house to someone from church. If she left Whidbey now, she wouldn't be tempted to break her agreement. She'd promised no contact. No matter what Clay had done, she had to keep that promise.

"Tell them two weeks from Monday."

CHAPTER THIRTY-EIGHT

Libby didn't understand, and she wouldn't listen. There was more to tell her, but when she'd asked Clay to leave, he'd honored her request and driven away.

Her phone call played in his memory. *Tell them two weeks from Monday.* She had taken the Bellingham job. She probably wouldn't have done that if he'd held off on his news another day, but he hated having this secret hanging over him. Now, whatever chance they'd had was gone.

His phone rang, and he pulled off the road to answer.

Kason's face flashed on the screen. "You headed this way?"

"Yeah."

"You don't sound good."

"Had an argument with Libby." Clay wouldn't tell his brother about Daisy. He'd keep his word.

"Oh, man. Listen, bad timing, I know. But Dad's at my kitchen table, and he needs to talk to you. Not that he said so himself, of course."

"I apologized to him the other day for the accident."

"Good job."

"Yeah, it didn't seem resolved though."

"Better come talk to him."

"Will do." They disconnected, and Clay got back on the road. He wasn't far from the farm. Weariness pressed him down.

"Unka Clay!" Muriel barreled toward him as soon as he got out of the truck. He barely had enough time to catch her after turning from closing his door.

He scooped up his four-year-old niece. "Puddin'." She threw her arms around his neck, and her blonde curls bounced in his face, tickling his nose. Daisy had been this small once, and he'd missed it. The thought grated over his heart like a rake leaving lines in soil. Changed. Marred. "I need to find Grandpa. Is he inside?"

"Yeah." Her lips pushed out in a pout. "He didn't wanna play."

Clay set her on the ground and gave her a bolstering smile. "Maybe he will later, kiddo." Clay waved at Brynn as she worked across the yard in her garden. He stepped into the farmhouse's kitchen. Sure enough, his dad sat at the table, slouched over an empty mug. The room was silent, except for the refrigerator's hum. His father appeared empty himself. A wave of compassion hit Clay, slowing his steps. He'd come dreading another fight, but Dad didn't look defiant right now.

Clay walked to the far counter, across from the table. "Hey." The word came out low.

His father straightened a bit. "Any more java in that thing?" He tipped his head toward the coffee pot waiting on its heated rest.

Clay would bide his time, let Dad begin when he wanted. The other day, Clay had said all he needed to say. It was Dad's turn. "About another mugful."

He held up his cup, and Clay obliged. The man's gray eyes looked weary. He grunted his thanks when Clay finished.

For years, Clay had avoided being alone with him, dodged all that yelling. Even now, as if by habit, he braced for a blowup. Would he always feel this way around his father?

Things are about to change. God's voice.

I hope so. Honestly, it's hard to believe that, Lord. Clay stared through the kitchen window, near the sink. Then he busied himself making a fresh pot of coffee. Kason and Brynn might appreciate it.

When Clay had cleaned the counter and even wiped down the double basins, and Dad had stewed for about fifteen minutes without saying another word, Clay sighed. His dad wasn't in a talking mood. So be it. Clay started toward the door. "I'd better go help Kason with the new orders."

Dad reached for his arm, stopping him with a firm grip. "Wait." His voice came out gravelly, though he didn't look up from the table.

Clay stilled.

"Have a seat?" A question rather than an order? This was new.

Sitting across from him, with nowhere else to look but into his eyes—Clay couldn't handle that. "I'd rather stand, but I can stick around a minute."

"Fair enough." Dad gave one nod while Clay moved back into his view across the small room.

Sunshine streamed in the windows, like God was trying to remind Clay to have hope.

"I want you to know, Son," Dad began and then paused.

From his peripheral vision, Clay knew his father was looking right at him, but he found a gouge in the old farmhouse's hardwood flooring and traced the groove with his eyes.

"You need to know that I accept your apology. In fact, I'm proud of you." His voice was still hoarse. "You're a good man."

Clay's attention shot to his father, and his heart seemed to stop. Wha—?

"And it's no thanks to me." He grimaced. "I've been a fool."

"I let you down. I get it." No one could blame Dad for condemning him, not even Clay.

"But you're making it right. I can see that."

"I'm trying."

Dad stood and grabbed his cane. Something had changed in his face, in his voice.

Ask him to forgive you.

Clay rubbed his jaw as God's directive hit him.

Trust Me.

Clay fidgeted. Finally, he forced himself to speak. "Can you forgive me?" He choked on the words.

A warm hand landed on Clay's shoulder, comforting and strong. "Only sorry it took me this long." He caught Clay in a hug and Clay checked his gut, fighting the emotion.

"I know you'll treat her right." Dad eyed him, almost in warning, but then his expression softened. "You're a different person now."

His acceptance and affirmation felt good, and Clay drank them in. But Dad didn't know the latest. "Except she's given up on us again." Should Clay confide in him? The rest of the family was still outside, which meant privacy. Clay could use fatherly advice, and his dad was the only one who knew about Daisy. "I might have done something stupid."

"Sit." Dad pointed at the chair Clay avoided earlier. "Talk."

He plunked himself down. "It's about our daughter." Liberty knew Dad was aware of her. Since he'd known all along, discussing this with Dad wouldn't break Clay's promise. "Liberty doesn't want me upsetting her."

Dad raised his brows but didn't speak, reminding Clay of his childhood confessions.

Libby had asked him not to interfere in Daisy's life, but he'd never promised that. He'd promised not to go see her. "And I haven't. Liberty's been so sad, which is understandable. I wanted to help her. I did some digging, got advice, found a little information."

"How much does she know?"

"She would only hear so much. Made me promise to keep my distance."

"And have you?"

"Physically, yes. But I did make a call."

"Son, you know I haven't been to church in a while, but since you go all the time, I gotta ask. What is God telling you?"

"Good question." Clay hadn't prayed about this enough. "Are *you* curious about her?"

"Yup. But I'm fine leavin' things as they are. Sounds like you aren't."

Clay drummed his fingers on the table. "Part of me wants to do whatever Liberty says, you know? Keep her from getting angry. Part of me... This is our daughter."

"You're taking a big risk. You could cut off any chance of Liberty ever talking to you again."

"I know."

"Are you willing to chance that?"

A question Clay had asked himself often. His answer came easily—if his search might help Libby heal while giving her peace of mind about their daughter, he had to try. Not for himself. If he was in this for himself, he could take the easy way out—give up on his search, honor what Libby sometimes said she wanted. But her words about her friends whose babies had died haunted him. Daisy wasn't lost to them, not truly.

Yes, he'd risk everything to give Libby a chance to see for herself that Daisy was okay.

"Absolutely."

Dad gave a decisive nod as though he read Clay's determination. "Okay, so what's next?"

"Before Libby decided to move away in a couple of weeks"— Clay held up a hand to stall Dad's question as he opened his mouth to speak—"I contacted our girl's adoptive father."

"Hoo, boy."

"Yeah, and I scheduled a meeting with him." A lead weight dropped in his gut. Had he gone too far? Libby was going to kill him when she found out. Dad was right. He needed to pray about this. It wasn't too late to cancel the meeting.

"Look, I get that you wanted to fix this 'not knowing,' but maybe you should have gotten on the same page first."

"She hasn't been willing to listen, but I hear what you're saying."

"My advice? Pray and then act. But only if you're sure."

Sunshine lit the yard as Liberty crossed to the house. She had to find her treasured hosts and tell them she'd accepted a job in Bellingham. Then she'd call her boss. She didn't relish either conversation, but what choice did she have? Shea would say she was acting rashly, that she shouldn't make such a drastic decision like relocating when she was this upset. But if her moving away meant Clay backed off his search for Daisy, if it meant Daisy's life didn't get interrupted, then wasn't that for the best? Clay kept saying he was searching for Daisy because he wanted to help Liberty. He couldn't help her if she moved away. With this decision, Liberty could protect their daughter one more time.

The moment she'd decided to try to trust God again, this

happened. Oh, and Clay. She'd thought he was trustworthy too now. But he kept pushing.

Gloria stood at the kitchen sink. She'd been baking today, and she scrubbed a mixing bowl as Liberty entered. "Hi, dear. I saw Clay leave. Everything all right?"

"Roy around?"

"He's out front. Do you need him?"

"I'll grab him. I'd like to talk to you both, if you have a minute."

"Of course."

Liberty found Roy outside waving the hose over the grass. They'd decided not to put in a sprinkler system out front because he enjoyed this process. After catching a glimpse of Liberty's face, and probably adding up clues like a disappearing Clay, he turned off the hose and rewound it before following her indoors.

"Something's on your mind," Roy said.

Gloria had warm slices of banana bread waiting in the kitchen with coffee and hot water for tea or cocoa. "Which flavor, dear?"

Blueberry tea this time. In her new Bellingham home, Liberty wouldn't even keep Earl Grey. It reminded her too much of Clay—that scent could get into her head. The thought brought a pang. Could she walk away from everyone here? From Clay after getting close to him again?

Gloria set their tea steeping, making a whole pot of blueberry.

Roy poured himself a cup of coffee. "Saw Clay leave a while ago. That was not a happy man."

"We had a disagreement." She still wouldn't share the details. "And it helped me make a decision."

At the table now, they all sat. Gloria poured tea. To keep her hands busy, Liberty spread a thin layer of butter on a slice of banana bread. The aromas of berries and bananas filled the dining area. A wind off the water kept the house cool this late July day, adding a salty hint to the air.

"Okay, dear. I have a bad feeling about this little chat. But we'll help you however we can."

Roy donned a mock-fierce expression. "You want me to rough the boy up?" He tapped a fist into his other palm, and Liberty laughed.

"That won't be necessary, but thanks, Roy."

He smiled and then sobered. "Seriously, what's going on?"

"You know I've been unsure about my future since Bainbridge."

They nodded, neither of them joking about the timing of their retirement. Such support. She hated what she had to say. But like giving Daisy up the first time, she must follow through. "I spent part of the summer job hunting... off-island."

Gloria set down her teacup with a light thud. "Off-island?" She reached for her husband's hand.

"And I wasn't sure. For a while I didn't hear back. Clay and I were doing so well. You both decided to buy me a house." She traced shapes on the table. "Which meant so much to me."

Now Roy's face wore concern, but Liberty guessed he wasn't worried about money.

"I'm so grateful to you, for everything. Especially"—her voice barely cooperated, but she forced the words—"how you've cared for me, for years. You've welcomed me as part of your family. You've helped me when I had no one. Thank you."

Roy stood. "I don't like this." He wasn't one to show his disagreement in a strong way. The man had principles and integrity. But Liberty rarely saw this side of him. Agitated. Assertive. "You know we consider you family, an honorary daughter. And I need to say something."

Gloria, in a rare moment herself, didn't interrupt.

"Fair enough." Liberty fought to keep her expression neutral when all she wanted was to cry. Clay had done this—forced her decision to move. Still, she couldn't hate him, even if she had to leave Birch Harbor once more because of one of his decisions.

"You are welcome here—you've always been. We'd hate to see you run away because of an argument with Clay. I have a feeling there's more between you two than we know. So I'll hold my piece on that front. But Liberty, your new house aside, I don't think you should leave."

"Right," Gloria said. "I agree. We'd miss you so much. Plus, we bought that house for you. I hate to see you not live there."

"You can take it with you. It's mobile," Roy said.

Liberty shook her head. These precious people were always thinking of her, even when they faced losing her. "I can't take it. And I need to get packing. I'm so sorry." Tears fell before she'd cleared the kitchen. She had plenty of time to gather her things since the move wasn't for two weeks, but she needed space from these precious people and their compassion and generosity.

Monday morning, she'd tell Elizabeth, give her two weeks' notice. For today, she'd hole up in her room and grieve her newest losses.

CHAPTER THIRTY-NINE

Dad had suggested Clay pray about whether he should meet with his daughter's adoptive father. For most of his search, Clay had avoided involving God. *What am I afraid of, Lord?*

He laced up his running shoes and headed out in the early morning fog. The wash of waves toward the left, behind the row of houses, the only sound this morning. A marine layer rested over the island, but no doubt it would burn off as the sun rose higher. The 6:00 a.m. chill pressed against his face as his feet pounded north on Beachside Road. The temperature would likely climb thirty degrees today—from the fifties to the eighties. An occasional car rumbled down the street, and Clay was glad he'd worn his reflective jacket.

Is it possible You'll shut this down? The conviction that he'd gone too far without God's approval returned, and his shoulders tensed. *I'm sorry I haven't asked You about doing this search or meeting with Daisy's dad until now.*

Daisy's dad. That dynamic confused him. But this wasn't about him. This was about Libby. *You get that, right God? That I'm trying to make things easier for her. I know it scares her in the short term. But our daughter lives nearby. I can't let this go. Please, show me what to do.*

Given the fog and his speed, houses blurred on the left. Joseph Whidbey State Park was coming up on that side of the street. He'd stop in and walk the beach for a few minutes. Maybe God would speak.

Yes, he was praying, but he was also running.

He slowed his speed and caught his breath. He'd been running this whole time. Running to see if Libby was okay. Running to find their daughter. Running from the possibility that God, like Libby, didn't want Clay to touch Daisy's current life.

The park stretched in a long beach of gray sand littered with large driftwood logs and rocks. No one else wandered out here this morning. Waves pushed in with a salty spray. Now that Clay was talking to God, God wasn't talking. Was He grieved, or worse, angry? Dad would be—would have been, before the recent changes. But maybe God, who never compromised, waited patiently for a moment like this with Clay, His heart open, His love reaching. No scowl in sight.

Clay stopped in the damp sand and faced the Sound. The fog clouded his view. On a normal day, he could see farther into the Strait. Not today. *Has my agenda clouded my perception of what You want, Lord?* Before he'd finished praying those words, the answer hit him. It had. Because Clay had decided to search and followed that plan, his view had been skewed.

He closed his eyes. *Please forgive me. Forgive me for charging ahead with my own plan. Forgive me for assuming that because I'm in Your family You're behind everything I do, even if it feels noble to me.* The presumption made him pause. *And if I've blown things with Libby, please forgive me for that, especially if it hurts her even more. You know my intentions.*

The last thing he wanted to do, beyond not hurting Libby, was hurt their daughter. *I'll stop if You want me to. I only want—*

Be still and know that I am God.

The verse rolled through his thoughts in the wake of his anxiousness. His words dried up, like the sand farthest from the tide.

No condemnation. Only an invitation to listen and receive peace. The marine layer peeled back a bit, and Clay gazed toward the open Strait. The powerful sea stretched beyond what he could see from here.

When Clay imagined Libby spending birthday after birthday in her camper, celebrating a daughter who couldn't come, his heart broke. Did God's? *Lord, You know how much pain she's been in.*

Like a fading cloud, the words of a verse went through his mind, something about if there's anything good you can do, you should do it.

Was that the Lord, trying to tell him where to go from here? He didn't hear words today, but peace had begun to settle inside after weeks of uncertainty and chasing leads. He tugged out his phone and ran a search for that verse. There. Proverbs 3:27. *Do not withhold good from those to whom it is due, when it is in the power of your hand to do so.*

She couldn't search because she'd signed papers. But Clay never had.

"Is that Your answer, Lord?"

No response, but no sense of God's irritation either. Instead, an increased feeling of peace, relief, and perhaps even joy. Clay didn't have to run from God's answer anymore.

He'd keep his meeting with Daisy's dad.

While Clay waited at Skye Café, a large group left. He appreciated the quiet in their wake. Nick was due soon—Daisy's dad. Clay had to remind himself not to call her that during their meeting. Her real name was Jaelyn. And for once, Clay was allowed to say it.

A tall man arrived, glancing around the hostess stand. Clay had a hunch and stood. "Nick?"

The man turned and faced him. "You must be Clay."

They shook hands, and the hostess led them to a table.

Once seated, questions came to mind. But Clay would go slowly. Had Libby been partly right? He couldn't deny how following through with this satisfied a deep need for answers and maybe closure. She'd moved two weeks ago and hadn't been in touch with him. "Thanks for meeting me."

"Yeah, no problem. We've been curious, you know." Nick wore a friendly smile. "Didn't think we'd ever learn anything about you. We signed papers. Never planned to search. I still can't believe you live on Whidbey. We only moved here a few years ago." Which made sense of the adoption agency's choice of placement. Of course they wouldn't put Jaelyn in her hometown right after birth.

"You didn't keep her photos off the church's website." Clay

wasn't accusing, only stating facts. He sure wasn't sorry Nick and his wife had given permission to share their names and photos in the directory.

"No, we didn't."

The server brought their drinks and took their orders.

Nick gulped his iced tea and set down his glass. "What do you want to know? I'm guessing you've seen the latest pictures."

"I have. You three seem happy. It was important to Dai— Jaelyn's birth mom and me to know that she was happy."

"Are you still in touch with her birth mother?"

Clay chose the short answer to that. No need to explain their long story. "Yes."

"It's the craziest thing. Jaelyn has your eyes."

Those words settled deep inside, and Clay welcomed them. He'd known this, but the confirmation strengthened him.

"Since we're talking about Jaelyn's moms, I need to tell you my wife—Amanda—isn't completely comfortable with this get-together. She has lived in fear of someone coming along one day and trying to take Jaelyn away."

Clay raised his hands. "Nothing like that. It's more worry for her wellbeing. In fact, Jaelyn's birth mom, I'll call her April, didn't want me to reach out to you."

"Fear?"

"Yes. We didn't know if you'd told Jaelyn that she was adopted."

The server brought their meals, and the conversation went silent.

Nick slapped the inverted ketchup bottle over his fries after the server walked away. "Their food is pretty good."

"You've eaten here before?"

"Yeah, brought the family in a few weeks ago." He bit into his hamburger.

"*April* and I were in recently too, with Jaelyn's grandmother— my mom."

"It's weird that we might have run into you and not known it. I'm guessing April has red hair, curls."

"Yup." Clay's appetite faded. "She isn't around anymore, so I may not be able to tell her we met, but it helps to know more about Jaelyn. Anything else you can tell me?"

"She loves music, and she is always creating. We gave her popsicle sticks when she was four, and she built a house of them. She's an only child because my wife and I can't have children and haven't felt the call to adopt again. But she keeps us busy. She has cousins and living grandparents, and we cherish her." He talked like he worried Clay *would* try to take her away, like Clay needed convincing to leave things alone.

"I am glad to hear it." He wished Liberty was here so she could know the same thing.

"We've always wanted to thank you both." He finished his meal and pushed his plate back. "In fact, I'm going to talk to my wife. Once I tell her how this went, she'll probably want to meet you in person. Any chance April could join us?"

Clay couldn't imagine Libby agreeing to come. He wouldn't promise that. "I don't know."

"Would you like to meet Jaelyn?"

The question caught Clay in the chest. "I would." But it would break his heart to meet their daughter without Libby present.

"You know, I can't guarantee anything." Nick checked his watch. "I'm sorry. I need to jet. Our church has a softball game in half an hour, and I'm on the team."

"Sure." Clay stood, shook Nick's hand. "This means a lot. Thanks again."

"You got it. I'll be in touch if Amanda feels comfortable. Otherwise, you take care."

Clay nodded. Nick pulled cash from his wallet and tossed it next to his plate before leaving.

Whether Libby liked it or not, Clay was getting closer to a possible meeting with their daughter. If Libby knew Jaelyn was aware of her history, and that everyone was at peace, would that ease her worries? Would she be willing to meet Jaelyn, Nick, and Amanda then?

It hit Clay—Nick had never answered his question about

whether Jaelyn knew she was adopted.

So far, Clay had kept his promise not to go see their daughter. Time was running out though.

He finished his burger and texted Libby: I KNOW YOU HATE THIS BUT I HAVE AN UPDATE. CAN WE TALK?

No response came. He pictured her getting settled into her new place as if the last several months hadn't happened, as if she didn't have a family here who missed her. When Clay saw the Archers at church, their heartache was obvious. Her news must have blindsided them. But Clay assumed she didn't mention Daisy.

He paid for his meal and headed to his truck. August's heat hung on, making the air muggy and the grass dry. Wildfire smoke tinged the air. Hopefully Bellingham's air quality was better than here since smoke bothered Libby.

Would he always worry about her?

His phone rang before he backed out of the space. He flicked the gear shift into Park. Nick. "Hey."

"Dude. My wife is so happy right now. She wants to meet you and April. We haven't talked to Jaelyn yet. We wanted to get your answer first. Don't want to get her hopes up if we all can't meet."

That was a quick turnaround. "What changed your wife's mind?"

"Amanda knows Charlie, and he vouched for you." Charlie had given his recommendation? He owed the man a favor for that. "But if you don't think it'll work, we'll leave Jaelyn out of it. She can visit her cousins, have a playdate while Amanda meets you."

"I need time to try to reach April. But I'm guessing this means Jaelyn knows she was adopted."

"Oh, yeah. We celebrate two special events with her—her birthday and her gotcha day two days later."

Two days. That's all the time Libby had had with her.

"Listen," Nick said, his voice quieter. Less background noise interfered with the call. "Do you think April will want to meet?"

"I'm hopeful but no guarantees." How was he going to convince Libby to do this? "I can tell you she doesn't live locally."

"Oh."

"It's not far, but it's a consideration." And saying so would buy him time.

"Please do whatever you can. Wow, this stuff is happening so quick. Thanks, man." Nick hung up, and Clay stared out his windshield. He fired up his truck to get the air moving and drove home, working on his pitch while praying again.

No one made Libby do what she didn't want to do.

CHAPTER FORTY

Liberty sipped tea in her apartment after work on Friday afternoon. She'd hoped to have settled in by now. To feel confident about her decision. That the excitement of her tuition-free art classes beginning in September would matter more than the loneliness suffocating her.

She hadn't cut off the Archers, but neither did she feel comfortable calling to talk. It wouldn't be fair to expect them to cheer her on when they didn't agree with her decision to leave. And Shea... Liberty hadn't given her much time to protest her decisions. Nor had she prayed about it. Deep inside she felt a tug, like God might be pulling the reins and trying to get her attention. The sensation was familiar from her teen years but submitting to it wasn't.

The scent of her tea filled her tiny kitchen space. All the dusty, aged furniture reminded her of her old camper. Was she doing it again? Settling for less, condemning herself? The test for giving advice to a fictional best friend in this situation came to mind. What would Liberty tell her best friend to do? *Go back to the people who love you. Live there. Make it work. Without an escape plan.*

Except Daisy. Liberty had to protect her. And if leaving Whidbey and Clay behind meant he'd give up his search—which he said he was doing for Liberty's benefit—then she had to leave. Had to make a fresh start somewhere else.

Clay. Before this summer, when it had been a decade since she'd seen him, she could avoid thoughts of him distracting her all day. Despite her decision not to buy it, she'd drank more Earl Grey tea since moving here than ever. Something about his unconditional acceptance, the way he seemed to care about her needs—housing, friends. Her heart didn't stumble over their history. She'd fallen for him again, for his kindness and his selflessness. And she'd had to walk away.

A knock at the door brought Liberty out of her sad thoughts. One peek showed a man standing in the outer hallway with a bouquet in his hands. She opened the door. In her work at Seaside Florist, she'd been the one bringing the flowers.

"Delivery for Libby Winfield," the man said. He wore a navy-blue uniform of one of the florists in town.

Libby. From here she could see the bouquet's type. Daisies. Cranberry gerbera daisies with baby's breath.

She accepted the flowers and pulled a buck from her pocket. She wasn't wealthy, but a small tip might be better than none. "Thank you."

"Have a good one."

Clay had sent flowers. Why? She pulled out the card. "Please talk to me. It's important. Love, Clay."

Did he have news about the Archers? They'd have let her know if something was wrong with them. Elizabeth, then? Or Jonathan? Searching for a vase in the apartment's cabinets and hoping this furnished place could accommodate her, she dialed Clay's number. Would the owners have thought to include a vase among the cups and glasses?

A click came from his end of the connection. "You got them."

Her eyes stung at hearing his voice. "Thanks. They're exquisite. What's happening? Why the note?" She hadn't taken his phone calls or returned his texts. So he figured out a way to get her attention. She found a tall tumbler and filled it with water.

"I have good news, actually. Very good news. Please hear me out."

After loosening the bouquet from its wrapping, she arranged the flowers in their makeshift vase. Then, she dropped into a hard chair at the kitchen table. "Okay." Perhaps loneliness had made her willing, but she'd listen today.

"First, tell me how things are going in Bellingham."

"I start classes next month." Her cheerfulness came out forced. "I love that it's free. The next best thing to a scholarship."

"I'm glad for you. I know you've always wanted to study art." His cheer sounded put on too.

If only she could be honest with him. At one time, they'd challenged each other to avoid façades between them. Those days were over now—a fact that pressed on her shoulders. Neither of them mentioned it.

"Thanks."

Lord, it feels like depression wants to weigh me down. She stood and searched the studio for the Bible Gloria had given her.

"What's going on, Clay?" She kept her voice light, curiosity prodding her to ask. "Why the flowers and phone chat?"

The Bible was in the nightstand drawer. Yeah, she'd hidden it when that tug kept harassing her insides. Was God trying to tell her something?

While Clay geared up to say whatever he had on his mind, Liberty sat at the table and let the book fall open. It landed on Jeremiah 31. *Yes, I have loved you with an everlasting love.*

"It's about Daisy. But remember, you promised to hear me out."

Therefore with lovingkindness I have drawn you.

"I'm listening." She set her fingertips on the verse and forced herself to relax.

"I met with Daisy's dad. His name is Nicholas Neill, goes by Nick. His wife's name is Amanda."

Adrenaline fired arrows in her veins. "Why are you telling me names?"

"Please listen, okay?"

"Fine." Maybe she should have opened to a psalm that called down fire from heaven. She flipped pages, half chuckling to herself. But seriously. Clay never could leave things alone.

"They want to meet you."

"What?"

"From their perspective, my finding them was a God thing."

"Well, they allowed her pictures on the church's website."

"Right. But what are the odds we'd—I'd—find them."

She appreciated that he'd corrected himself. She had never wanted to interrupt Daisy's world. What was her real name again? Jaelyn.

The gerberas on the table seemed too sunny in the small room. Too hopeful. Their symbol of Clay's care challenged the dreariness in here.

"Jaelyn grew up knowing she was adopted. Nick said she cries for us sometimes because they believed they'd never be able to find us. He's such a cool guy, Libby. He's friendly, kind. Jaelyn's their only child. His wife was scared like you, but she's on board now." The words gushed out as if Clay were afraid Liberty would hang up.

Daisy knew? She cried for Liberty and Clay? This project of Clay's might have been a mission of mercy all along.

"It would mean everything to them if we'd agree to get together."

"She wants to meet us?" Her voice broke. After all this time, she might get her heart's desire, without breaking any laws. "What about our signed documents?"

"There was a stipulation that if neither of the parties broke the agreement, if somehow a meeting happened anyway, that was fine."

Her lawyer must have made that provision. "So, the only way for this to have worked was if you, because you never signed any paperwork, were the one to make it happen?"

Clay stayed silent, as if letting her process her own revelation.

"Clay?"

"Yeah."

"Did you know that all along?"

"No."

"But you couldn't leave it alone?"

He gave a light chuckle. "No."

Her fingers traced the words on the page. *I have drawn you.*

The news was too kind. Too merciful. She might get to see her daughter. This opportunity was overwhelming in what it told her about how God treated her. How He cared. She studied the ceiling. *Thank You.* A tear leaked toward her ear, and she reached for a tissue from the box on the counter.

"You still there?" Clay's intimate tone told her he got it. And that he wasn't going anywhere. She'd moved an hour north, but he wasn't going anywhere.

"When? When can we meet them?" Joy bullied the darkness away. "I can drive down tomorrow morning, first thing."

"They'll be glad to hear it. How about Skye Café at ten?"

"I'll be there at 9:30."

He laughed again. "Can't wait to see you. And to meet our daughter."

"You kept your promise? You didn't see her yet?"

"Correct."

She loved him. Only the strongest restraint kept her from blurting it out right then on the phone. But heaven help him when she threw herself into his arms the following morning. "Clay? Thanks."

"You're welcome."

CHAPTER FORTY-ONE

Who needed sleep? After a restless night, Clay had shown up at the café by 8:45 and sat there by the front window, sipping coffee, praying. Watching. He'd called the Neills right after his chat with Libby to give them the good news. Nick answered his phone, listened, and finally cheered. Amanda whooped in the background, and they saved telling Jaelyn until after they were off the phone.

Seeing his daughter in person? Hearing her voice? Noticing her inherited traits? Clay could hardly stay in his seat. Pushing his cup of java back, he jostled his leg as he waited. Enough caffeine.

At 9:20, Libby pulled up out front, her brow creased with a hint of worry. When she spotted him through the window, her face brightened, and she hurried to gather her bag and climb out. He'd missed her. Seeing her this morning sent his heart beating double-time. Something had switched between them last night. From distrust to trust, maybe? He hoped so. He hadn't set out to change her mind, only to follow Roy's advice and show her he cared about her. Hadn't been hard. He'd never stopped caring for her.

He met her at the door, and she pulled him from the entrance and threw herself into his arms. He grunted and wrapped her up. Yeah, things had changed between them. "Hey, Libby." He tightened one arm, stroking her hair with his other hand. She trembled, and he kept her there while people entered the café around them. "Hey, it's okay."

She pulled back enough to meet his eyes. "Thank you." The sheen in her pale blues prompted his own to tear up.

"You're welcome."

She examined the area. "They aren't here yet?"

"We are so early."

She giggled. "I couldn't help it. I'm surprised I didn't get a speeding ticket driving down here."

He peered behind her at her car. Hope knocked into him. "Are those boxes in your back seat?"

"I have a lot to tell you. Where are you sitting?"

He held the door open to the café, and she ordered a cocoa and slice of banana bread at the counter. He ordered a muffin. His old coffee cup had already been cleared, so he also bought a bottled water. They found a table in the back.

In about a half hour their daughter would walk in. Though Libby seemed nervous, she was willing to update him first. The old Libby would have watched the door, paced out front, tried to control every aspect so she wouldn't be surprised or miss anything. This change seemed much healthier.

She reached across the table, took his hand. "You have been so great this summer. Like a good friend."

His muffin lost its flavor. *A friend?*

She studied his face. "Hear me this out this time?"

He waved a hand. "You have the floor."

"All those times you showed consideration for me. Thinking about it, talking to Shea, I feel selfish and self-absorbed, that I was so needy. Shea said sometimes we need a season off from helping others, a time of focusing on ourselves. After we get healing and have our needs met, we can serve again. That sounds simplistic, but you get the gist. From the very beginning, I could see you were a different man. This time your affection seemed real."

He ran his thumb over her hand.

"And I realized something else. I don't want to live in Bellingham. I don't care about free art classes. I can earn the tuition and take courses here. I called the Archers, and they haven't sold or rented out the tiny house." Her face beamed. "I'm moving back."

He stood and pulled her into his arms, his heart thumping. "I'm glad." She hadn't said what he'd hoped she would. Hadn't made any further comments about their relationship. But he wouldn't push. She was moving back. That was what mattered.

Nick entered the café, hand-in-hand with his wife—a tall brunette. And Clay froze. A redheaded girl who probably came up to Libby's shoulder in height joined them.

"Hey, sweetheart," Clay whispered in Libby's ear. "They're

here."

She pulled away, wiping under her eyes, keeping her back to the entrance for a second longer.

"They know you as April, but you can fix that."

She gave a fast series of nods.

"We got this."

Libby turned, and Clay heard her catch a small gasp before her fingertips went to her mouth. His own attention locked on their daughter. Daisy—Jaelyn, looking a bit shy, with her red hair braided in a side braid, joined them near their table. Amanda rested her palms on Jaelyn's shoulders, standing close behind her.

Clay shook Nick's hand. "Hey."

Nick's smile, like before, shone. "How ya doin'? This is my wife, Amanda." Clay silently greeted her. "And this is Jaelyn."

"Nice to meet you, Jaelyn." Clay gave her hand a light squeeze. Was this actually happening? "This is..." He checked in with Libby to get her permission to share her real name and when she nodded, he continued. "This is Liberty."

Jaelyn stepped away from her adoptive mother. "Liberty?"

Libby held her fingers over trembling lips. Everyone else went still. Libby opened her arms, and Jaelyn stepped right in as if she'd been doing that all her life. Amanda seemed a little nervous and yet determined to see this through. Nick ducked his head momentarily. When Libby opened her eyes and peered up at Clay, he gave her a smile.

After a few more moments, they sat at the table. Clay couldn't tear his attention from their daughter. She'd worn her hair the same as Libby's and when Amanda pointed it out, everyone chuckled.

Jaelyn faced him, and awe stole over him. "Dad says you run a nursery."

"My family does."

"I love to grow things. I've always got new seeds going in the kitchen window. In the summer, I redo all the garden beds."

Nick sipped the coffee he'd ordered. "Sounds like it runs in the family."

"And you do artistic things, like build?" she asked Libby.

"I do. In fact, I have something for you. Do you mind if I go get it?"

"I wanna come." Jaelyn checked in with her parents. "That okay?"

"Of course." Amanda waved them outside.

Once they'd walked away, talking excitedly, heads together, Clay sat back in a bit of shock. "It's incredible. She looks exactly like her."

Amanda gripped her coffee mug. "We can't thank you enough for making this happen. I'm sure you know by now how Jaelyn has longed for more information. I'd find her crying in her room and ask her about it. She tells me her feelings of fear she'd been abandoned or rejected and that if she could only meet her birth parents, she could have her questions answered." She paused. "I couldn't deny her that."

"We'd be happy to answer her questions whenever she feels comfortable enough to ask them," Clay said. "I think God orchestrated this, but for my part, you're welcome."

Nick's brow furrowed, which was rare for him. "We're only sorry this is a once and done. If only April—I mean Liberty—lived on the island."

"Oh, I didn't tell you yet. She's moving back."

"Really? She'll be local?" Amanda's face lit. "It's been such a tough time for Jaelyn. I mean, she's at an age where answered questions aren't always enough, you know? But meeting her birth mom now, maybe having a relationship with her? That's everything when you're searching for your identity."

Amanda's courage amazed Clay. She didn't seem overly threatened by Libby's presence in her daughter's life.

"It sounds silly now, but I've been afraid you would try to take her away from us."

"I understand. And we would never do that. Liberty's biggest concern was not wanting to upset your lives. Not wanting to hurt Jaelyn."

Nick tipped his mug in a mock toast. "I could tell that from the first time we met. That's why we trust you. But let's take this at her pace. Sound good?"

Clay and Amanda both nodded as Libby and Jaelyn rejoined them. Her hands were full of that fairy house from June's birthday celebration. The gift Libby had made for her.

"I've got eight more gifts to give you. One for each birthday I missed." The words flowed smoothly as if the deep sadness and grief of loss no longer held on. She must have stored the gifts in a safe place because they'd survived her camper's crushing.

"Ooh, presents." Jaelyn traced the fairy house's roof with a fingertip. "This is perfect." She met Libby's eyes. "Thank you."

"My pleasure."

Before they left, they set up another meeting the following day. Libby wanted to show everyone her new house. Of course, since the space was limited, they'd gather outside. Had she been over there today? Probably not.

Her new house waited with gifts from Clay to Libby.

When the family of three had backed out, Clay took Libby's hand. "That was incredible." He waved through the window one more time.

"Wow. I still can't believe it." She kissed his cheek. "I'm glad now that you set that up. I feel like I'm always thanking you for helping me. Now that I'm moving back, you tell me what you need, and I'll help however I can."

"Kourtney's been harassing me about her wedding. Want to jump into planning that again? We're at two months and counting, and she's turning into a sci-fi villain."

"Ha. I'd be glad to. Your mom took me back at the flower shop, with a raise. I'm going to take art classes here this fall."

He walked her to her car. "You're getting all you've ever wanted."

"Almost." Her eyes held a mystery. "Hey, come over to the

Archers with me?"

"Okay. I'll follow you in my truck."

"Great."

At her new driveway, she turned in and headed straight back to her house. What did she think of the changes?

The new shrubs were in place, and the hydrangeas bloomed in pale blue, like her eyes. The pathway to her tiny house's porch was flanked in lavender vincas. A window box decorated the house with overflowing petunias. He'd even squeezed a flowerpot with colorful annuals into the corner of her porch. A hanging basket balanced it out, full of sunset begonias and cherry red calibrachoa draping over the sides.

For the yard, he'd put in a winding dry creek bed which featured a walking bridge, as part of a path to a two-person garden swing.

She parked and closed her car door. He joined her near the beginning of the path. "It's a fairy house." Her voice held awe. "Did you do this?"

"There are daisies growing on the waterside."

She grabbed his hand and tugged him down the path toward the house then pulled him over the bridge and around to the back of the house. He laughed as he kept up. Tall daisies swayed in the breeze off the water. One more tug and she was right in front of him. "I love you."

He'd barely had time to hear her before she pressed her lips to his. The world stopped spinning. His hands came up her back and though he could feel her fire, he wanted to take things slow. She broke the kiss, and he lifted her off the ground to spin her around. She squealed, and he laughed.

Setting her in front of him, he ran his fingers into the wisps of hair that had escaped her braid. "I love you too."

Yeah, things had definitely changed between them.

CHAPTER FORTY-TWO

"You shouldn't have to work this hard at your daughter's wedding." Liberty tried to snag the bouquet of mums and roses in white, lavender, and burgundy hues.

Elizabeth relinquished it. "I want everything to go smoothly."

"It will. I'm here to make sure of it. But you should enjoy being mother of the bride."

"We're at two hours and counting. What else is left to do?"

"We finished decorating the sanctuary." Kourtney and Fletcher were going to wed in the main auditorium at the family's church. Liberty had worked with a few assistants to ensure the large room looked perfect for this fall wedding. "Go and check in on the bridesmaids or the groomsmen." Clay was one of them.

"Kourt already shooed me out of the bridal room." Elizabeth gave a nervous giggle. "Said I was fluttering too much."

Maybe Elizabeth needed a job. "Okay, let's see. How about you pass out the flowers to everyone in the wedding party, including family. Start with the men, and we'll save the bride's and her ladies' bouquets in cold water a bit longer."

"Oh, yes. Good idea." Elizabeth grabbed the box of boutonnieres and made her way out into the hall.

A hand came to rest on Liberty's shoulder as a familiar scent surrounded her. She turned into Clay's arms. "Hey."

"Hey." He wore his suit, complete with boutonniere. Handsome, competent, and at peace.

She was on duty, so she let him kiss her cheek. He groaned in playful disappointment and pulled back. "How's it going? I see Mom's on her best behavior."

"She is freaking out, but otherwise, we have everything under control. Have you seen your sister yet today?"

"She's in hiding. Doesn't want old Fletch to catch even a glimpse of her." He squeezed Liberty's hand. "The flowers look amazing."

"We try." She couldn't take all the credit, of course. But satisfaction filled her.

"For our wedding, let's fill the chapel with daisies in every shade." He'd been kidding lately about their wedding, saying things like, "When it's our turn," or "Let's have red velvet cake."

"Of course." Liberty glanced around. For the moment, no flurry of activity. The rest of the floral shop's team was loading out boxes and cleaning up scraps in the sanctuary. This back room, off the kitchen gave them privacy. "Are you enjoying our visits with Daisy?" Jaelyn had liked the nickname and agreed they could use it for her. To honor her adoptive parents, they called her Jaelyn when everyone was together.

"I think it's cool her parents are fine with it. They let their daughter decide how often we meet."

"You were right. We're getting everything we ever wanted."

He took both of her hands. "Except one thing."

"What's that?"

He dropped to his knee. "I know it's not the most romantic spot, but then again, maybe it is."

She grinned down at him, kneeling there.

"And I know we've only recently gotten back together. But I can't let you get away this time. Libby, will you marry me?"

"Yes." She drew him up, and this time she kissed him. Who cared who was watching?

She'd seen she could trust him, knew he cared deeply for her. She'd spent the last couple of months focusing on helping others and found joy in doing that. They'd started doing outreaches at church again, including a backpack drive for local school children last month. Daisy had helped.

He scooped her up and spun her around. "Think two of us can fit in your tiny house?"

She resettled on her feet as he set her down. "Might be close quarters."

"I'm fine with that." His delicious smile captured her heart again.

This time, she didn't need an escape plan.

She was home.

And she and Clay would make their own family, full of honorary members and hopefully, a sister or brother for Daisy one day. Their life together was complicated, and their history was messy, but now that they were together, it'd been worth it.

Clay fished something out if his pocket. A ring. There was a center stone, perhaps close to a carat in weight and two smaller stones on each side. He held it up to her hand. "May I?"

"Of course." It looked like his mother's, but that couldn't be. He slipped it on her finger, and she marveled. Last summer, she'd worn one like this for their photo shoot and now she could wear her own? It symbolized the past, present, and future. A perfect fit.

Elizabeth peeked into the room, smiling ear to ear. Ring in place on her own finger, she clapped her hands together. "Do we get to plan another wedding?"

Clay laughed. "Yes."

Liberty reached for her phone to call Shea, but her friend ducked into the room at that moment. "Hey. I didn't know you were coming." The two friends hugged. A few feet away, Clay's face showed guilt. He'd invited her because he'd planned this proposal all along.

Shea pulled back. "Let me see it." Liberty showed her the ring. "Stunning. I'm so happy for you—both of you."

Gloria and Roy appeared in the hall and stepped through the doorway. "What's going on in here?"

Had Clay told everyone his plan? Didn't matter. She wanted to share this moment with them. As her honorary parents, she hoped they'd participate in the wedding. Positive her face was beaming, she raised her hand, wiggled her fingers, and flashed her ring at them.

Gloria shrieked and scooted over to them for hugs. Roy clapped Clay on the back and shook his hand.

Jonathan joined them in the room, his face wreathed in pride. "I take it this means my boy popped the question?"

"Yes, he did, and I couldn't be happier."

Jonathan gave Liberty a light hug and then she teared up when he embraced his son. God had restored their relationship. In fact, He'd restored a lot of relationships in this room.

When Kason and Brynn walked in, kids in tow, the gathering morphed into an impromptu party.

"Hey, we have a wedding to put on," Elizabeth finally said, clapping her hands together. "Let's go." She waved everyone out. "I'll give you guys a minute." With a blush, she closed the door.

Clay drew Liberty close. "Is this really happening?"

"Absolutely."

"Long engagement?"

"Definitely not."

He chuckled. "Good."

"Think Kourtney will mind our news today?"

"She's going to be thrilled for us. You know she's wanted us together all along."

"Like the Archers, Shea, your parents—well, your mom, and a hundred other people."

"Yup. I can't wait." He lowered his head and kissed her, reminding her of the past, while grounding her in the present, and pointing with hope toward their future.

She couldn't wait to start the next chapter. Together.

Author Note

Dear Reader,

For thirty years, I've enjoyed visiting Puget Sound beaches. When I walk the sand and smell the sea air, stories run through my mind. It's been a pleasure to share three of those with you in this Washington Island Romance series. If you're like me, you enjoy an escape when you read. Writing these novels has been an escape of sorts. I lose myself in the settings and strive to bring you with me.

I've recently begun studying genealogy. There are a couple of TV programs that feed my inner genealogist. One of them is a reality show about finding long-lost family members. Say, a mom gave up her daughter for adoption forty years ago. They've spent the last four decades wondering about the other person. For the child, I've learned the questions center on identity and whether or not she/he was wanted. For the mother, she tends to worry if the child had a safe and happy childhood and whether she made the right decision. These real-life accounts pull me in, and I consider the bigger stories around them. This Whidbey Island novel is not based on any of the stories I saw, but I was certainly inspired.

Doesn't it sometimes feel like the Christian life is a roller-coaster, with opportunities to trust the engineers that yes, you will arrive safely at the end? We can't understand why God allows what He does in the world. We can only trust that He is sovereign, that He has a plan, and that He will bring us to Himself when our ride ends. It's my prayer that you have that assurance.

Until next time, friends.
All His best,
Annette

If you've enjoyed my stories, I hope you'll consider leaving a review wherever you purchased it, or on Amazon, BarnesAndNoble.com, ChristianBook.com, etc. Also, if you'd like to connect with me, you can find me at the following places:

My website: www.AnnetteMIrby.com
My blog: www.AnnetteIrbyReviews.blogspot.com
Facebook group:
www.facebook.com/groups/252272708574760
Twitter: @AnnetteMIrby
Amazon Author Page:
www.amazon.com/author/annette_m_irby
Bookbub: www.bookbub.com/authors/annette-m-irby or @AnnetteMIrby

In case you missed it—the first
chapter of book one

*Finding Love in
Friday Harbor*

CHAPTER ONE

Rain drizzled over the empty parking lot at Lime Kiln Point State Park, well north of Seattle. This close to the Salish Sea, the mercury floated near fifty degrees, despite the calendar's June date. Only one other vehicle—a scuffed pickup—sat abandoned near the trails this early. Professor Mikaela Rhoades could have the place to herself. But it wouldn't have mattered if there were hordes of people. She'd find a spot to pray, contend for peace.

Her lungs squeezed in her chest. Did Hunter know yet?

Cold wind pitched mist at her face. She ducked under her raincoat's hood, scooting across the parking lot, past the closed gift shop/interpretive center and orca sculpture. The scent of salty air reminded her of why she loved the water, her career path.

Was it a mistake to be here?

Oh, Lord, help. You brought me here. Please make this work.

She just had to remember to breathe. There were three reactions to fearful things—fight, flight, or freeze. Her reflex, almost every time, was to freeze. If she held her breath, the proverbial monster wouldn't find her. She could hide. Evade. But always, she had to then face whatever the fearsome situation was and overcome. Otherwise, she'd never have gotten this far. Never suggested this plan.

Never come this close to a collision with her past.

I'm going to see him again. Something she'd been avoiding for over a decade.

Her phone buzzed against her leg. She'd just talked with her family, updating them, sending Dad love on his special day. He'd called her Kayla, making her remember how Hunter had always called her Miki, after the first part of her name, while her dad preferred the latter part.

Maybe this was her boss calling.

She scurried under the slight overhang of the map wall and pulled out her vibrating phone. Dr. Amelia Wren's photo gazed up at her. Mikaela corralled her thoughts and connected the call. Wind buffeted her from behind, rousing a shiver while her eyes reviewed the image of her favorite place on earth—the Salish Sea all dotted with islands.

"Hello, Dr. Rhoades." Amelia was using her "all-business" voice. She sounded healthy today. Mikaela pictured her salt-and-pepper curls, intelligent eyes, and laugh lines. The years hadn't diminished her zest for life, or authority. Too bad zeal hadn't healed her. Another thing for Mikaela to pray about. "All settled in?"

Tucking her phone against her ear inside her hood, Mikaela rounded the map area and started down the evergreen-surrounded path between her and Haro Strait. Hopefully, the rain would let up soon. "Yes, thank you."

"And the accommodations?"

"I found a rental overlooking Griffin Bay." The department chairwoman wouldn't like this. The university had offered housing, but Mikaela couldn't see herself in dorm-like accommodations all summer. She didn't mention her beach cottage was one she'd always had in mind if she ever returned. Amelia needn't worry. Mikaela would be nearby and could easily access the grounds and faculty at the labs. Plus, Mikaela's not living in the dorms meant more room for students.

The other option had been to move in with her grandmother, but Granny rented rooms to several students, and Mikaela preferred downtime at day's end. She should, however, get over to see her soon. Granny Belle might have some wisdom to help Mikaela through the summer. Maybe she'd recite a verse, like *"Cast all your cares on Him because He cares for you."*

Yes, that one.

He cares for me. He cares.

"If I'm able," Amelia was saying, "I plan to visit in a few weeks, and perhaps bring the funding representative with me." Mikaela heard snipping and pictured her boss navigating the balcony of her Seattle condo tending her plants, broomstick skirt fluttering around her ankles. Must not be raining there.

"I'd be happy to have you." So long as she found her footing first. Best to look competent when they visited. The funding rep? She didn't look forward to welcoming him. Theirs was an arrangement that kept the rep at arm's length, for at least a little while. One saving grace in this endeavor. He could just stay in Seattle for now.

"Have you been to Cahill Touring since you've been back?"

"Not yet. I'll be there Tuesday." Too soon to come face-to-face with Hunter.

Coward. Probably.

This brainchild had been Mikaela's. After learning from Hunter's mom how much they could use the help, Mikaela had nudged the department's chairwoman into supporting her crazy notion, touting how the program would benefit both the University of Seattle and its students, as well as Cahill Touring. Then, she'd found funding. Since this was an extra program, the students paid for the privilege of being here during summer term. But ongoing, Mikaela still had to appease the funding representative, Dr. Denver Smythe. His family's foundation would fund the research in the pilot program, the new lab in Hawaii. This summer's project proved the next one was viable.

"Oh, that's right. It's Sunday." Silence rolled along between them like slow-moving water down a rocky creek bed—familiar territory, but nonetheless rife with sharp obstacles. Dr. Wren had no room in her life for church or God or taking a Sabbath, though

Mikaela had spoken to Amelia of her relationship with God. "Well, Tuesday is soon enough. I know you realize all that is at stake."

Mikaela knew once a person gained Amelia's support, she'd cheer them to the finish, like she'd faithfully done in Mikaela's life and short career so far. Amelia had once been friends with Reid Cahill, so when Mikaela pitched the idea, Amelia had appreciated the opportunity to help. But Dr. Wren had never known everything about the connection.

Mikaela broke free from the madrone trees just as the wind kicked up. The sight of Haro Strait arrested her. Even oppressed by clouds like today, the view of rushing gray water between here and Vancouver Island captured her like few other locales. The lighthouse lay in the distance, a bit more of a hike. "Now that I'm onsite, I'm more convinced than ever this will be one of our best endeavors, hopefully continuing for years." Of course, she'd be gone by fall. But that's what Hunter preferred, according to their last conversation twelve years ago. By autumn, the benefits would be obvious for the Cahills. Mikaela could walk away knowing she'd tried, and hopefully helped. Then someone else could step in here while she took what she'd learned over to Hawaii.

"One more accomplishment before the Big Island, right?" Amelia's voice sounded wistful. Maybe she'd rather be the one spearheading the Hawaii pilot. "Still, I'd love for you to settle down someday."

Ah, it had only taken ten minutes to arrive here again— Amelia's favorite topic lately. Sure, Mikaela longed for a husband to share her life. But she wouldn't divulge that to her boss and give her more ammunition. "There's too much yet to do."

Several secrets pressed for release to her mentor, including candidness about the conflict of interest between her and Captain Hunter. She stuffed those thoughts and put a smile into her voice. "Maybe one day, when I meet *the one*." Dr. Wren didn't need to know Mikaela had stopped looking years ago. Back to this summer's project. "Don't worry. I won't let you down."

Or the Cahills, for that matter.

Hunter Cahill dug his oar into the strait. Biting wind threw water at his face, burrowing into his street clothes. No wetsuit or even a lifejacket today. He'd been in too much of a rush to get here. Out of habit, he scanned the waters for signs of life. A short, dark gray dorsal surfaced a couple hundred yards toward the center of the channel. Harbor porpoise usually traveled in pods of three to six animals. Dall's porpoise the same. Without seeing any other fins, he couldn't be sure what he'd seen. Not that he was on duty right now.

He paddled north, toward Lime Kiln Lighthouse. As he predicted, the churning tossed him like a cork today, and the current dragged on his boat.

If his dad knew he was kayaking alone in these conditions, he'd have said, *"What are you thinking, Son? Always take a partner in choppy weather. Where's your life jacket? I raised you to have more water smarts than that."* But then Dad would ease up, seeing the way Hunter wrestled. He'd know just how to help, what advice to offer.

Too bad he couldn't advise him anymore.

This time Hunter wasn't imagining the presence of harbor porpoise. Their grayish dorsals pierced the surface in a pod of five just off to his left as they raced north.

A mottled Pacific harbor seal twisted up to the surface next to his kayak before dashing back under. Sea otters poked their velvet noses out, watching him. Dad would have loved this, despite the mist. If he were here, he'd talk about the wind velocity and predict orca activity.

Then he'd tell Hunter what he'd told him since that summer— that he'd made a mistake all those years ago when he let Mikaela go.

A huge mistake.

Hunter's chest ached. Relinquishing his dad was hard enough. Death hadn't given Hunter a choice. But Hunter was the one who'd chosen to release Miki.

And he was drowning because of it.

His abs burned and sweat broke out on his face, mixing with the mist. He considered shedding a layer but didn't want to lose his momentum. Stroke right, then left, right, then left. Pause.

How often had his dad challenged him about giving up on Miki? The last time they'd been together on the water, they'd discussed her . . .

Wind bullied the clouds across the early autumn sky that day. Dad breathed deep, working his kayak closer. "You've never cared for anybody like you care for her." Present tense because Dad knew Hunter'd never gotten over her. They proceeded along in tandem, talking above the wind.

"True." His gut clenched just thinking about her. "But it's been over ten years. She's probably married with six kids by now, all of them non-fish eating and not a landlubber among them." He grinned as the image of Miki with an imaginary gaggle of blond offspring finding green shore crabs under every rock, worked him over.

"And I loved her like a daughter." Aw, Dad. "I understand why you went on with your life, Son." His dad stilled his oar and rested a fisted hand on his thigh. "But if she ever comes back to the island single, if you ever get another chance, promise me you'll pursue her—romance her. Promise me you'll give it one more try."

Maybe Hunter had sensed it was the last time they'd talk like that. Maybe he realized how much it meant to his father for him to agree. Whatever the reason, fool that he was, Hunter caved. "I will, Dad."

Of course Miki had never returned.

So here he was, alone and off the hook, trying to keep his dad's business afloat. Maybe the new arrangement with the University of Seattle's marine bio department would help. Professor Matthews, or Michaels, or whatever his name was—Mom hadn't given Hunter all the details—was due to arrive this week. Hunter would have to tolerate college students on his bridge, asking questions, trying his patience. But he'd do it. Anything to keep Cahill Touring open. For Dad.

Hunter watched two black dorsals slice through the water dead ahead about ten yards—one higher and straighter than the other. Never got old. He held his breath and stilled his oar. A smaller, curved fin joined them, surfacing momentarily before arcing back into the strait. Their offspring. Dad would have talked nonstop about the pod, but he'd always been so hyped about marine life. Just like Miki.

There was one more thing Hunter had to do before he pulled his kayak from the channel. For the rest of his life, his hero would no longer be here to offer advice or direction or affirmation. Hunter's throat burned, and he tightened his jaw against the quivering in his chin.

A wet gust of wind blew at him, and he faced it, arms still for a moment. Waves tossed him side to side. He sucked in a ragged breath, sighted a mighty eagle soaring over the water, hovering near the tall Douglas firs.

"Happy Father's Day, Dad."

He gave himself one moment . . . to picture Dad, see his smiling face as he captained the *Millennium*. His eyes always shone with light and warmth, but you wouldn't want to cross him. He was a good captain.

Hunter shook off the memories rolling through his mind, worked the kayak forward. Something caught his attention on shore. One person stood alone on the rocks, peering out, binocs raised. The on-again, off-again rains had glazed every surface. Not even tourists had ventured out this morning. Just that lone figure up there, too close to the edge. A single slip and he'd be a goner.

Yellow slicker. Long legs, lean build. Escaping strands of dark blonde hair flipped in the wind. Wait.

Hunter had grown up here. The island's residents were mostly familiar—even at a distance. No local would stand there in this weather. They'd choose a better time. Tourists might, but today's conditions must've chased them away because he hadn't seen a single soul until now. Only one person he knew would brave it. Someone so crazy about whale sightings she'd risk climbing slippery boulders and reject the buddy system, just to get close to the water. His heart thumped.

Miki.

The First Chapter of Book Two

Finding Love on Bainbridge Island, Washington

CHAPTER ONE

Liam Barrett could use some fresh air.

The red-eye from Hawaii to Seattle seemed unending, especially with this snoring guy next to him smelling of curry. Before the flight crew requested that he pocket his phone, he wanted to check on his great-aunt. So long as she kept uploading pictures of her pets or the stormy June weather on Puget Sound, he knew she was okay. But any lag in her online activity and he got worried. His zany great-aunt Matilda was a social butterfly, but she could also be a bit … eccentric. The shorter her leash—and his absences from her vicinity—the better.

A vintage photo of a father, mother, and children was captioned in Auntie Mat's latest upload: *Family is everything. Make peace.* He shook his head, though it wasn't surprising she would post something odd. The point was—he had confirmation she was fine. A relief after everything she'd done for him.

The phone buzzed in his hand as another Facebook notification popped up: *New friend request from Jack Barrett.*

His heart stuttered. Wha—?

An image flashed in his mind of his mother and him alone in the house. She wouldn't stop crying. Preschooler Liam standing at her bedroom doorway, watching. *"You okay, Mommy?"* He'd rubbed his stomach where it hurt. Should he run to her? Hold her hand?

Could he hug her and make it better like she did for him? He darted to her side. *"Mommy, are you broken?"*

Now at age thirty-three, his thumb shook as he pressed the power button and turned off his phone. He should've deleted it immediately. Blocked him. Rejection would send a message without having to type a message. He wanted to throw his cell. Or maybe hurl himself off something for the adrenaline fix. How soon could he and his buddies schedule another getaway full of daredevil stunts?

"We are now beginning our descent into SeaTac International Airport. Local weather in Seattle is fifty-six degrees and cloudy with a 70 percent chance of rain this afternoon. Local time is 6:35 a.m." The flight attendant went on to list the various end-of-flight things, like raised tray tables and final trash collection, and Liam tuned him out.

Jack Barrett.

Liam hadn't seen that name for at least two years. Back then, he'd run an online search, as if compelled to track down the man and prove Liam was no longer helpless to fix Mom's pain. Half hating his curiosity, he'd scrolled links. He hadn't done this research as a child, hadn't asked his mom any questions so he wouldn't upset her. The name *Jack Barrett* wasn't uncommon in the Northwest. But, heart thumping, Liam had narrowed it down to those born in Bremerton, Washington around fifty-five years ago.

Best match for the Jack he researched? A felon, busted for armed robbery, grand theft auto, drug possession, and several DUIs. No wonder Mom never mentioned him. Stellar guy. Role model material. Liam didn't drink, didn't use drugs. *He'd* never chased the next high—outside of adrenaline. Or been pulled over by the police. Not even so much as a parking ticket. No, in those ways he was nothing like Jack.

It was the similarities that troubled Liam.

Shake it off, dude.

The plane touched down, and most passengers squeezed into the aisle as soon as the fasten seat belt light went out. Liam let the guy in his row pass, glad to put distance between them. As much as he wanted to bail, he'd be last off today. He and his three buddies would exit after the final passenger—one member of the group moving much slower since the "incident." Poor Hitch.

Liam had a role with his buddies—easygoing. Jack Barrett's name could cancel that part of Liam. The part that had learned to move forward, avoid being too serious.

Around him, his buddies roused. Across the aisle, Isaac "Jinx" Tabor stood and reached overhead. Liam playfully bumped him, though he had plenty of room above his own seat. "Hurry up, Jinx."

Jinx laughed and reached into the compartment. "Shoot, Liam, hang on! I'm grabbing our newly disabled guy's bag too."

"Disabled? Thanks for that. It's only a broken bone." Clark Hanson, known to the group as Hitch since he'd recently gotten married, waited behind them near the lav doors, crutches rammed under his pits. "Flying was sure easier before I needed these." He nodded toward the new accessories.

"We didn't tell you to break your ankle." Liam tugged down his duffel bag. This was good. *Forget the notification.*

"Get a move on, will you?" This from Dylan "Burr" Burgess at the tail of the plane.

Liam marched toward the now-open cockpit. Another adventure in the books. They'd dived with sharks—terrifying and exhilarating—and gone cliff diving.

Out in the concourse, the four of them lined up. Hitch hobbled along and without him asking, the others slowed their pace. The guy's foot must be throbbing after the six-hour flight with no way to elevate it. Still, his buddies teased him about the new *hitch* in his step.

"You're all gonna get it. Line up, and I'll whack you with one of my crutches!"

"Who knew those things made good weapons? Maybe we should alert security." Liam laughed. "You know your wife is going to kill you, right?" Heaven help Liam, but having a wife who could insist he avoid adventures wasn't for him. Good luck, Hitch, and no thanks.

Liam caught his sheepish expression before Hitch answered.

"Yes, she is."

"See, that's why I'm not getting married." Burr yanked his duffel strap higher up his shoulder.

"Nah," Jinx joked, "no one'll have you!" He darted away before Burr could punch him. "There's a reason we call you *Burr*."

This earned him a scowl.

The troops went quiet while they waited for the elevator to take them to baggage claim where Hitch's wife and father would meet them. Soon, Jinx and Burr would head back to the Eastside, and Liam would return to Bainbridge Island—something his buddies would never forgive for how posh the island was. Didn't matter that Liam lived in an aged tiny house—not the cool kind— inland, which meant no water view. Or that the roof leaked after the last rainstorm.

At baggage claim, gorgeous Fiona Hanson approached the group. Hitch wore the dopiest of grins. She beelined to him as if she didn't want him to take another step and break something else. "Oh, Clark! Are you all right?" The guys elbowed each other over that name, while Fiona examined him, probably looking for more injuries.

All that fussing—Hitch could keep it. Except, what would it be like to come home to someone? He had a sudden image of Jenna-Shea Brown, the only person he'd ever wanted to come home to. But, she'd made it clear long ago that he'd blown his one chance with her.

All her fuss aside, no one had ever looked at Liam like Fiona looked at Hitch.

"Hey, everyone!" Hitch's dad stepped into the group. Elijah Hanson was a solid guy. He'd personally taken them up in his plane for a few skydives over the years. Seeing Hitch like this, Elijah didn't fret over his son, merely patted his shoulder. "Glad to see you're still with us."

"Hey, Dad." Hitch tilted his head down, but then he raised it and met his father's eyes, as if seeking approval or something, even though he was a grown man. But the looks they exchanged—silent communication from knowing each other so well. Shoot. What was that like? To have someone trustworthy who worked to protect you and build you up?

A dad. Not that Liam would know much about that.

Eli eyed his son's gimpy limb—the cast the Hawaiian doc had put on him, anchoring his ankle to his shin. "You're okay?"

Hitch nodded. "Yup."

"Good. Let's get you home. I'm here to carry this." He reached toward the duffel bag Fiona held, which she happily handed over with a "thanks." Fiona smiled at her father-in-law. Yeah, everyone got along well with Eli. The rest of the guys greeted him, shaking his hand and guy-hugging him with their other arms. He brought respect out of you, and you couldn't object to his warmth or the way he genuinely cared for his son and his family, as well as this foursome who grew up raising Cain together.

They still enjoyed their adventures, but the clock was ticking for Hitch. His days of cliff diving, skydiving, and shark diving were about to end.

A few see-ya-laters after that and Hitch hobbled off with his wife and dad while Liam watched them.

"You coming, Liam?" Jinx asked from several feet away, and Liam meandered in his direction. They fell into step side by side—a faster pace now. "How's your beach-house project?"

Cool, moist air hit as soon as they entered the sky bridge that led to SeaTac's parking structure and the taxi line. Raindrops streaked the tinted plexiglass, rushing down the sides of the elevated transparent tunnel perched over the harried traffic below. Yeah, Hawaii in June beat Seattle hands down.

"Electrical this week. Glad the Browns don't need the house for another few weeks. It's been one thing after another."

Burr nudged Jinx. "Yeah, we feel sorry for you. All that suffering at the beach."

"I don't live at the beach, Burr." *He* could volunteer to trek over and help, but nope. Whatever it was Burr did all day kept him too busy to lend a hand.

Burr grunted again.

For once, Liam was fighting to succeed at something, but all

Burr could do was badger him. Enough. "No, I get it. You don't have your life together, so you can't respect that that's what I'm trying to do." Ever since Liam had learned of Jack Barrett's criminal record, he'd determined not to be like him. To keep avoiding brushes with the law, of course, but also to thrive at work, be dependable. To prove he was nothing like Jack.

At the walk-up parking payment booths, Burr stopped. "Yeah? Is that what you think? Working on my sobriety doesn't matter?"

"Dude, it matters," Jinx spoke up—ever the peacemaker. "C'mon, Liam."

Liam ground his jaw. No matter what he did, Burr always seemed ticked at him, which pushed Liam's buttons and made him overreact. "Knock it off, Burr." Everyone had seen Burr their last night in Hawaii. Nobody said anything, but everybody saw. The guy was spiraling again, without a chute. It wasn't like the four of them to sit around in a circle and spill their guts to each other. So no one really knew what was eating Burr—what secret, or regret, or whatever. The way Burr could push Liam's hot buttons made Liam keep his distance.

Except Liam did owe him.

Burr pivoted away. "See ya, Islander."

There it was. His nickname. Liam clenched his jaw. He didn't hate the moniker, but he knew Burr meant it as a dig—implying Liam was always on vacation or that he was lazy. Burr stalked off. Liam looked at Jinx. "Keep an eye on him, okay?"

A fast sigh. "Yeah. I always do." Jinx lived near Burr, so it fell to him to play babysitter of the tribe's weakest member.

"Jinx!" Burr called from the elevator bank, elbow locked while he held the door.

Jinx was not only the peacemaker, he was the klutz. Eccentric himself in some ways. He jumped, but then shifted into the put-together façade no one ever bought. "Gotta run. Give your auntie Mat a kiss for me!" Because he tried so hard to fake competence in everyday life, he often tripped or sabotaged himself—thus the name Jinx.

But if anyone could figure out what was up with Burr, it was Jinx. For some reason, Burr didn't bark at him.

Liam watched him lope off toward the brooding Burr and felt that sense of aloneness that always followed the high of the guys' getaways. Hitch with his family, Jinx and Burr driving back to the Eastside, and Liam stuffing his parking stub into the automated booth, followed by his credit card, before scuffing toward his parked truck. It was cheaper to leave his beat-up truck here for a few days than to pay a ride service the fare both ways for the distance to Bainbridge from this airport.

He'd head back to his house—alone—and try not to think of how good Hitch had it.

Oh, and Jack Barrett. Liam would rather never think of him again.

Matilda Hartwell held her breath for a second. Liam was going to kill her.

She clicked on the active message box in Facebook and let herself exhale. *I THINK HE MIGHT BE READY TO AT LEAST LISTEN TO WHAT YOU HAVE TO SAY.*

The response was quick. *ALL I CAN DO IS HOPE.*

AND PRAY.

Their conversation went still for several moments, and Matilda wondered if the other writer had stopped to do just that. She'd heard he'd changed, but what if he wasn't a good guy, even now? She wanted to write a new message immediately and demand to know if he'd truly changed. Get him to promise only good would come of this contact attempt. Thing was—Liam was no longer a child under her protection. Not that she would ever put him in harm's way, of course, not even emotionally. Not after all Liam had been through. But something in her gut told her this was the right path—and that it would be hard for her nephew. Plus, the man had found her message, though they weren't friends on Facebook yet.

She wouldn't even consider messaging him today if she wasn't utterly convinced this road was best for Liam. Her nephew carried too much baggage from the past. Too much hurt—and anger, probably—though he covered it well. Most of the time.

Minutes had passed now, and still no activity on the other message-sender's end. Matilda clicked into the message box once more and typed: *It might be time to try.* Gulp. *Send him a friend request. See what happens.*

Again, silence. Had he left his computer, or pocketed his phone? The site's note said he'd "seen" it, but that could just result from an open computer. No guarantees he was there.

She'd take a break and check if her gull friend was visiting her water-side deck. Perhaps he was hungry. She grabbed some berries for him. Sure, part of her knew she should let him fend for himself, but he kept her company while she gardened. For that, he deserved a treat. Plus, she enjoyed singing with him. And he didn't mind performing for an old lady.

Ten minutes later, she returned to her laptop. Still nothing. And then, motion. He was typing.

Already done . . .

Matilda's nails clicked as she responded: *Then, we wait.*

Terrifying.

I know.

Liam would have a few choices when he found the friend request. He could delete it right away. He could block the sender. And if God was working miracles at this moment, Liam could consider at least talking to him. Matilda pressed her lips together. No doubt God *was* working miracles somewhere, but Liam had decisions to make and God wouldn't force him.

For as long as Matilda had been Liam's guardian, and even before, she'd tried to teach him the freedom of forgiveness, and how not forgiving brought regret, anger, even rage to the surface. Hopefully, he'd keep those truths in mind when he saw the name pop up in his friend requests. What would he think of her family picture post and the subtle suggestion about making peace?

She clicked on the genealogy site and opened the Search box. She knew the details around Liam's generation and a few names from the previous generation, but the one before that—almost nothing. Later today, she'd try to find Liam's paternal grandparents' names. But for now... She clicked into the new family tree she was creating and pressed Liam's name. Then she clicked on Add Father.

There she typed: *Jack Barrett.*